Mrs Snow and the Colonel

'That old cow Mrs Southover who fell downstairs and died last week. Well, it wasn't any accident. I pushed her.'

Since Mrs Southover was a good candidate for sudden demise, being over-weight and with high blood pressure, Phyllis Bolter, the Home's long-standing lay visitor, wasn't immediately ready to believe Mrs Snow's outrageous confession. Perhaps she was rapidly heading for another sojourn in the happy farm? The Home's enigmatic Colonel, Mrs Snow's friend and fellow resident, was already a candidate, forever apparently loading an imaginary clip of ammunition in his walking stick to fight some bloody war single-handed.

But when Miss Green, one of the longest-stay residents, became the next fatal 'incident', then a plan began to form in Phyllis's mind . . .

After years of married misery there seemed no way of freeing herself from the coarse and paunchy Mr Bolter. Not even Councillor Bob Roberts, ably equipped at least to satisfy her most urgent need, could compensate for her present unhappy state. So, when Mrs Snow agreed to consider giving a hand with Mr Bolter, a new future for Phyllis seemed to dawn.

As the fatalities mount up the pressure on Phyllis Bolter, burdened with the complexity of her own domestic situation and finding it difficult to grasp the reality of her involvement in the murderous machinations of her confidante Mrs Snow, tightens to breaking point.

With immense skill and a rare precision Julian Day has portrayed in chilling but humorous and compassionate terms the terminal state of the human condition.

MRS SNOW
AND THE COLONEL

Julian Day

Constable London

First published in Great Britain 1990
by Constable & Company Ltd
10 Orange Street London WC2H 7EG
Copyright © 1990 Julian Day
ISBN 0 09 469910 0
Set in Linotron Palatino 11pt by
CentraCet, Cambridge
Printed in Great Britain by
St Edmundsbury Press Ltd
Bury St Edmunds, Suffolk

A CIP catalogue record for this book
is available from the British Library

1

Mrs Bolter left quietly by the back door of the Home without saying goodbye to anyone and sat in her car, looking across the short stretch of patchy grass and the low wall at the traffic which crawled purposefully and noisily along the main road. But she was not aware of it. She gripped the steering wheel tightly, then suddenly picked up her handbag and rummaged through it for her diary and a pen. She found the day's page, then, resting the diary on her knees, clicked the pen and wrote firmly 'Today Mrs Snow told me that she had killed Mrs South-over'. She replaced the pen and her diary, started the car and strapped herself in. I must forget about it, she thought, put it out of my mind. She's old and she's going mad. She *is* mad. She couldn't possibly be so wicked. I must concentrate on the traffic.

It was at the first set of traffic lights that the indescribable sense of panic took over. She looked up at the signal and stopped; Mrs Snow ought to be draped with red warning lights, she said to herself, she ought to have 'danger, keep away, keep your distance' written all over her. She'd met her in the room kept for visitors to the Home, a place away from the main rooms where tea could be made and sandwiches or cakes eaten after a journey. Mrs Snow had asked to see her there, and when she went in the old woman was seated at the table with cups and saucers arranged in front of her, her walking frame parked by her chair.

'Hallo, Mrs Snow, I'm here,' she said breezily.

'I can see that, dear. Perhaps you'd put the kettle on.'

'We shouldn't be here really. This place is meant for visiting relatives.'

'It's meant for visitors. You visit. We're entitled.'

'But I visit everybody, every day.'

'Well then, like I asked you, visit me; make some tea, there's a dear.'

She watched as Mrs Bolter plugged in the kettle, put tea in the pot, milk in the cups.

'I've got cake here,' she said.

Mrs Bolter poured the tea, cut the cake and put a slice on each of the two plates.

'What did you want to see me about, Mrs Snow? Do you want me to do some special shopping for you?'

'No. I don't want no shopping done, dear. I want to tell you something.' She paused. 'That old cow Mrs Southover who fell downstairs and died last week,' she went on. 'Well, it wasn't any accident.' She paused again for a few seconds. 'I pushed her.'

'You really mustn't say such things, Mrs Snow.' Mrs Bolter was surprised how calm her voice sounded.

'I can say it because it's true, and I'm telling you, not anyone else, so if I get into trouble from them it'll be your fault, not mine.' Mrs Snow was equally calm. 'And watch those crumbs you're putting on the carpet,' she added.

Mrs Bolter looked down at the threadbare imitation Persian square. It's a hessian nightmare, she thought. Carpet, indeed! Watch the crumbs, indeed! She shuddered and looked up at Mrs Snow, who was still looking at her intently.

'It's not true, Mrs Snow. It can't be true. And if it is true, why are you telling me?'

The old woman continued to eat, staring. The pink lids of her unwavering eyes were loose, as if several sizes too large for the sharp bright eyes beneath them. The fingers of her left hand stroked and pushed the squares of cake on her plate into handy morsels, patted them into firm cubes which would not shed crumbs on the short but uncertain journey to her mouth. Her right hand clutched an enormous soft leather handbag which rested on the table, and all the time the dark eyes set in their deep sockets watched and waited. Suddenly her right hand ceased guarding the handbag and moved to brush the thin lips.

'I'm old but I'm not senile,' said Mrs Snow. 'It *is* true and I'm telling you, and you can do what you like about it. I can't help it if you don't want to believe what you hear.'

Mrs Bolter shuddered again and looked away.

'A few crumbs on the floor aren't going to be noticed,' she said inconsequentially. 'Everybody knows that Mrs Southover fell accidentally. Matron herself told me that she had fainted and slipped. It really is very wicked of you to tell such lies.'

She had seen the visiting doctor soon after Mrs South-over's accident just over a week ago. There had been no inquest. Like all the other residents, the unfortunate lady had been in the care of the part-time doctor, newly qualified and heavily pregnant. 'It's my first death since I took the job', Dr Jackson had said; 'one in eight months is well within the range of statistical probability for a Home of this kind – I checked. The majority of the patients are just about ticking over anyway, and a light fall or even a sudden change of temperature could be sufficient to finish them off. Mrs Southover was a good candidate for early demise, overweight and with high blood pressure. She must have fainted and fallen and that was that. Shock is a most effective killer of the elderly.'

Mrs Snow's voice broke into her thoughts.

'All right,' she said. 'I didn't mean to kill her. But she'd been getting on my nerves. A greedy old person she was.' She paused. 'I caught her in my room. Hands in my locker, if you please, and my things all over the floor. She

7

hadn't seen me, so I didn't say anything, not then. Waited until she was outside. Walked along the corridor to the lift with her. When we got to the staircase I said to her "You've been at my things." She was always taking stuff – not only mine – mostly underwear. She should have worn napkins, always wetting herself. It was disgusting. Anyway, she stopped and looked at me. A biggish woman, she was. "And what are you going to do about it, you no account old cow?" she said to me. "Prove it." And I was so incensed I lifted up my frame and knocked her walking stick away. She fell arse over tip down both flights of stairs right to the bottom. Nobody saw. Serves her right too. As she went down I could see that she was wearing a pair of my new long knickers.' Mrs Snow took a long sighing breath, sat back and sipped at her tea.

'It's better than the muck the staff make for us,' she said appreciatively. 'I've always said that they put stuff in the tea to keep us quiet. And they steal our food.' She smiled, the thin lips parting reluctantly and the ill-fitting dentures clicking and sagging ominously. 'Maybe I'll put something in their tea,' she added. 'That'll give them a nice surprise.'

Mrs Bolter grimaced again. 'I don't know if you're making this all up, and I don't wish to know. You really are a very naughty woman, Mrs Snow.'

'I've been watching you visiting; I reckon there's a few sticks you wouldn't mind knocking, eh? Think about it. We could help each other.'

The traffic lights changed and she moved off. Had it really happened? That extraordinary old woman! What on earth did she mean when she said that there were a few sticks you wouldn't mind knocking? And that laugh! She was so frail that she could hardly move without her frame. The frame itself was burdened with her bulbous handbag and a plastic shopping bag stuffed with unfinished knitting. Several times Mrs Bolter had seen her making her way from the Television Room to the Dining Room, always alone. The task took so much effort she must always have been the last to be seated at her table, the last to be served, the last to finish and to return along the corridor. Two hands on the frame, up with it a few inches forward. First one foot and then the other brought up in line with it and then again up with the frame and forward. Moving along the corridor she looked broken, pathetic, but closer her eyes reflected back light like two jet buttons, hard, bright, dangerous. And her voice was impressively strong.

Why pick on me? Mrs Bolter thought resentfully. God alone knows, I do enough for them. And it's a good job I don't expect gratitude because there's precious little of that. Shopping, writing letters, running errands of all kinds, standing up to Matron for them – subsidising them – even placing bets for some of the incorrigible old men. I'll be buggered if I act as Mother Confessor as well. Supposing Mrs Snow's confession was true, how could it be proved if subsequently she denied ever making it? And supposing that it could be proved? Would they take the old dear away in handcuffs and send her to some awful prison for the rest of her days? Not that she's got too many of those to come. And why does she think I'd like to do the same to someone?

She was still asking herself questions when she parked the car outside her house and walked down the path with the empty shopping bags dangling from her wrists and flapping against her knees. Every day, for months, she had gone up there to the Home, sometimes twice a day, weekends too, without a break. You went in through the main entrance to encounter the sour smell of stale urine underlying the cloyingly sweet antiseptic smell of Dettol and the complementary odour of newly wiped backsides and unwashed underwear. The floors of the communal rooms were set with plastic tiling, wiped almost continuously by two very black ladies of West Indian origin wielding grey cloths on the end of long poles. Most of the

9

residents sat around all day, in high-backed chairs, day-dreaming, twitching, belching and breaking wind, the long hours broken only by the routine of meal-times, bath-times, sing-song times, television-times, pill-times, bed-times; the thoughts no higher than the sagging bellies and what next was to be shoved into them. But of course they weren't all like that. So why had Mrs Snow chosen to unburden herself on her, when there were several of the residents to whom she could have turned for a sympathetic hearing?

'I don't propose to listen to another word, Mrs Snow,' she had said, standing up, brushing her lap. 'Not another word.'

The old woman's eyes did not leave hers.

'I told you because it's no use doing things if nobody else knows,' she said. The old hand came up slowly and tapped the sharp nose. 'Matron might believe me, but she wouldn't help. She'd probably have me put away somewhere.'

'What do you mean, wouldn't help you?'

'Wouldn't help me tap some more sticks, of course.' Mrs Snow grinned an infinitely mischievous grin, the button eyes alive. 'I'm going to do some more. You'll help. Miss Green's next. She should be pleased to get away from herself after all these years. And if she isn't pleased, everyone else will be.'

Mrs Bolter knew Miss Green as one of the longest-stay residents. She'd had a colostomy many years ago and had been fitted up with a series of ill-fitting plastic bags ever since. Nobody would sit next to her. Miss Green's end would be a merciful release; but at the thought of being involved in it she had stormed out of the visiting room and out through the back door. How did one cope with that unspeakable old woman and with this unspeakable panic? No one could seriously have said what Mrs Snow had just said. She had a sudden vision of Mrs Southover tumbling softly downstairs, over and over, in slow motion, coming to an abrupt and untidy halt on the corridor floor. Above, Mrs Snow looked down, pointing triumphantly at the long knee-length knickers which the late Mrs Southover was displaying so immodestly. 'I told you so,' she was shrieking. 'I told you so, the thieving old cow.'

As Mrs Bolter put the key in her front-door lock she shook her head from side to side like a dog emerging from water. The old woman had gone mad. Right over the top. She would speak to Matron about her tomorrow. If what she said was true she should be locked up. If it wasn't then at least she should be watched, just in case she decided to act out these fantasies. Going around upsetting people with her mad notions. It wasn't fair. She had more than enough on her plate to cope with.

2

Mr Bolter arrived home and parked untidily, one wheel up on the kerb and the front fender half an inch away from the trunk of the flowering cherry-tree. He stopped to lock the car door, his eyes blinking behind the thick lenses of his spectacles, a premature paunch half-mooning across the belt encircling his trousers. He gave the belt a hitch and turned, walked solemnly up the path, wishing that the path would go on for ever, that the door would shrink and disappear or that the keyhole would close up, or the key melt, disintegrate, explode, anything to delay entry, as he inserted it. But nothing like that happened, it never did. He opened the door and then shut it noisily behind him. She was in, then, cooking for a change; he could smell onions burning, dear God, and thought briefly about going out again. But he was tired. One day I'll come home and all this bloody junk will have been thrown out, he told himself; the piles of newspapers transported to the tip, the clothing collected for jumble sales sent to some unsuspecting charity, and the toe-rag on the floor, over which he tripped daily, placed reverently on some bonfire. He tripped over it on cue and fell forward, heavily, crashing into the table which supported telephone, pencils, pads, directories and various specimens of chipped and broken china; figures, pots, small useless dishes and a weary looking pot plant.

Mrs Bolter came out of the kitchen still holding the knife with which she had been prodding the fast disintegrating lumps in the frying pan which a short while ago had been freshly frozen hamburger patties, 100% pure beef with onion. Too good for him.

'Drunk again?,' she enquired politely.

'Sod off,' he said wearily, and hauled himself upright. He pushed the table back against the staircase as she went back into the kitchen and then replaced the telephone. The other debris looked better on the floor. Not out of place anyway, hardly noticeable in fact. He gave a deep sigh and went into the back room. He wasn't really drunk. There'd been a couple of gins before lunch and a bottle of wine with it – you had to keep the clients happy – and not a thimbleful after. Well, he'd had a couple of fingers of Scotch from his reserve stock – it wasn't every afternoon that one of his juniors announced that he was getting married. He was a promising lad. At least he had been until then. 'This calls for a drink, young Michael,' he remembered saying, 'and if we stick at it – drinking, I mean – we might even persuade you to change your mind.'

Inside the back room he sank into his chair and lit another cigarette.

'Phyllis,' he yelled. What does she do all day? Whatever it was, it wasn't housework. That bottle under the TV was where he had left it last night. All this bloody charity stuff. Visiting old sods. He shrugged his shoulders and eased his belt two holes. We all have to get old, he conceded that, especially if we live long enough, but you had to be a bit queer to fuss around geriatrics the way she did.

'Phyllis,' he called again.

She came to the door, still holding the knife.

'Your meal will be ready in a few minutes,' she said.

He waved his hand deprecatingly, the cigarette describing glowing arcs. Look at the ash, she thought despairingly. I'll kill him.

'It's Michael,' he said. 'He's getting married.'

'Michael who?'

'You met him last year. My number two, area three. At the Dorchester dinner.'

'Why do you always talk in riddles? I haven't the faintest idea who you mean.'

'You've met him! For heaven's sake take an interest, woman.' He dragged desperately at his cigarette and then reached down by the side of his chair for one of the bottles which he kept for such emergencies. 'For Heaven's sake,' he repeated wearily.

'I'll get your food,' she said.

In the kitchen she picked her way to the cooker through the accumulated obstacles of chairs, boxes, tables, a wooden horse festooned with damp clothes, a black plastic sack filled with inanimate things which nevertheless at times seemed to wobble about as if endowed with malevolent life. Must get rid of it tomorrow, she thought. And, stabbing desperately at the contents of the frying pan, I must do something about those empty margarine tubs. The surface of the table, in the middle of the room, on which she prepared food, was reduced effectively to a small square at one end of it. Most of its area was occupied by bottles and jars of one kind or another; one large jar held freshly cut mint, another contained flowers gathered at least a week ago, which were spreading specks of pollen or whatever over a wide area. Adds a welcome touch of horticulture to the diet, she thought, her eyes

13

studiously avoiding the contents of the basket of laundry waiting to be put into the washing machine. She knew she should do something about that but despite her good intentions it seemed daily to get larger and more formidable.

I must talk to him about Mrs Snow, she thought, whatever state he was in – and there was nothing unusual about his present condition. He was her husband, after all. Husbands were to be available for talking over things, problems, things of all kinds.

She transferred the crisped-up crumbles of meat patty on to a plate, added a small mountain of mashed potato which she had prepared from a handy packet in another saucepan and took it into the dining room.

Already he was fast asleep, legs sprawled, jacket off, waistcoat and trouser buttons undone and collar loosened. His head had fallen back and his heavy features glistened with perspiration, his mouth wide open, snoring. She put the plate on the table and stood over him.

Why don't you expire? she thought bitterly; she could hear the pain in her voice as she spoke out loud. 'You've had my youth, my love, the best years of my life and you've ruined the lot. And now there's nothing left. Nothing left but sterile indifference. You want Mrs Snow in here knocking your stick.' Instantly the thought took root and was irresistible. Mrs Snow will see to you, she thought, between the two of us we'll think up something. She knew that she would not need much persuasion to accept that Mrs Snow was one of the world's great benefactors; that one might have a very interesting conversation indeed with that remarkable old lady.

14

3

Ranji Patel lay still in the semi-darkness of his room in the
staff quarters of the Home. Close by, on his bedside table,
his alarm bell began to ring. He got out of bed, fixed the
alarm, went over to the window, pulled back the curtains
to let in the light and leaned against the heavy cast iron
radiator, cold in the early summer morning, staring out at
the traffic which was already gathering in density if not
speed.

It was a long way from his birthplace, his home, in
Bombay. Here there was no material poverty. The old
people were fed and clothed, entertained and given
money. But they had no purpose in life. No function. No
place in the scheme of things. They were a nuisance, an
embarrassment. There were poor people at home; at night
they stretched themselves out on the pavements. They
went to sleep hungry and they got up hungry. At night
they looked up at the warm, star-studded sky and saw
only darkness. Perhaps they drew nourishment from the
smell of the place, rich, thick, foetid; or, as they slept,
from the dreams of the life they would have when they
were next on this earth. But whilst they were alive they
were part of the accepted pattern of things, not put out of
the way, disregarded, unregarded. If they died hungry it
was because the living had little to spare, and life was
hard, and a thankfully short episode in one's spiritual
development.

He turned back into the room and filled the wash-hand
basin in the corner with hot water. The pipes groaned and
knocked as he splashed his face and then rubbed his teeth
with his pink-lined forefinger. He dried himself and went
back to the bed, stripping off his pyjamas, then stretched

15

himself out on the bed, naked, his dark olive skin alien on the crumpled sheets. Mrs Bolter, now, what did she want? What was her game? He smiled to himself. Maybe he would invite her to his room – or perhaps take something to her house. His smile broadened and his tongue tipped the edges of his mouth. She was rich. Must be rich. She ran a good car, dressed in quality clothes. Rarely took money from the old people for the things she bought for them. But there was undoubtedly an air of tension about her, a dangerous air of unpredictability. It added spice to the prospect of a seduction, for a game of humiliation – perhaps for him, maybe for her – it did not matter. Next time she came he would invite her into the visitors' room to take tea, tea brewed from a blend sent to him specially from Sri Lanka, and to try some of the sweet cakes bought in the Indian Emporium which had opened up recently down the road. And then, sooner or later, he could ask her into his room, or make some excuse to call on her. There were things he could show her in private. He laughed out loud.

He got up and dressed quickly, pulling on jeans and a sweat shirt. Along the corridor Matron would be padding about in her self-contained flat; someone would be taking her tea on a tray. He could have morning tea brought to his room too, but the West Indian women stewards had an odour about them which offended the nostrils of a high-class Hindu, BA English (failed) Bombay University. Most women gave off strange smells, but the bandy-legged black women with their frizzy hair and strange accents were beyond the pale, old boy.

Mrs Snow, already washed and dressed and seated strategically as close as possible to the entrance to the dining hall, watched him as he came down the stairs towards her. Slim, tall, straight black hair, handsome profile, dark olive-brown skin and beautiful teeth. Bloody wog, she thought, there was something really crafty about him, something that made her hackles rise whenever he

16

came close. What was a man like that doing in a place like this? Assistant Matron indeed! She clutched her handbag more firmly. He extracted the mail from the inside letter box, unbolted the front door and then went over to her.

'Good morning, Mrs Snow,' he said. 'Up early as usual?' The white teeth flashed in the dark face. With that cough, he thought, and the way she smokes, wouldn't give her another winter. No relatives as far as he knew. Some rings, a chain, could be gold. His eyes flickered over her tiny body. Hardly enough of her to make a decent bonfire. That watch looked like a good one too.

'I slept well, thank you,' she said. 'Any letters for me?' He shuffled the morning's delivery.

'Nothing today, I'm afraid. Perhaps something to-morrow?' He moved on, still smiling.

He knows bloody well nobody ever writes to me, she thought. She opened her handbag and took out her shopping notepad. I'll put him on the list too, she thought as she turned over the well-thumbed pages. In firm flowing script she wrote 'Assistant Matron R. Patel'. He was young and fit and didn't need a walking-stick or frame to keep his balance. It wouldn't be easy but planning it would provide many hours of pleasurable fantasy.

She looked up; fellow residents were beginning to make their way to the dining hall. Some could still manage the stairs. Others emerged from the lift. There were grunts of acknowledgement, some embarrassment – as if the one was surprised that the other had survived the night again, making it more likely statistically that they themselves would soon be answering the last call of nature. There was old Mrs Davies, at ninety-three the oldest resident, hanging on grimly until she got her telegram from the Queen and her picture in the paper. She was a stuck-up old madam, but it wasn't sensible to put her on the list. Him upstairs had already marked her card. Mrs Snow grunted and hauled herself upright to begin the slow laboured procession to her table. Tea, that was all she wanted, she was always dry, and bread and butter. They could keep their cereals and fried stuff, she grimaced, greasy muck. Just a decent cup of tea and a bit of crusty bread and some best butter – not that they ever got either – to chew on, and she'd be happy. Her mouth began watering. Out of the corner of her eye she saw Matron hurrying downstairs and then turn and run, almost, in the direction of her office. She smiled to herself. A boiled egg wouldn't come amiss some mornings, either. She reached her chair and manoeuvred herself safely into it. Somebody from behind – she guessed by the way it splashed into the saucer as well as the cup that it was Pearl rather than Sadie – poured tea, already milked, into the white cups and pushed one towards her. She reached for it eagerly. Already, a couple of minutes from the time breakfast should start, the tables were all fully occupied as far as she could see, except the one in the corner where Miss Green usually ate in solitary state. Mrs Snow's smile manifested itself and widened. Perhaps she would have a sausage this morning, or a bit of bacon, if it was on offer, with a dab of mustard to make it tasty. No harm in dreaming, was there? She sipped her tea. Wait till Mrs Bolter turned up; she had that one's number all right, she'd help sure enough. Together they'd have some fun, talking and planning, and a good laugh. It was better than waiting for pneumonia to get you, whichever way you looked at it.

4

Mrs Bolter twitched once and woke up. She reached for her glasses by the side of the bed and saw that the clock showed eight-thirty. He'd be gone by now. He hadn't come up to bed again – it was getting to be a rare event indeed when he did. How he could sleep down there all night in that uncomfortable chair was beyond her. She shivered; if it wasn't so bloody insulting she'd be laughing. On the few occasions when he did come up, smelling of drink and stale cigarette smoke, swearing and lurching about, knocking things over, his crude fumblings and the sheer grunting weight of him were unbearably degrading. He'd never been much good that way and she had had to turn elsewhere early on in their marriage for what should have been her marital pleasures. She smiled and lay back, began stroking herself and, half dreaming, conjured up a vision of the new young manager in the paper shop in the parade. She dressed him in a splendid uniform with epaulettes which went on for ever and masses of gold braid and buttons on a plum velvet tunic. He had shiny black riding boots with white riding breeches, which had a button-down flap in front. He smiled at her. 'My darling,' he said, 'you are so beautiful, your skin so white, so smooth,' and cupped her breasts with his enormous hands. She groaned and lifted her arms to welcome him. There was a sudden noise downstairs and she sat up, startled, listening, the vision banished. There were grunts and more thuds. She got up and put on a dressing-gown and went to investigate.

Mr Bolter, still slightly befuddled with a hangover, was in the kitchen shaving in front of a scrap of mirror propped up on the kitchen-sink taps. There were patches of blood on his chin and he had the desperate air of a man who was late for an important meeting, trying to claw back lost time and succeeding only in making life even more tiresome.

'You're late,' she said.

'I don't need you to tell me that I'm late. I know I'm late. And now you're up, why don't you do something about this place? It's not fit for a pig.'

She drew her dressing-gown tightly around her.

'And why don't you shave in the bathroom? This is my kitchen.'

'Your kitchen? No one else would want your bloody kitchen, that's for certain. Can you at least put on the kettle? Make some tea or something?'

She plugged in and switched on the kettle.

'That's the most useful thing you've done all week,' he grunted. 'How you can cook anything in here is beyond belief. Not that you could cook anywhere else either.' He wiped his face and splashed on some powerfully smelling after-shave lotion which he kept under the sink with his shaving gear, next to the Vim, a scummy-looking plunger and a box of rusting Brillo pads.

'How you can go on the way you do is beyond me,' he went on. The kettle spouted steam already. She unplugged it and shook it. It was almost empty. 'Can't even boil a kettle of water.' He shook his head in mock disbelief. 'For Chrissake get yourself organised, you dozy woman,' he shouted.

She stared at him. He was a large man. In singlet and trousers his paunch, noticeably larger in girth than when she had last observed it at close quarters, was sagging aggressively. She smiled. An aggressive sag to his paunch. Not a bad description, that. His paunch threatened her, she said to herself, more than half pleased with her flight of fancy.

'For Chrissake,' he said bitterly. 'Forever mooning about.' Then his face crimsoned. 'All this bloody stuff on the draining board.' With a sudden wide gesture he swept an assorted array of cartons, dirty dishes, utensils, a soapdish filled with the slimy ends of bars, and a potted plant, crashing into the sink. 'And this!' He charged over to the corner and kicked her neat stack of margarine tubs into a shapeless pile of plastic. 'And all this rotten germ-ridden rubbish.' With another grand sweep a row of potted plants rattled noisily to the floor. 'Now perhaps you'll tidy up,' he shouted, and stamped out of the room.

20

She stared around her in total disbelief. Before, it had been admittedly chaotic, but at least she knew where everything was and what she planned to do with it – if not right now, then sometime, as soon as she could get round to it. But now it looked as if some wild animal had been let loose and had rampaged about. She went to the kitchen door. He was halfway up the stairs, which were creaking noisily under the weight of his furious ascent.

'Come back here,' she screamed up at him. 'Come back here. How dare you! Come back here at once and clear up this mess.'

She could hear him in the bathroom overhead. Although he slept in his day clothes and never, these days, as far as she could tell, changed his underwear during the week, every day he put on a clean shirt over the deodorants and after-shave lotions which were his usual method of making his physical presence acceptable in an air-conditioned office with no windows. By Saturday he stank, on Sunday he'd take a bath and the process would begin all over again. Like a good wife, she washed and ironed his shirts and the week's supply was draped, each Monday, on hangers on the towel rail over the bathroom radiator. 'Must have my shirts well aired,' he informed her. 'We're subject to arthritis in my family. Sod the towels, you can dry them off somewhere else.'

Clean shirt, she thought desperately. I'll give him clean shirt. She heard muffled oaths as he dressed himself, then more footsteps as he came out of the bathroom and made his way downstairs.

'Is that bloody tea ready yet?' he demanded.

'Get your own bloody tea,' she shouted, 'and your own bloody dinner and bloody everything else from now on. Get out and don't bother to come back.' She moved towards him with clenched fists.

He adjusted his glasses and stared at her coldly. 'So you want to settle things physically, do you? Reverting to type, is it? And if I'm so unbearable, you get out, go on, leave.'

She thumped him on the chest, unable to speak, her face contorted.

'Feel better does it?' he enquired soothingly. 'What about a goodbye kiss then?' His hands closed over hers and she felt trapped, helpless.

'Look at this mess. I hate you,' she managed to sob. He pushed her to the side of the hall and went into the kitchen again. She heard him walking about, crunching things underfoot, and she held herself tightly as he came out.

'Mess?' he said jovially. 'What mess? Doesn't look any different from usual to me.'

He opened the front door and then came back and chucked her under the chin.

'I'll be in late tonight,' he said. 'Don't bother to wait up for me.' The door slammed behind him. A few seconds later she heard the sound of his car starting and then, above it, his voice calling to someone, a near neighbour perhaps, as if there were no problems, the sun was shining and everything in the garden was absolutely bloody lovely.

'Be late. I'll be waiting up for you. I hate you, you bastard, I hate you,' she screamed at the closed door.

Stupid cow, he thought as he drove to the top of the road and paused to light a cigarette, the second of the day, before pointing the nose of his car into the stream of traffic along the main road. Only one way to make a right-hand turn, he said to himself as he gulped down a lungful of smoke; shut your eyes and get stuck in. There was a shrieking of brakes behind him and he waved non-chalantly as the driver swerved past him angrily, shaking a clenched fist.

Another stupid sod, he thought, weekend driver. Not like us daily commuters, know what to expect, cut and thrust, had every inch of the road between home and office mapped out, knew to a tyre's width where to position the car at every crossing and every set of lights. Bet the car could find its own way there and back if he was blindfolded. It certainly seemed to know where to go when he drove home at night after taking a few drinks. He patted the dash board affectionately. 'You and me,' he said out loud. 'Come shit come snow, we can make it together.' He took another pull on his cigarette and the smoke caught in his throat. He coughed and hacked and bent over involuntarily with the suddenness of it. Almost at the same time there was a sickening crunch as his car was struck squarely in the middle from the off side and slewed around. He stood on the brakes and switched off the engine. There was another crunch almost immediately as the car behind him skidded to a halt by slamming into him, jerking him back hard against his seat and neck rest.

'You stupid bastards,' he yelled, and struggled out of his belt and seat and forced his way out of the nearside door. Already, within the space of a few seconds, a queue of stationary traffic had formed behind him and the line was building up.

The woman driver of the car which had first hit him sat white-faced, clutching the driving wheel of her car tightly as if for protection. His angry face, contorted and working furiously, pressed against her nearside window. 'Open up,' he shouted, 'open up. Let's see your licence and insurance. Look at the damage you've done.'

She wound down the window.

'You should have let me in,' she protested. 'I gave you plenty of warning.'

Mr Bolter spluttered. The driver of the car behind came into view, fumbling unsteadily for his identification.

'Terribly sorry old boy,' he said. 'There just wasn't time to dodge you. Take one of my cards. It was all this stupid woman's fault. You must take my name as a witness.'

Mr Bolter managed a grunt, feeling slightly mollified at this unexpected support.

23

'Women,' he said despairingly.

The other driver nodded. 'Shouldn't be on the road, most of them,' he said. Together they turned on the unfortunate lady.

'You ought to have your licence suspended,' snarled Mr Bolter, 'and if I have anything to do with it, it will be.'

'A fine's not sufficient for dangerous drivers like you,' chimed in the other driver. 'You should be locked up. You're lucky this gentleman wasn't fatally injured.'

Mr Bolter nodded his complete agreement. As far as he could see, the damage was fairly superficial and the car could be driven. He was unhurt. He had read somewhere that drivers in London could expect to be involved in at least one accident a year, and he'd had more than his share. But, touch wood, they had all been in the mornings when he was sober, never at night when he might have been guilty of a spot of over-indulgence. Insurance would take care of the damage and his firm paid the premiums. Let her sweat a bit, he thought, beginning to enjoy himself. The day, which had started out so unpleasantly, was unfolding rather more to his liking. Across the street he saw a policeman threading his way through the lighter traffic on the other side of the road.

'Over here, officer,' he called, waving his hands in the air. 'The culprit's right here.' He reached in through the open window of her car, removed the keys from the ignition and dangled them triumphantly in the air. 'She won't get away,' he called. 'We'll see to that.'

His newly found friend nodded approvingly. 'Good for you, old boy,' he said. 'Have a cigarette.'

Mr Bolter lit up. Pity he wouldn't be home until late tonight, he thought, he'd enjoy telling this tale to his ever-loving. Providing of course she'd cleared up that appalling mess she had the cheek to call her kitchen.

Mrs Bolter had in fact cleared away the debris in her kitchen and had carried out her morning's shopping in a complete daze, filling her trolley from the list without

24

even bothering to check the prices or the sell-by dates on the packets. He's insulted me for the last time, she thought, slamming cans on top of egg cartons and bottles of tonic water on top of everything. At the Home there was a bar run by Matron, but it was poorly stocked and the prices were high. Those who could afford it had bottles of spirits brought in and got Mrs Bolter to top up their supplies of tonic water or ginger ale as required. She bought whatever fruit was being offered at bargain prices and in the evenings went from one resident to another offering it at less than cost. Secretly she imagined herself to be some kind of superior Nell Gwynne – and look whose bed she had ended up in.

Her shopping somehow done, she drove home and unloaded her bags. Perhaps the house was in a bit of a mess. Life itself was more than a bit of a mess and very confusing at times. He was a mess himself and had no grounds for criticising it or her. And he was going to get what he deserved. She found the prospect of something dreadful happening to him to be infinitely exhilarating. 'Freedom from that lout,' she said out loud. She hugged herself. Dear God, she thought, all those wasted years. Were they really coming to an end at last? And what did Mrs Snow get out of it? A modicum of sweet revenge on society in the closing years of a life which clearly had not been an easy one? She needed to talk to her some more.

But what about Mrs Southover? she thought. Whatever the quality of her life had been, just as clearly she must have been reluctant to depart prematurely for higher planes, since she had clung to her empty existence so tenaciously, thieving to the last. What did she gain? And what was in it for the others on Mrs Snow's list? But it was nonsense thinking like this. It was all a game, a kind of amateur theatricals, none of it was real or existed outside Mrs Snow's warped imagination. She went upstairs, changed her dress and made up her face. Mrs

Snow has such an interesting face, she thought. I'll go and talk to her, see how she is today.

As she neared the Home she saw an ambulance come out of the drive-in. There were no flashing lights and she had heard no obnoxious wailing noises, so it couldn't be an emergency. Someone being taken to an out-patient's appointment at the hospital, perhaps, or a new resident transferred from hospital. She parked her car and walked in, carrying the errands she'd bought that morning. It all seemed to be as peacefully odorous as usual, with sounds coming from the TV room along the corridor and cluttering and banging noises from the direction of the kitchen. Matron came out of her office as she passed the door. She was holding a clipboard and her sallow face wore a seriously important expression.

'Can't stop now, Mrs Bolter,' she said. 'There's been another incident, I'm afraid.'

Mrs Bolter knew that an incident in Matron's vocabulary was a sad event in hers.

'Sorry to hear that,' she said. 'I'll just cut along and distribute these errands.'

Matron paused. 'Did Miss Green ever ask you to fetch anything for her?' she asked. 'Any drinks, spirits for example?'

Mrs Bolter shook her head. 'She rarely asked me to get anything for her. A packet of Kleenex occasionally. Never any drink of any kind. Why do you ask?'

'I'm afraid she's no longer with us, that's all. And it's a bit of a mystery really where she got hold of it. We wondered if she'd suddenly been asking you to buy her drink.' She sniffed. 'She's certainly not been patronising the bar, I can tell you.'

'She surely hasn't drunk herself to death then?'

Matron shook her head. 'Nothing like that,' she said. 'But I must be off. You'll be in as usual tonight? We'll have a talk then.'

Mrs Bolter nodded. 'Yes, of course,' she said automatically. Don't like that bossy little woman, she said to herself for the hundredth time as Matron hurried away. She was an ex-army sister with all the proper qualifications and had spent years abroad looking after our servicemen. 'I was an officer of course – Queen Alexandra's Nursing Corps. Devoted my life to the army . . .' And to the bottle, she should have added, thought Mrs Bolter, who drank moderate quantities of cheap sherry as a 'tonic', and who couldn't abide women who drank. She shuddered. Mrs Snow had said that Miss Green would be next, and Miss Green was now, in Matron's words, an incident. Perhaps it was her body that the ambulance had come to collect. 'I must talk to Mrs Snow,' she said out loud.

She stopped by the door of the TV lounge as the Home's enigmatic Colonel emerged. He nodded gravely, his tall figure bent over the too-short walking stick. He was in one of his lucid moods.

'Good morning,' he said politely.

Mrs Bolter nodded. 'Is Mrs Snow in there?' she asked, peering into the half-darkened room.

'I fear not,' he said. 'But I know where she is. In the visiting room. She's expecting a visitor.'

'Oh, good.' She thrust the errand bags into his unoccupied hand. 'Be a dear,' she said. 'Here's a list and there's the errands. Would you mind awfully handing them out? Don't bother about the money. I'll see to that later.'

She left him and almost ran down the corridor. There was only one visitor Mrs Snow expected, and her name was Phyllis Bolter.

Mrs Snow was indeed waiting, impatiently expectant.

'I thought you might be coming in this morning,' she said, 'so I came down here in case you wanted to talk.' The sharp eyes revealed nothing.

Mrs Bolter filled and plugged in the kettle.

'There's a dear,' said Mrs Snow. 'A nice cup of tea. You must have heard the news. Poor Miss Green. Funny we

27

should have been talking about her only yesterday. A merciful release.'

Mrs Bolter nodded her agreement. 'I've just seen Matron,' she said.

'And what did she say?'

'She implied that Miss Green had been drinking secretly and asked if I had been bringing in any alcohol for her.'

'Silly old cow,' commented Mrs Snow.

'You had nothing to do with it, did you?'

Mrs Snow allowed herself a grin. 'Whatever do you mean?' she said. Her bent claw-like finger touched her nose and then tapped it. Mrs Bolter felt her blood run cold.

'Well, if it's of interest to you,' said Mrs Bolter, 'I don't believe that you had anything to do with either Mrs Southover or Miss Green.'

'Of course, my dear,' said Mrs Snow. 'You believe what you like. It's a free country.' Then she added, 'But I know what I know.'

Mrs Bolter made the tea and sat down.

'So tell me what you know,' she said.

Mrs Snow's smile faded. 'Matron's nearly got it right,' she said flatly. 'Miss Green's been in a state for years. She's put up with her lot, no grumbles, but there's a limit to the amount of suffering and indignity one can take and she finally ran out of patience. What's strange is that she didn't make an effort to go years ago. Perhaps she did, but there was nobody around to help her. And maybe she was used to those plastic bags. Maybe she didn't even smell them. But I did. I have a very sharp sense of smell.'

'And you helped her?'

Mrs Snow ignored the interruption. 'She took stuff to help her sleep,' she went on. 'They gave her a couple of tablets every night, strong ones, but they never stayed to see if she took them. Perhaps she saved up a week's doses, or more, and took them all at once. And if she

28

washed them down with a tot of whisky, or even a couple of tots for luck, it could be fatal, couldn't it?'

Mrs Bolter poured the tea and pushed a cup towards Mrs Snow.

'That's one explanation,' she said. 'Another might be that some kind friend took her a tot of whisky some nights to help her sleep and that one night, last night in fact, it was an extra big tot and had something else added to it.'

Mrs Snow nodded sagely. 'Could be,' she said, 'especially if that friend had been doing the same thing with her own sleeping pills. But we'll never know, will we? We all need a helping hand occasionally.' She paused. 'But I've decided that it's best for you not to know everything. You do what I ask and no questions, then you don't need to worry about things. If you worry, you might blab. To your husband perhaps. And he might tell someone else, and before you know what's what, it'll be in the Daily Mirror . . . and then there'll be nothing to look forward to, if you get my meaning.'

'You needn't worry about Mr Bolter,' said Mrs Bolter. Then she added, as lightly as she dared, 'Put him on the list too.'

Mrs Snow picked up the tea cup and slowly the cup found her mouth. She made loud sucking noises as she sipped the tea.

'Give us a biscuit then, will you, dear,' she said after a few seconds. 'I thought that you might help me,' she said slowly, 'but I didn't really think that you might want me to help you. That's a turn up and no mistake.'

Mrs Bolter moved closer. 'I'll help you,' she whispered. 'All I want from you is a bit of moral support. And maybe some ideas. And I'll visit you here and we can plan and talk about it. And I'll take you to my place and we can talk about it there. You can meet Mr Bolter. When you've met him you'll understand more. You'll be on my side, I know. I'll go mad if I have to put up with him any longer.'

Mrs Snow finished demolishing her biscuit.

29

'I'll certainly need to know why you want your husband on the list before I can work up any enthusiasm for it,' she said. 'I've never met the man. There's enough to do thinking about people here without bothering about someone I don't even know. But I'm willing to consider it for your sake. You fetch me for lunch next Sunday – you'll have a bit of roast meat for lunch on Sunday, I'm sure, I'd like that. I'll come and case the joint.' She laughed, a choking, neighing sound as if she was flexing some little-used part of her vocal chords and wasn't certain that the exercise was all that worthwhile. 'Case the joint,' she repeated and Mrs Bolter didn't quite know whether to laugh or to cry. Mrs Snow's good humour evaporated suddenly. With an air of infinite innocence she said 'And next time you come perhaps you might bring me in a nice bottle of whisky, dear, for medicinal purposes only of course. I'm clean out of it. Somebody seems to have purloined my last lot – it's all gone, anyway – and I'm sure I only had a mouthful of it.'

5

Assistant Matron Patel watched Mrs Bolter close the door of the visitors' room behind her. She stood for a few seconds, apparently staring into space. He walked softly along the corridor. He was aware that Mrs Snow had manoeuvred her way into the room that morning, and that it was the second time within a few days that Mrs Bolter had gone along there too. What were they up to? Whilst there were no rules or regulations to say that the room should not be used in that way, it was unusual, almost a breach of privilege in his view. Mrs Bolter had no official standing. It might be a good opportunity to remind

30

her of that fact and then to gloss over it, making her feel obligated to him.

'Good morning, Mrs Bolter,' he said, his white teeth flashing.

Mrs Bolter snapped to. 'Good morning, Mr Patel,' she said nervously. 'You startled me.'

'All the time I ask you to call me Ranji, and all the time it is Mr Patel.' His smile widened. 'I hope there is nothing wrong? Mrs Snow is a very difficult resident. She makes trouble, you know. A most aggressive old lady.'

'Nothing wrong at all, nothing. She's got nobody else. If I give her a bit more attention now and then it's because she's never had an outside visitor. Most of the others have someone, sometime, and if she's difficult, what can you expect?'

'What indeed, dear lady,' he said smoothly. 'We would miss having you call so regularly. I was saying only yesterday to Matron what a wonderful person you are, spending so much of your time here, day after day, and these old people are really greatly appreciative, as we all are.'

'I don't know about that. Sometimes I think that they think I'm making a fortune out of them. They don't understand how prices rise all the time and how little their money buys now compared with a few years ago. I subsidise them quite substantially, I'm afraid.'

He nodded in sympathy. 'You are a good person,' he said. 'A good woman.' They began walking in the direction of the main entrance, which was reached through a lounge area furnished with an assortment of high-back and easy chairs which were clearly well used. There were a few shelves under the side window carrying an assortment of books, paperbacks and magazines. At right angles to the wall there was an old piano, a dark-stained and well-thumped upright which was the focal point for the afternoon entertainment times.

'We know very well what you do for them,' he went

31

on. 'People would not believe that it costs you good money to do these things. They talk nonsense to each other. Gossips. It would be such a pity if we had to stop or curtail your visits. They would be the losers. Very much so the losers.'

She halted in her tracks. 'Stop my visits? Why should anyone want to do that?'

'Nobody wants to, dear lady. You are very privileged, rightly so, and nobody wishes to see these privileges taken away. But others see you visit Mrs Snow in the visitors' room and are jealous. They talk. Get upset. This is bad for them. As I was saying to Matron, what an exceedingly good tonic for our residents you are, and how you would be missed.'

'There's no question of that,' she snapped. 'And if anyone here suggests that I should stop coming, Councillor Roberts would want some very compelling reasons indeed.'

'You are a friend of Councillor Roberts?' He knew that Mr Roberts was chairman of the Council's Social Services and Welfare Committee, and as such took a very active interest in the running of the three old people's homes in the district. He was also tipped as being likely to be the next mayor. A useful person to know indeed. His manner changed subtly and although he said nothing his smile widened even further.

'We were at school together, as a matter of fact,' she said, 'and it was he who suggested that I should take on this kind of voluntary work after my breakdown. But that was long before you were appointed here,' she added quickly, hoping that he hadn't noticed what she had said. Not many people knew about her breakdown, the dreadful time which her dear husband was pleased to call her 'puggled' period, an experience from which, he had repeatedly assured her, nobody every wholly recovered. But Ranji did not pursue that point; he merely noted it for future reference.

32

'Any friend of Councillor Roberts is a friend of ours,' he said. 'And of course we would not listen to any ridiculous suggestion that your visits here should stop, whoever made it. If it was made, I, we, would not allow it.'

His smile was infinitely non-reassuring, thought Mrs Bolter.

'And you will be particularly early on Saturday for Open Day?' he asked.

'Of course,' said Mrs Bolter. 'Haven't I practically organised Open Day for the past few years? There's no chance that I'm going to be late.'

'I shall be off duty,' he said, 'but I will come down and see how I can help. Please assume that I, and my car, will be entirely at your service in the morning.'

'I'll let you know,' said Mrs Bolter, still very much on her dignity. Perhaps he hadn't noticed what she had said about her breakdown. Or perhaps everybody he knew had breakdowns; it wouldn't be surprising if the whole of the Council's staff on social and welfare work had breakdowns, the amount and type of work that was put on them.

'Yes, I'll certainly let you know,' she repeated.

'Please remember me to Councillor Roberts and give him my regards.'

She inclined her head graciously.

She was good at remembrances . . .

She remembered very well indeed when Bob Roberts suggested that she might do some voluntary work in the Borough. 'There's a whole heap of things you could do,' he had said. They were in bed at the time, she recalled, and he had been trying, one way or another, without success, to satisfy her for well over half an hour.

'You should relax more,' he had complained bitterly. 'I've never had this trouble before – you ought to do something to take your mind off things. Get you out of yourself. Make a new woman of yourself, and a new life for yourself, instead of worrying about him.' By 'him' she inferred that he meant her husband. 'And that little bitch of yours,' an apt description of her adopted daughter.

He was a big man, and he had been a very large youth. During their last term at school together – how many years since? – he had acquired a well-deserved reputation as the school's randiest ram. He had tried dating her several times, but she had already decided which of her contemporaries was to relieve her of the burden of her virginity. The chosen one was a tall gangling youth, very shy, very reserved. She remembered still the startled expression on his face when she had sought him out in the school library. They were both working on the same subjects for their Advanced Levels and she had laid her plans after some months of observing him at close proximity. He was refreshingly cerebral and old-fashioned, someone she could manage.

'I can't seem to get the hang of this Old Chaucerian English, Philip,' she recalled saying. 'Of all the nonsense – "a poore wydwye woman, somnel stappe haste" – I ask you!'

He coloured up. 'It isn't easy,' he admitted. 'The only way I can get round it is to try and imagine that I'm back in the period, with all the odd people Chaucer wrote about, and then to say the words out loud and listen to them and then to try and think in them. It makes it so much more real, somehow.'

'Sounds a good idea,' she said, 'but we can't chatter away in mediaeval English in here.' Then she added, as if the thought had just struck her, 'Come over to my place on Saturday afternoon. We can have tea in the garden and maybe you can help me to improve my vocabulary; you can tell me all you know about Chaucer. How about it?'

'If you like. I'll bring my notes. And maybe we can do a spot of biology as well. I'm well behind with my reading and I know you're on top with it.'

34

She smiled serenely. 'See you about three o'clock, then.'
She'd give him a biology lesson to remember, she thought.

He stood up and smiled in return. He really had a very
interesting face, she thought, with those high cheekbones,
that strong nose and chin and that great domed forehead.
But he was very young for his age, very serious, always
working. Pity his father was only a bus-driver, she could
have made a very big play for him.

On the Saturday she had watched from her bedroom
window high up in the front of the house, hoping to see
him climbing the hill towards it. Her father was a bank
executive and her mother owned and ran an expensive
Beauty Salon in the suburb. At weekends he played golf
and she worked. Sometimes her mother would look at her
and sigh and suggest that she might like to make an
appointment at the Salon for some advice. 'Do something
about your hair, dear . . . And you really should be
wearing a bra.' Coming up for eighteen, she was a large,
disorganised, well-built young woman who led the
school's debating team earnestly and with passion, played
chess very badly and wrote inferior poetry incessantly. At
that time, she recalled, she was on her vegetarian kick,
and with it went one or two other expressions of her
growing individuality. She would cycle for miles with her
friend Maude, who was undergoing the same kind of
changes in attitude and conviction with equal fervour.
They talked almost without taking breath, and without
apparently listening to each other – except for the weekend when Maude had confessed that the night before she
had sacrificed her maidenhead, quite voluntarily and
almost, she said, without premeditation, to a young man
her brother had brought down with him from University
for the weekend. Maude's version of the event had left
nothing in the telling and it was all very curious.

She watched all afternoon, almost without moving,
staring at the point where Philip should first appear.

But he didn't come.

It was the following Monday, after brooding about her unhappy non-experience, and after a long bike ride on the Sunday when Maude had persuaded her not to commit suicide, that she put into operation the new plan of compaign they had worked out together. She walked out of school with Bob Roberts; even then he was big and beefy, in his last year. Their parents were golf acquaintances and their houses a few streets from each other.

'Walk through the park with me, Robert,' she said.

He grinned. 'If I carry your books, what sort of reward do I get?'

'What sort do you want?'

'You know me.'

She smiled at him, provocatively, she hoped.

'Yes, I know all about you,' she said. 'You take girls to the cinema and expect them to let you do it as part of the evening's entertainment.'

'You've got it all wrong,' he protested. 'Girls take me to the cinema and it's only fair that I should give them the benefit of my experience. They expect it.'

'You're a conceited pig.'

'I know. When are you going to take me to the cinema?'

'I wouldn't waste my time and money,' she said. 'Have you ever done it here, in the park?'

'Want me to show you my favourite place?'

They walked along in silence for a few minutes.

Conceited pig was just about right, she thought.

Play my cards and here's another one for my little black book, he thought. Perhaps next weekend. There was a good film due on at the local Gaumont. He'd even sport the price of a couple of seats to get across her – one of the few to resist his enterprise and youthful charms so far.

The gravelled path followed the meanderings of a small stream which rumour had it emptied eventually into the Thames. On the other side of the stream there was an embankment which carried the local railway line used by commuters to the City. The trains were infrequent, but regular; one could almost set one's watch by them. Between the path and the stream there were several clumps of hawthorns and elderberries, a scattering of horse-chestnut trees which boys ill-treated unmercifully in the autumn in their search for conkers. Behind one of the groups of trees and bushes there was a solitary bench, hidden from view from any casual path walker but known to all the locals as the site of much nocturnal hanky-panky. At night it seated courting couples and lovers who over the years in the full frenzy of their transient passions has hacked messages of love and hope, hearts and arrows, all over it. In more recent times it had been over-sprayed liberally with Glo-paint by lovesick and not obviously talented artists. The seat could be seen, from the other side of the stream, from the windows of trains passing by on the embankment, but at night that was clearly of little consequence.

She nodded towards the bushes.

'I'll bet that's one of your places,' she said. 'Let's have a tour of inspection.'

At the seat she turned and looked at him challengingly. 'I'll bet you've never done it here in daylight.'

He fingered his collar.

'You're right,' he said. 'I believe there's a bye-law about it.'

'You're scared.'

He stared at her. 'Well, I'll be blowed,' he said. A sly grin crept across his face. He looked around. 'I'll tell you what,' he said. 'I'm game if you are.'

He dropped the books he was carrying and sat on the bench. 'Come and sit down,' he said.

She sat next to him and he kissed her roughly. At the same time his hand slid up her skirt, breaching the elastic of her knickers and she wriggled so that he could get at her more easily.

He came up for air, stood up and loosened his belt and unzipped his fly. She scrambled out of her knickers and

37

stuffed them into her blazer pocket. She tried to stretch out full length on the bench, but the seat was curved and there was the remains of an iron divider in the centre of it.

'No, no,' he said urgently. 'Sit up, lean back, that's right.'

He eased down his pants and underpants.

'Be careful,' she said breathlessly. 'It's the first time.'

He seemed to be smothering her completely and she gasped as he broke into her and began pumping away enthusiastically. 'It won't be the last,' she heard him mutter, and then she gasped again as she felt him rising in her and filling her. At that moment, precisely on time, the 3.45 pm train sauntered past on the embankment. As she buried her head in his shoulder, whilst he carried on relentlessly, she caught glimpses of anonymous, startled faces behind the carriage windows.

It's the last time here, that's for sure, she thought. And if this is what it's all about, the next time will be a long way off. She tapped him on the shoulder as the end carriage disappeared out of sight.

'That's enough,' she grunted. 'Off with you.'

But there was no holding him back now. She reached around his backside and gripped his appendages. They were soft and tight and heavy and she squeezed them, hard. He reared up and she slipped away from him sideways. She saw him glaring at her, his face brick red with frustration and anger and pain.

'That's a bit thick,' he managed to mumble.

'So is that,' she said, pointing. 'Put it away.'

He still looked mortally offended, but he began to hitch up his trousers.

'You put it away,' he challenged.

She finished putting back her knickers, smoothed her skirt, then reached in her pocket for a handkerchief. With a shudder she covered his manhood with it and then, without bothering to pull up his underpants, zipped up his fly. A tuft of pubic hair came up with the zip and he leaped into the air, clutching himself and moaning loudly.

'Why don't you castrate me while you're about it?' he yelled.

She picked up her books, smoothed her hair and looked at his woebegone face as he bent over double on the seat, still holding himself. He looked back at her, furious.

'I'm off home,' she said. Then took pity on him. 'I'm sorry it wasn't good for you,' she said. 'But the train put me right off.'

'And you can bugger off,' he said. 'It's the last time I walk through the park with you. You give me the ballsache.'

She patted his head. 'Come up to the house next Saturday,' she said. 'About three o'clock. There's no trains there.'

It was the beginning of a relationship that was still going strong. They had both married, produced or adopted children, remained in the same locality and they still made love; not as frequently now as they had done decades ago, but regularly. It was an oddly comfortable relationship based, she mused, on a kind of perverted mutual respect. He understood and appreciated her need for sexual fulfilment which he prided himself he had both awakened and satisfied. On her part, she admired his undiminished enthusiasm and the superb technique and control which he had developed over the years; the way in which he had rarely failed to bring her to a very vocal climax. And despite their respective marriages, they had remained firm friends; let anyone, particularly this Asian smoothy, even suggest that her visits to the Home should be rationed; she'd have Bob Roberts down on him so effectively that he'd wish he was back in Bombay and no mistake.

*

39

Ranji Patel watched her closely. For a few seconds she clearly had been mentally somewhere else, had drifted off into some other private existence of her own, although he had been even more aware of her physical presence as a woman. There was something oddly sensual about her, he thought, despite her generally other-world air, her plain skirts and blouses and her sensible low-heeled shoes. In fact her clothes effectively hid a figure which still made Bob Roberts suck his teeth in appreciation when it was revealed to him. I must see what I can do about her very soon, thought Ranji, she reminded him so much of the pictures he had seen of the Hindu Temple in Madras, the stone figures, melon-breasted, acrobatic, graceful, copulating gleefully in every direction. Instead of thick tweedy stuff she should be dressed in diaphanous trousers, with dangling ear-rings and an egg-sized ruby stuck in her navel. He licked his thin brown lips.

She came to with a brief shudder.

'You're looking most odd, Mr Patel,' she said. 'Most odd indeed.'

He smiled. 'We'll see you bright and early on Saturday morning then?'

'Never fear,' she said. 'Let's hope that we have some decent weather. The old ones do so like sitting in the sun.'

6

Mrs Snow stirred uneasily in her sleep and awoke in the semi-darkness of the early hours of Saturday morning. Sleep came reluctantly these days and then returned whence it came at the slightest excuse. What was it this time? she asked herself. First, she listened to herself, to the strong slow beat of her ancient heart, then to the various familiar and comforting gurglings and rumblings from other parts of her. Then she checked the pains; behind the eyes, behind the forehead, in her back, and radiating from the stainless steel hip-joint which had improved her mobility by about five per cent and had not ceased to give her trouble and discomfort since it was first fitted. Slowly she finished pushing and poking and probing her frail body. It all seemed to be no worse than usual. She was still alive, then. She opened her eyes. Someone was in her room; the shape outlined against the window. She made no sound; her eyes felt heavy and sore, and she allowed her lids to slide together again as if sleep had reclaimed her. Momentarily the shape had reminded her of her daughter, now getting old herself, so many miles away, and of her children and the children's children, known only through photographs.

It was becoming more and more difficult now to tell whether one was awake or dreaming. And yet at other times her mind was as sharp and as clear as ever, a match for anyone. If she had only known then what she knew now, life would have been very different for her. Ending her days in a Home full of catty old women was a disgusting finale. The men weren't much better, but then they were after all only men. The Colonel was different, bless him, a clever man and the master of many practical skills when he was rational, but hopelessly confused when he wasn't. Do anything for her, that was a fact. The shape against the window had gone when she opened her eyes again. Perhaps it had never been there in the first place. It didn't matter much anyway. She sighed. Soon it would be Open Day, another penance for unmentionable sins committed in her youth, she thought. Was I really that bad? She smiled to herself and went back to sleep.

When he heard her breathing regularly again, Ranji Patel left her room and paused outside it, listening to make quite certain that she had gone back to sleep, and then moved on, reassured. Every night he walked through each of the rooms in the Home at least twice, checking to

41

see that everything was in order, quietly moving like a tall, thin wraith, melting into the darkness when necessary to avoid being seen, disappearing around corners and vanishing, it seemed, into thin air. It was not part of his duties; there was a night team always on call from 7 p.m. to 7 a.m. But the Home was his domain, the residents were his people, and there was a not-to-be-denied compulsion to look after them. And their things. It was his duty, his right. They and theirs were his.

Mrs Snow was awake again; she knew that it was probably his presence that she had sensed in her room earlier, that it was his outline she had half seen. She was fully awake now. Curiosity killed the cat, she said to herself, and smiled. He'd come to no good, sneaking in and out of people's rooms uninvited – especially hers. He was a nuisance, prowling about all night. With the night staff you knew where you were. Two patrols before midnight, then they too got their heads down and slept, sensibly.

Light was beginning to creep into the corner of her room. It was early morning, and she felt good, because she knew that before the end of the day, a day which would be stuffed with the appalling tribulations and humiliations of Open Day, the solution to the problem of what to do about Mr Ranji Patel would suddenly pop into her head, ready made, foolproof and within her restricted ability to bring about. She'd had the feeling before. A kind of divine inspiration, not voices exactly but a sudden shaft of illumination which revealed to her what she must do and how to do it.

Breakfast was a slow and painful affair, mainly of boiled egg. By the time Pearl had got around to taking off the top of her egg for her, most of the bread and butter had gone. By the time she'd managed a couple of spoonsful of egg, the three greedy sods with whom she shared the table had finished stuffing themselves and had gone and there

42

was nothing but half a cupful of pale milky tea to get down and she was in a thoroughly bad temper.

'Come along, Mrs Snow,' called Matron from the doorway. 'We must get tidied up for our visitors. Open Day, you remember.'

Not likely to forget it, are we, you stupid cow, thought Mrs Snow. She struggled to her feet, gripping the table to steady herself as she reached for her walking-frame. If that was breakfast, then I've had it. Her dentures clicked as she directed a malevolent glance at Matron. Only one good thing about it, there hadn't been enough food in her mouth to make a problem with bits under her plate. If you thought about things hard enough there was always a good point to offset the bad. You had to think hard though, sometimes.

'Come along, dear, best foot forward.' Matron disappeared from the door in a rustle of perma-pleated nylon skirt, pleased with her parting shot.

She wants to watch out too, thought Mrs Snow darkly, projecting a mental image of her list in front of her. If these others weren't occupying my attention right now, I'd put her on the list too. She'd have to wait her turn, though. She inched her way to the reception area by the front door where she could see Mrs Bolter busily piling things on a trestle table covered with a white sheet. Some of the things were the fruits of many hours of painful labour in the therapy classes. Embroidered oven-cloths, knitted soft toys, baby mittens and bootees, tray-cloths and table-cloths. The late Miss Green had been very good at table-cloths, she remembered. They'd make nice winding-sheets, she thought, how about a nice shroud as a souvenir, going cheap, what could be more appropriate? On another table Mr Patel was arranging various junky-looking items collected by the Friends of the Home from anyone in the neighbourhood who could be persuaded to part with ornaments and bric-à-brac, most of which had been produced, it seemed, for the sole purpose of donating to such worthy causes. Every year the same items turned up.

Matron was supervising the laying out of the bottle stall, which was usually run by the visiting clergyman. If the number on the ticket, which cost 25p and was drawn out of a drum, coincided with the number on a bottle it was yours, unless the priest could persuade you to put it aside 'for the old folk's comfort'. Which was another way of saying 'for Matron's private stock'. And when Matron had guzzled it she didn't even come down and tell you how much she'd enjoyed it, thought Mrs Snow, who had never had a drop of the stuff so donated. She was convinced that the priest was in on the fiddle and, moreover, that he had taken up priesting solely because it gave him unfettered access to cellars full of free communion wine. He looked perpetually drunk to her. She sniffed.

Cook had baked and iced an enormous cake. Its weight could be guessed for a small fee; the prize for the winner was the honour of cutting the first slice from it, and having one's photograph taken doing so for the local paper. The cake would then be distributed to the residents at supper-time for the next few days.

Mrs Bolter flitted fussily from one side of the room to the other, dressed in what Mrs Snow thought looked like a badly tailored length of hessian. Her feet were strapped into Roman-style sandals and when her skirt whirled up as she swung around or changed direction suddenly, you could see that she wore silly little stockings that ended just below her knees. Mrs Snow reached her chair, next to the Colonel, at last. He looked at her vacantly. One of his off days, she decided, poor man. Mrs Bolter stopped in front of her.

'Good morning, Mrs Snow,' she said briskly.

Mrs Snow nodded non-committally.

'The Mayor and Lady Mayoress are due soon, with Councillor Roberts. It's a beautiful day outside.'

44

Mrs Snow allowed herself to smile. 'Did you get my whisky?' she asked.

Mrs Bolter shot a look at the Colonel, who was apparently loading an imaginary clip of ammunition in his walking-stick, taking aim and firing at the bottle stall. He smiled gently at Mrs Bolter.

'No need to bother about him,' said Mrs Snow. 'He's fighting some bloody war all by himself today. Looks like he's winning, too.'

Mrs Bolter leaned over and spoke confidentially. 'It's in my car,' she said. 'I'll fetch it for you before the day's finished. And I'm taking you home tomorrow, for lunch.'

'And what does Mr Bolter think about that?'

'He was in a good mood. He'd upset me in the morning and then got some poor woman into trouble in a traffic accident.'

Mrs Snow digested this information.

'I think I could list him without seeing him,' she said finally. 'But we'll wait until after the roast tomorrow.'

'I must be off then,' said Mrs Bolter. 'So much to do.'

Mrs Snow half closed her eyes. From beneath her hooded lids she could see the Bolter continue her rushing about, her arms waving and her hands flapping. She addressed herself to the Colonel.

'She knows about as much about organising an Open Day as my backside knows about snipe shooting,' she said.

The Colonel looked up, a glimmer of comprehension in his eye.

'Organisation? Ah-ah-logistics?' he queried. 'Not one of my strong points. Fighting man myself.'

'With big guns?' she asked politely.

'Regiment of the line, madam, small arms and bayonets. Jack of all trades in the infantry, weapons, fortifications, transport.'

She looked away as he droned on and on about sorties and recces and raids and crossfire, wondering how much

45

of it was true. She remembered quite suddenly the young New Zealand soldier she'd met in Joe Lyons Corner House in the Strand during the First World War. He'd got blown to pieces the first day his unit had taken up position in the trenches, the great new future they had planned together after the war blown sky high with him. She had often wondered what life would have been like if he'd come back and they'd married and gone to live on his farm. All those woolly sheep, no music halls, no queuing in line for a seat in the gods at a West End theatre, no buskers, no fun. Perhaps she'd have learned to ride a horse and done a bit of shearing; one thing was certain, she wouldn't have ended up in a place like this. Life was queer all right.

Mr Patel was opening the double doors from the entrance area which led out into a small paved courtyard. There were wooden seats and a few dejected-looking trees which had only partly adapted to the pollution which wafted over the wall across the car park from the main road. Already the traffic was heavy on it, and noisy; a great site for an Old Folk's Home, thought Mrs Snow. If the years don't get you, the diesel fumes will. Some of the more mobile residents got up and made for the seats in the pale sunshine. Mrs Bolter was outside tying notices with 'Open Day' crayoned on them to the trees. The odorous air from inside the Home began to filter out, to be replaced by the slightly more poisonous fumes from outside, and Mrs Snow sneezed. Mrs Bolter came charging back and stood at the door counting the residents left inside. 'Thirty-one,' she calculated breathlessly. 'Me, Matron, Mr Patel, two or three of the staff, the rest outside.'

'The Mayor should come straight in,' she said to Matron. 'There's more people inside than out, as well as the stalls. And there'll be some visitors.'

Mrs Snow grunted and her half-closed eyes shut fractionally closer. Maybe I'll sleep, she thought. Or dream something nice while I'm awake. Time must be getting on, they should be bringing tea around soon.

But it wasn't break-time yet. There was a flurry of activity outside. People were coming in through the double doors and there were cars parking and manoeuvring. Then there were large red-faced men and women, some young people, all able-bodied, healthy and well-dressed, giggling away in an embarrassed fashion and goggling at the U-shaped line of olds sitting there. Who asked them? thought Mrs Snow resentfully. We don't go marching into their homes, pushing and poking noses and patronising. Mrs Bolter was in the forefront, of course, like a bloody collie-dog worrying sheep into some kind of order. The dignitaries lined up. The Mayor had his heavy gold chain round his neck. A gold lavatory chain, thought Mrs Snow. She'd like to pull it and flush him away, along with that painted old tart next to him with the lesser chain who she guessed was his wife. The Mayor began to speak; there were other men with cameras and flash lights. We'll all be in the local paper next week and maybe one or two of the olds with dodgy tickers will have heart attacks with all the excitement and pop off. Then we'll make the National Press. 'Mayor speaks in local Home for old people. Three dead.' Boredom rather than excitement would be a more likely cause of death, she thought.

There was a brief pause in the Mayor's smooth flow of words, and in the sudden silence someone along the row from her farted, a great rumbling noise that seemed to go on forever before it finally shuddered to a halt. The Mayor pretended not to notice. Councillor Roberts, next to him, had trouble with what seemed to be an unexpected restriction to his throat which caused the veins in his neck to stand out and his eyes to bulge. Mrs Bolter and the Mayoress blushed; Matron's eyes, like cold slate in her sallow face, pin-pointed the offender with an icy glare. The offender promptly responded nervously with another louder but less extended performance. Mrs Snow cackled. The Colonel in a very loud voice said, 'By Jove, snipe shooting, what!' and took aim with his walking-stick, following the flight of an imaginary bird across the room before he shouted 'Bang!' Mrs Snow cackled again. This was more like it, she thought. Councillor Roberts backed out through the open doors, his seizure obviously getting worse, and the Mayor finished his speech rather more quickly than he had planned.

'. . . and I have great pleasure in declaring this Open Day, er, Open,' he concluded.

'Just like that old cow's bowels,' commented Mrs Snow.

Matron glared at her and moved to speak to her across the row.

'It's one thing for someone to break wind in company when they're old and senile,' she said, her voice grating, 'but that remark was disgusting. And stop encouraging the Colonel.'

'They came for entertainment,' said Mrs Snow, 'and that's what they've got.'

'Just behave yourself,' hissed Matron and stalked back to her distinguished visitors.

'Stupid old faggot,' said Mrs Snow.

The Colonel smiled. 'I got that snipe right between the eyes, dead centre,' he said.

She returned his smile encouragingly. The immediate excitements over, she could see that Mrs Bolter was now in her element and enjoying herself hugely. The Mayor was photographed with her guessing the weight of the cake, with her talking to the oldest resident. If that didn't kill off the old hag she'd be good for her century, the way she ate and took care of herself and the way people fussed over her. Who wanted to live that long anyway? It was unnatural. She saw Mr Assistant Matron slide up to Mrs Bolter, talking fifteen to the dozen and smiling away at her. Crafty sod. What was his game, then?

Mrs Bolter was susceptible to flattery, he had decided.

48

'It looks as if it is going to be a most successful day. You are to be congratulated, my dear lady,' he said. 'Despite the disgraceful interruptions to his worship's speech.'

'Thank you,' she said. 'There's always something unexpected with the olds.'

'A farting is never welcome,' said Mr Patel gravely. He wrinkled his nose. 'Always a bad sign, too.'

'Well,' said Mrs Bolter hurriedly, 'it all passed off very well, I think.'

'And your good friend Councillor Roberts. He is better now?'

'Better? I see what you mean. Recovered well, I'm sure.'

'Perhaps you will introduce us, before I go off on my weekend? We have not met socially.'

'Of course,' said Mrs Bolter. 'But be a good soul first and go and fix those Open Day notices properly. The breeze is playing havoc with them.'

She glanced around. She'd have to watch him, she thought. No wonder he was happy to work on his day off. Introduce me to Councillor Roberts, indeed! What cheek! She took two beakers of coffee from the stall staffed by two volunteer Friends and went back to Mrs Snow, who was deep in conversation with the Colonel.

'Off you go, Colonel,' she said. 'They'll give you coffee over there.'

The Colonel got up, saluted and moved off, his walking-stick in the trail position; a man with a mission.

Mrs Bolter sat down next to Mrs Snow and handed her one of the beakers.

'I'm going to be quite busy for the rest of the day,' she said. 'I'll put the whisky bottle in your room, under the pillow.'

Mrs Snow took her first sip of coffee. 'Make sure nobody sees you go in or come out of the room,' she said.

'I'll be careful. And I'll collect you tomorrow morning about midday.'

'I'll be ready. Mind you're not late.'

49

Mrs Bolter looked around furtively. 'Have you decided who is going to be next?' she whispered.

Mrs Snow tapped her nose. 'Best you shouldn't know,' she said. 'What can't speak can't lie. Off you go and enjoy yourself with your friends. See you tomorrow.'

Mrs Bolter stood up and shook herself. I don't really believe it, she thought. Everything seemed normal, just like Open Day every year, the olds sitting there and people moving about, buying things at the stalls, taking the refreshments, chatting nicely to the residents, and we're plotting to do someone in. At least she is, and I'm helping her. Who would believe it? How did I get involved? It would be simple enough to get out of it all. Just walk away. Don't collect her tomorrow. But she only half believed that the old woman had done what she claimed, and did she really want proof, one way or another? Was it the prospect, however faint, of freedom from that pig she lived with, or even the simple pleasure of planning the event, however unlikely its execution? Was that the reason why she went along with it all? One thing was certain, she couldn't face the trauma of divorce. She sighed. It was all very difficult. Best not to think about it.

'Tomorrow at noon, then,' she said brightly.

Mrs Snow watched as she hurried across the room to speak to the priest, who, she had observed, had already stowed away half a dozen bottles or so under the table. Mrs Bolter turned and waved to her, a kind of forlorn gesture somehow before she was whisked off somewhere out of sight.

That night in her room Mrs Snow undressed and washed herself meticulously as usual before putting on her nightdress. Seated on the bed she slid her hand under the pillow and withdrew the bottle of Scotch which, as she had promised, Mrs Bolter had hidden there. She unscrewed the cap, poured a liberal measure into her tooth-mug and got into bed, with difficulty. Turning out the light from the bedside switch, she sat up in the near darkness sipping the neat whisky and savouring the strength of the raw spirit as she swilled it around her mouth before swallowing it. There's nothing quite like it, she thought. Not that she was a drinking woman, but if you're going to have a drink you should be able to taste it. It made you forget, and at the same time everything became clear and made sense. She took another sip and tried to concentrate on the problem of Mr Patel. It wasn't an immediate problem, now, more like your difficult conundrum type of thing actually, but she didn't propose to worry too much about it, and this whisky was sending her right off. She up-ended the mug and replaced it carefully on her bedside table. Her head eased back on the pillow and her teeth, which vanity would not allow her to remove at night, clicked peacefully. Haven't felt so good in years, she thought. For once her hip wasn't giving her any pain, and surprisingly her back too was pain-free. Everything was quiet and calm and peaceful. She'd go off to sleep without the aid of one of her stock of pills and dream of marvellous things to eat and to drink, and perhaps of her late husbands, all three of them. Did they allow husbands and wives to live together in Heaven? In all those mansions in the sky we've been promised? Would we all be young again and be able to enjoy ourselves? Would she live with all three of her former partners, or would they come and visit her in turn? If they had different arrangements, like ladies one side of para-dise and gents on the other, perhaps she should be making enquiries about the alternative place. You couldn't roast forever, and it couldn't be much worse than being a convict in Australia in the old days. Kangaroos were queer creatures all right. She'd seen one in a travelling circus years ago. It sat back on its enormous tail and had boxing-gloves on its front paws, and boxed with anyone stupid enough to take it on. Funny place. All upside down and sunshine. She smiled at the thought of the antipodean sun which seemed to be coursing through her veins, warming and soothing and extraordinarily pleasant. The Colonel had been funny this morning. They'd had a long and involved talk, and he seemed to understand everything she said. Still smiling, she drifted off quietly to sleep.

7

Mr Bolter looked out of the lounge window from behind the security of the net curtains at his wife, who was helping some wizened old crone along the garden path. He looked at his watch. Just after midday. Soon be lunchtime. And then he remembered. One of the old people from Bob Roberts' Homes was coming for Sunday lunch. He racked his brains furiously, trying to recall why he had agreed to such a monstrous breach of the unwritten laws which governed his household. He'd been in the middle of recounting to her how he'd reduced the stupid woman who had run into his car that morning to a quivering jelly, and had had the pleasure of seeing her led away, all tears and shaking, by the policeman he'd whistled up, when she said something about bringing in someone for lunch. He'd sort of waved general assent, thinking that she'd forget about it, and, anxious to get on with his story, he'd not followed it up for his usual second thoughts and the straight veto.

Funny-looking old bird, he thought. Well on her last legs. Why her? She'd often talked about having one or two selected 'olds', as she called them, for a meal or something, but he had assumed, if it ever came about, that it would be a man. Some of the old men were right villains, plenty of go left in them, and who knew what they got up to? Intrigued, he went to the front door and flung it open. Might as well make the most of it, seeing

52

that it was inevitable. But Sunday lunch. It was a bit much. There'd be a few words said when the old dear went back.

The two of them reached the front door eventually. Mrs Snow paused, leaned on her frame and looked up at her host. She saw a large, paunchy middle-aged man with brown curly hair going grey at the sides, a high forehead and heavily jowled face. He had on grey slacks and a yellow shirt and he was smoking a cigarette. She gave him her best coquettish smile. He saw a tiny figure half bent over her aluminium walking-frame. She had on a bright blue two-piece suit with a freshly laundered white blouse pinned at the neck with a large cameo brooch. The skirt came down almost to her ankles and to his surprise he saw that she was wearing shiny high-heeled shoes. But it was her head that caused him to look twice. It was small and beautifully balanced on her long neck. Her hair was still dark – must be tinted, he thought – longish, plaited and wound around her head. The sharp-bridged nose and the hawk-like mouth and chin beneath, and those dark eyes, deep violet in the morning light, in their sunken sockets. Phew, he thought, fancy having you as a mother-in-law. He took a last puff on his cigarette, tossed the butt into the herbaceous border and swaggered down the steps. Mrs Bolter stepped forward hastily.

'Mrs Snow, my husband,' she said.

Mrs Snow inclined her head graciously.

'Mrs Snow will be staying for lunch,' added Mrs Bolter. 'As we discussed.'

Mr Bolter gave his famous boyish grin.

'Of course. You're very welcome, Mrs Snow,' he said. 'Why haven't you paid us a visit before?'

Smarmy sod, thought Mrs Snow. But I like it.

'I've never been bloody asked,' she said primly.

'It's her fault, is it?' he chortled, waving at a distracted Mrs Bolter. 'It usually is, but not many people tell her so.'

'I'll bet you do,' said Mrs Snow.

53

He hooted again. 'I like you,' he said. 'Here,' he said to his wife, 'catch hold of this good lady's frame and bring it in. I'll take Mrs Snow in, otherwise we'll be out here all day chatting and hobbling about.'

Before Mrs Bolter's incredulous eyes, he picked up Mrs Snow complete with handbag and voluminous Sunday papers and disappeared into the house with her. She shook her head, hoping that the neighbours had missed the excessively overdone welcoming ceremony. It was one thing to make a guest feel at home, but there were limits. He didn't seem to understand that. But then he never had done. She picked up the walking-frame with its impedimenta, followed them inside and shut the front door behind her. She'd been out of bed early that morning and before going to church she'd made an attempt to tidy up the entrance hall. But there were so many things there, all of which were useful or could be, or were awaiting collection for one charity or another, that her efforts to order the chaos had not been noticeably effective. He'd been gardening whilst she was out and must have been called to the telephone in the middle of it, since next to it, newly arrived in her absence, were a rake and a pair of mud-caked wellington boots. She parked the walking-frame next to them and went on into the kitchen.

The breakfast dishes and frying-pan were still piled up in the sink – he might at least have done those, she thought resentfully – and the round of beef which she had taken from the fridge earlier was still on the draining-board oozing blood. She shuddered as she began working. Vegetables to prepare, a Yorkshire pudding to mix and bake. It was enough to drive anyone to drink. There were sounds of raucous laughter coming from the front room as she stepped outside briefly to listen. She went back into the kitchen, closed the door and took out from the back of the larder a bottle labelled 'Sarson's Malt Vinegar', into which she had decanted her supermarket sherry, and poured out half a mugful. She took a deep draught of it.

I'd go mad without it, she thought; I don't drink – this is food and it steadies the nerves, and so far she hadn't been caught . . . Sainsbury's cream sherry looked like cold tea in her mug and like vinegar in the vinegar bottle. It also had the added attraction that it could be bought with the groceries, and the only way she could be found out was if she was caught at the check-out stuffing the bottles into one of her plastic carriers. And then of course she could always say that she was buying it for one of the old people at the Home. She took another swig. Here's to lunch, she thought, here's to a good business lunch with arrangements concluded satisfactorily and a contract in the bag at the end of it. She put the meat into a roasting-tin, shoved it on to the top shelf of the oven and banged the oven door to with a satisfactory clang.

Mrs Snow and Mr Bolter sat facing each other on either side of the fireplace in the front room. Both held large schooners of sherry and newly lighted full-strength king-size cigarettes of the brand which Mr Bolter bought by the carton and charged to his firm as an entertainment expense. Smoking in the front room, which Mrs Bolter insisted on calling the drawing-room, was normally forbidden, but, with guests in the house, just about tolerated by Mrs Bolter. Mr Bolter was beginning to enjoy himself.

'Tell me something about yourself,' he invited, settling himself back in his armchair.

Mrs Snow sipped her sherry, then took a deep lungful of cigarette smoke. She waved the hand holding the cigarette, and small particles of ash fluttered noiselessly on to the washed Chinese rug on the floor. She put on her best come-hither look.

'I'm an old woman,' she said simply. Her eyes invited him to dispute the fact. 'Tell me something about yourself instead.'

'Nothing much to tell,' he said readily. 'My father was a professional cricketer for Yorkshire County – and if you know anything about cricket you'll know that that means

55

he had to be good. When he finished playing they gave him a benefit match and with the proceeds he set himself up in the village as a baker. I had two brothers and two sisters. We all went to University, but I was the only one to go to Cambridge. There's where I met Phyllis.'

'Phyllis?'

'Mrs Bolter. My wife. She was an Arts Student. All Arts Students are superior people and despise technocrats like me. Scientists, physicists, engineers – they're all beyond the pale in her book. She used to mess about in amateur dramatics, spout reams of ancient Greek, dressing up and going about with a lot of cream puffs in boaters.'

Mrs Snow registered her disgust with a snort and took some more sherry. Mr Bolter's own sherry was disappearing rapidly. He settled back more comfortably.

'Anyway, to cut a long story short,' he went on, 'we got married despite her parents' opposition, and they still think that I'm some kind of northern hick with a spanner in one hand and an oily rag in the other because I'm an engineer, and proud of it. It's slide rules and computers these days, economics and management.' He finished his glass, refilled it and topped up Mrs Snow's.

'Don't expect me to feel sorry for you,' said Mrs Snow. 'I've lived through two major wars, three husbands and three children of my own plus three my third husband brought with him. I'm the oldest of twelve children and I'm the last of them to die. I've been nowhere but I've seen a lot. I should have been an actress but it wasn't quite respectable when I was a young woman, and the nearest I got to acting was when my third husband proposed to me. I'll give you the last ten years of my life, I told him. He was younger than me, and that's all you need to know about how old I am. I brought up his three young children – he was a widower and, would you believe it, ten years after we were married, almost to the day, he dropped dead at work, lifting a crate of Guinness.

56

And it's supposed to be good for you.' She laughed; it was the sound of Hallowe'en.

'Supposed to be good for you,' he repeated, then he laughed and slapped his thigh. 'Dropped dead under a crate of Guinness eh! What a gas!'

'I've been in some of the finest houses in England,' she went on, ignoring his interruption. 'My first husband was a valet, in service like myself. We had to get permission to marry, and it wasn't until I was pregnant that I got approval, and a nice little dowry, from the Master. Twenty-five golden sovereigns. Worth a tidy bit in those days. He thought he was the father.'

'And was he?'

'He could have been.'

'Really?'

'Or his son.'

Mr Bolter roared with laughter. 'And what happened to your own children?' he prompted.

'I had three of my own. The eldest was a girl, my favourite. She was so beautiful. She married young and went off to Australia to live. Her children are grown up, and I've grandchildren and great-grandchildren I've never seen except in photos. My two sons were a bit slow. One was mad about machines, went into the army and got killed in a tank. Never saw a shot fired in anger, that boy. The other one was a farm labourer. Still up north some-where, must be retired by now I reckon. Never married, always mooning about, scribbling, writing poetry, gloomy sort of stuff. Like a bit of life myself. My Anna was like me, a bit wild, but she was so lovely. I could have killed that sod when he took her to the other side of the world. I told them at the time. You'll break your father's heart, I said to them, but you won't break mine. And don't expect me to follow you out there with all those blackamoors and kangaroos. Ugh. He died soon after, her father, and when my boys went away I left service and became a waitress for a while. Did all kinds of things. When the second war

57

came I worked in a factory, made good money; I nearly left when I married the works foreman, but it was a good job I didn't. We were making tents, thousands of them. We had to go on different shifts and I didn't see all that much of him, which was why I wanted to leave. It was a beautiful September morning when I got home from the night shift and there was no bloody house there. Just a gap and a pile of smoke and rubble and wardens digging in it. My home up in smoke and him in there under it all. Couldn't have known what hit him, just bricks and rubble and Civil Defence men and police and firemen scrambling about all over it.'

Mr Bolter made what he hoped were sympathetic noises.

'And then number three came along?'

She drained her glass. 'I haven't talked so much in years,' she said. He refilled her glass again and she sipped at it.

'He was after the war,' she said. 'Much younger than me, although you'd never believe it. He'd been called up, went in as a private and came out as a private. Before the war he used to hump coal around the streets. All he could think about was getting enough money to pay the rent and get a couple of pints a night. He expected his wife to go to work to find the money for food and everything else. Funny bugger. But I was lonely and I thought I'd change him after we were married. It was hard work. He was on the war damage for a bit, nailing on slates, but he wasn't all that strong and I made him try for a postman but he didn't pass the reading test. Then I got him a job in the canteen of the factory where I worked. We'd gone into making hiking gear and real army-surplus stuff by then, and it sold like hot cakes. In the evening the canteen was used by the workers for social events like bingo, dancing, drinking, darts, and he used to help out there, in the bar, collecting glasses, humping crates, that sort of thing. And that's how he came to be lifting crates of stout.

He'd had a few pints himself at the time too, and a heavy meal, and he lifted up the crate, fell down and went blue in the face.' She took a deep breath, and some more sherry.

In the kitchen Mrs Bolter could hear their voices but not the words as she set about peeling potatoes, cutting into them deeply. The Sainsbury's sherry didn't seem to be working as quickly as it did usually. Her cheeks were flushed but there was none of the slow spreading euphoria and calmness which normally came with the first mugful. It was probably a mistake bringing home that old cat, she thought. From the sound of it they were well on the way to getting drunk, loud voices, all blurred and fuzzy. She clumped around the kitchen, lifted a utensil and put it down in a different place, stared vacantly at the dials on the cooker. She disliked red meat and rarely bought it. When she did she cooked it badly, since she knew that whether it was raw or perfectly done or burnt, she would not enjoy it. So she was quite indifferent as to whether the oven was pre-heated, the temperature set correctly – stuff it – like a lot of savages, cannibals, ugh.

She poured herself some more refreshing cold tea from the vinegar bottle and had another large swig of it. She beat the eggs and flour and milk, sprinkled in salt. Shove that in the oven as well, she thought, can't overcook Yorkshire pudding, and slammed the oven door on it with another satisfying clang. She looked around, trying to avoid seeing the piles of debris; she certainly had to admit that it looked like debris to the critical eye. 'Better do some dishes,' she said out loud and turned on the hot water tap. A tepid stream of water came out. Bloody hell, that sod had used it all. She took another swig of sherry, tied on an apron and marched into the drawing-room. Mrs Snow and her husband both turned to look at her, staring, glasses clutched firmly. She felt alienated, a stranger in her own home. The spectre at the feast. The air was thick with cigarette smoke and she coughed, waving her hands about in front of her face.

'There's no hot water,' she said accusingly.

'I had a bath this morning, remember?'

'That's no reason why the water shouldn't be hot.'

'You altered the timer on the boiler last week, remember that too?' He sat back, smiling smugly, and winked at Mrs Snow who grimaced in response.

'Well then, perhaps you'd alter it back so that there's hot water for less essential things, like dishes, as well as your weekly bath.'

He smiled at her, shrugged his shoulders, reached for the decanter and refilled his glass, waved the decanter at Mrs Snow and leaned forward and filled her glass again.

'Thank you, dear,' said Mrs Snow.

'Mrs Snow and I are having a very interesting conversation,' he said reasonably. 'Why don't you go and fiddle with the necessary knobs on the boiler? And I hope you're seeing to the knobs on the cooker, they must be fiddled with too if we're to have lunch today.'

Mrs Snow cackled. 'You are a caution,' she said coyly.

Mrs Bolter flushed.

'Well,' she said, 'I'll go and fiddle, as you call it. And if I blow up the bloody place whilst you're having interesting conversations, don't be surprised, will you.' She swept out of the room, her hands plucking nervously at her apron strings. I'll go out, she thought desperately, let them stew in it. She could hear them, talking still.

'You go straight to heaven if you get blown up on a Sunday,' said Mrs Snow.

'It's about the only way I'd get in.'

'Who wants to, anyway?'

She heard them dissolve into great hoots of laughter. If I hear any more I'll be sick, she thought. Mrs Snow was taking liberties, getting drunk, fraternising in the most outrageous manner. Couldn't expect anything better from him. He'd take every opportunity he could to humiliate

60

her. She recalled what her father had said when she'd taken him home and announced that they were getting engaged. 'Now tell us the good news,' he had said. She'd had him home before, during the previous long vacation, and he'd not gone down too well. His manners even then had been appalling. His father was a tradesman, too, so what could you expect? Mummy wasn't amused, either. 'You'll live to rue the day,' she had said afterwards. 'You should listen to your mother just for once, break it off.' But opposition had only made her even more determined. The deed had been done and her mother's prophecy had come true. She had done a lot of rueing over the years since.

She opened the oven door and then closed it quickly. No need to bother with that at the moment. Perhaps Mrs Snow was working on some extraordinarily devious plan to gain his confidence, that was it; was she ever devious! She went into the dining-room, feeling slightly better. Dear God, what a mess, she thought. Another swig of cold tea was called for before she tackled that lot. She set the table, cloth serviettes, heavy family silver cutlery, cut glass tumblers for water. I must get some air, she thought when she'd finished, and went through the French doors into the garden. He'd cut the grass the day before and it didn't look too bad. The warm air seemed to be doing things to her eyes, making it impossibly difficult to keep them open, and she sat down on the wooden bench on the paving outside the kitchen door. There were birds singing in the trees all over the place. Perhaps if I shut my eyes for a few seconds, when I open them this nightmare will be over. Was this really what life was all about? If it wasn't for Bob Roberts I'd go mad, mad, mad, she thought. And even he, dear Bob, was no more than an oversexed, overhung specimen who turned up these days when it suited him, not her, and she was almost certain that she was only one of several neglected females he was doing his best for. His poor wife! Perhaps she had visits

61

from other gentlemen who obliged her in turn. Or perhaps she wasn't interested. Oblige me, oblige me not. What did she sprinkle on his corn flakes in the morning? Portland cement? She smiled at the thought as she dropped off into sleep.

Mr Bolter came through the French doors about an hour later. There was a charnel house smell about the place which was detectable even through the cigarette-smoke haze in the lounge. Mrs Snow, in the middle of an anecdote about how in her early days in service she had escaped from a particularly nasty employer in a block of flats in Maida Vale, had dropped off, fast asleep, her story unfinished, her glass in one hand thankfully almost empty and her umpteenth cigarette wedged firmly between first and second nicotine-stained fingers. He got up and peered at her. Funny old tart, he thought. What a life. What a survivor! He felt quite woozy. Sherry on an empty stomach was deadly. When the hell were we going to eat? He took the cigarette from Mrs Snow's fingers and removed the glass to safety. By God, he was hungry.

'Phyllis,' he called, and stumped out into the kitchen. Something was going on in there, something that was suspiciously like arson and anarchy. Saucepans were boiling furiously, one of them had boiled over and the gas under it, although still turned on, was not alight. He turned it off quickly, cursing. It looked as if smoke was coming out of the oven and he turned that off too.

'Phyllis,' he called again, and went out through the kitchen door, blinking in the sunlight. There she was, fast a-bloody sleep, leaving him to see to everything as usual. It was a bit bloody thick, after all, work all week, all the hours God made. A man was entitled to expect a bit of rest at weekends, and a decent Sunday lunch. And here she was, asleep. He poked her shoulder resentfully. She shivered and jerked awake.

'What is it, what is it?' she demanded.

'What is it? The joint's only burning in the oven, that's

62

all. There's gas all over the place and it's a bloody marvel the place is still here. The old hag's gone sleepy-byes and yours bloody truly is starving, that's what it is.'

She got to her feet, smoothing her apron.

'I must have nodded off,' she said. She looked at her watch and with a mounting sense of panic, as she realised what the time was, added 'Oh Jesus' and was off back into the house.

Women, he said to himself in despair. He wandered off into the garden. Looking up at the sky. There was plenty of it.

'We are not alone,' he said out loud. 'Out there are other good men chained to stupid dithering women, women who go bonkers at the drop of a hat, burning good beef and Yorkshire puddings, giving us a hard time. You knew what you were doing when you created yourself male,' he addressed some lofty presence which he imagined might be lurking, dressed in a long white sheet, behind one of those soft fluffy clouds. 'Too right. And if you can still do miracles for a fellow-man in dire discomfort, let there be lunch today.'

Mrs Bolter hastily withdrew the joint, somewhat shrivelled at the edges, from the oven. The Yorkshire pudding looked beyond redemption, having risen beyond her highest expectations, and then, during its long sojourn in the very hot oven, flopped over and burnt – the source of much of the smoke which had billowed into the room when she opened the oven door. The roast potatoes were an interesting shade of very deep brown. The cauliflower had boiled over before it was properly cooked and was still raw; al dente, she comforted herself, even if the aroma was nothing less than insanitary. The carrots were overcooked, but they would be fine, if a bit limp, dished up and glazed with a knob of margarine. She got down the large meat dish with the channels for the blood to run into and the little reservoir in which it collected, and from which it could be spooned on to the servings. The tiny

63

joint was lost in the middle of it, and it was extremely doubtful that any blood would run out when it was sliced, always providing that the knife was sharp enough to cut into it. Nevertheless she pressed on, heaping the vegetables around it in the manner illustrated in the cookery supplement of last week's *Woman*. 'Tempt your man with this mouth-watering presentation', the caption had read. 'Tickle his olfactory and visual senses and make a meal for him to remember'. She took the results of her morning's culinary efforts into the dining-room and placed the dish in the centre of the table. A meal to remember, she thought, and managed to suppress a near hysterical bout of laughter.

'It's ready,' she called. 'Will you carve?'

Down at the bottom of the garden Mr Bolter heard the challenge and gave thanks for prayers answered. Will you carve? he repeated. Then he remembered the size of the joint. Carve what? There's more meat on a nine-year-old skeleton, he muttered to himself. He meandered reluctantly back to the house.

There was something missing, thought Mrs Bolter. She checked the dish. Everything she'd cooked was there; mustard, horseradish, condiments, all were present and correct. She focused on the table settings. Three. But why three? Claire was away and not expected home this weekend. Then she remembered her guest; she dashed back into the drawing-room. Mrs Snow, now wide awake, sat back in her chair regarding her with a look that could only be described as distinctly hostile.

'So sorry, Mrs Snow,' she said breathlessly. 'An unfortunate accident in the kitchen. I do hope that my husband has been looking after you.'

Mrs Snow snorted. 'I'm full of sherry,' she announced, 'and I feel mean. Where's the lavatory?'

'There's one in the hall. Can you manage?'

Mrs Snow reached for her walking-frame, looking

smaller and more evil than ever before as she hunched over it, gripping it tightly.

'Of course I can manage,' she snapped. 'It isn't easy but I manage. Every day of the week I manage, no thanks to anybody.' She heaved up her frame, which brushed awkwardly against a faded silk screen standing to one side of her chair, knocking it over. As it toppled over, so did she, pushing the frame to one side as she went down, knocking over the wine-table as well, the empty sherry glass on it describing a graceful arc through the air before it hit the carpet and slid safely into a corner. She herself fell on her side and then rolled on her back, quite helpless.

'Don't stand there gawping,' she shouted. 'Help me.'

Mrs Bolter picked up the wine-table, retrieved the glass and then knelt down by the side of her guest.

'I can see where your priorities are,' snarled Mrs Snow. 'Help me up before I wet on the floor.'

Mrs Bolter tried to pull her up but succeeded only in lifting her shoulders a couple of inches from the floor.

'I can't seem to lift you,' she said. 'You're so much heavier than I thought you would be.' She leaned over further and tried again. Mrs Snow twisted her head to one side and took a blast of Mrs Bolter's breath full in the face.

'You're drunk,' she shouted accusingly. 'Mrs Bloody Goody Bolter, never touched a drop in her life. I can smell it!'

Mrs Bolter reeled back.

'It's you that's drunk,' she retorted. She put her hand over her mouth to prevent confirmation of Mrs Snow's loudly voiced suspicion. 'Stay there,' she added. 'I'll get my husband.'

'I'm not likely to go far,' Mrs Snow said bitterly.

Mrs Bolter drew herself up, her cheeks flaming. Nobody had ever before accused her of being drunk, and she had never claimed to be teetotal. She felt a deep resentful hurtful feeling spreading over her. The old ingrate, she thought. At the door she blundered into Mr Bolter, who had wandered in from the garden. He looked from one to the other, open-mouthed.

'Help Mrs Snow, will you,' she said with as much dignity as she could muster, and brushed past him. Then she called back. 'Don't be long, lunch is on the table.'

Mr Bolter looked at Mrs Snow with an expression of complete disbelief.

'And what are you doing down there?' he enquired.

'Don't be stupid,' said Mrs Snow. 'Be so good as to help me to my walking frame and direct me to the lavatory.'

'I beg your pardon, madam,' said Mr Bolter, heavily sarcastic. 'Tell you what though, you're not such a speedy mover on that thing.' He bent down and picked her up as if she were a not very full sack of potatoes, carried her outside and deposited her by the cloakroom door.

'I trust I'm not too late,' he said.

When she emerged, feeling better and, unusually for her, hungry, the frame was in position outside the door. She reached for it, thankfully.

'In here, Mrs Snow,' she heard Mrs Bolter call, and she headed for the dining-room. At the door she paused. She'd been in some odd places in her time, but this was in a different league. On two walls, books from floor to ceiling. In one corner, hi-fi equipment stacked tier upon tier, wires protruding from all angles. A large TV set. Opposite it, on the other side of the fireplace, an old, worn-out armchair. There were heavy dining-room chairs of the kind one had to pay to have taken away and strange posters tacked on the wall over a sideboard which looked as if it had been hewn from a solid block of oak in Tudor times. French doors opening on the garden, and tattered tapestry curtains; a round table in the centre of the room, set for the meal. On the floor a threadbare carpet, not too clean. But the oddest thing was the two of them each side of the enormous silver dish in the centre of the table. Mr Bolter to one side, holding a carving-knife and fork poised over a blackened bit of meat surounded by limp vegetables. On the other side, Mrs Bolter standing guard over the batter pudding, or what was left of it, the burnt circumference having been removed and discarded in the kitchen. What an unholy mess, she thought.

Mrs Bolter moved around the table to help her to her seat.

'We've put you here,' she said, indicating the chair facing the French doors. 'You can see the garden from here.'

Mrs Snow grunted and made her way to her seat. Mr Bolter stuck his fork into the joint and met with some resistance. He adjusted his spectacles and tried again, this time plunging down with some determination. The fork slipped and the meat reared up, scattering some of the vegetables, then spun around and across the table, landing at the foot of Mrs Snow's frame.

Mrs Bolter flushed, reached for a serviette and picked it up.

'You clumsy idiot,' she hissed at Mr Bolter. And then more loudly. 'I've spent all morning preparing this and all you can do is ruin it.' She stamped her foot, her face flushed and her mouth quivering. 'I'm finished,' she shouted, 'get your own bloody lunch.' She flung both meat and serviette at Mr Bolter and ran out of the room.

Mr Bolter saw the objects coming and dodged. The serviette fluttered to the floor and the meat hit one of the book shelves behind him and fell harmlessly to the floor. In the silence which followed his wife's exit she could be heard sobbing all the way up the stairs.

'And what does she do for an encore?' asked Mrs Snow.

Mr Bolter sat down. Suddenly he began to laugh.

'Mrs Snow,' he said, 'I've got to hand it to you. Do you know what I'm going to do? I'm going to take you out to lunch.'

Mrs Snow grunted. 'The way today's going,' she said,

67

'if you find a place that's open, everything will be off. Except corned beef.'

Mrs Bolter, recovering rapidly upstairs, heard the front door slam to and from behind the curtains watched in disbelief the spectacle of her husband carrying Mrs Snow down the path to the street where his car was parked. He opened the car door with one hand, deposited Mrs Snow in the passenger seat, walked unsteadily around to his side, got in and drove off with a positive smirk on his face. Well, she thought, well. She went downstairs and viewed the scene from the dining-room door. Mrs Snow's frame was still there. She'd taken her handbag, but had left behind the plastic carrier bag with life's other necessities in it. Sunday lunch was either on the table or on the floor. I'll give her lunch, she thought. She must be coming back, she'd be lost without a frame. What a fool she had been to entertain the thought that Mrs Snow was going to help her. Take liberties was more like it. It was all lies, lies, lies. She'd made it all up just to get attention and sympathy and a trip out from the Home.

She made herself a pot of tea and broke open a new packet of digestive biscuits. Bob Roberts was due to call tomorrow, she reminded herself, and her tongue moved softly outside her lips. Thank God for Bob Roberts, she thought, I'd go mad without him. Her body arched gently at the thought of him. At least he knew she was good for something, good at something, and appreciated her. Would she make a play for him if she ever became free? Became free unexpectedly in the near future? She nibbled at another biscuit. Probably not. She'd go for somebody younger, younger than herself anyway, that was fashionable now. And if the rest of the world was critical it was because it was green with envy. She cast her mind's eye over some of the young men her adopted daughter had brought home since senior school. I could teach them a thing or two, oh yes, with great pleasure, she thought.

One at a time or two or three together. Make a party of it. She took another biscuit.

By the time Mr Bolter returned – she heard the car door slam somewhere outside the steaming cloud of her thoughts – she discovered to her horror that she had almost demolished the new pack of biscuits and was feeling more than slightly nauseated. How could I think such sick-making thoughts? she said to herself. Or was it the biscuits?

He opened the front door. She heard him go back down and path and imagined him carrying Mrs Snow back into the house. Pull yourself together, she said to herself. Don't let them see that you've been upset. She got up and took Mrs Snow's frame into the hall, staying well behind it. She heard them talking in the solemn tones that people adopt when they've taken too much drink and are doing their best not to slur their words, but not succeeding.

He brought her in and set her down.

'Told you everything would be all right,' he said.

Mrs Snow swayed slightly. 'Thank you for a most entertaining meal. Much appreciated.'

He waved his hands airily. 'Think nothing of it. It's all on the firm anyway. Expenses. Entertainment.'

He came into the house and went over to Mrs Bolter.

'Glad you're OK,' he said. He patted her shoulder. 'Don't worry about lunch. We've done very well.'

'Did you have anything to eat with it?'

'Bless you my dear, of course we did,' he said jovially. 'Go and put the kettle on eh? There's a dear.'

'Take Mrs Snow into the drawing-room, will you,' said Mrs Bolter icily, 'before she has another accident, and then perhaps we might have a word. In private.'

Mr Bolter picked up Mrs Snow under one arm and with her walking-frame on his other sauntered into the lounge, where he deposited both. Mrs Bolter went into the dining-room and he followed her in.

'Before you start anything,' he said, swaying solemnly,

pointing his finger and at the same time trying to light a cigarette, 'I just want to say that I know it's not your fault that the meal was buggered up, and we've eaten anyway, so there's no harm done and nothing to get mad about. I'm not mad at you for throwing the meat at me, it missed anyway.'

'I know you've eaten,' said Mrs Bolter. 'I just want you to know that next time, if there is a next time, if I don't get you with the joint I will with the cutlery.'

'Is that it? Is there any more?' He blinked at her.

'You are quite impossible,' she said. 'Nothing is ever your fault. There's literally and metaphorically no point of contact between us. We're finished and I mean it and I'm going to do something about it.'

He flicked some ash on to the floor.

'What's new?' he enquired. 'But we've been together for too long to break up now.' He groped his way towards his chair. 'Besides, I like it here. It's home. It suits me. Plenty to moan about.' He reached his chair and slumped down into it. In a kind of reflex action his legs unfolded and his feet found their way up on the mantelshelf.

'I'll have my tea in here,' he added. 'The old biddy is fantastic, but enough's enough. Be a good girl, will you?'

She watched, incredulously, as behind the thick glasses his lids came slowly together, met, and then his body seemed to settle and nestle in the shape of the chair; he grunted, and in a few more seconds his mouth was open and his right arm dropped from his lap, the hand still holding the cigarette almost touching the floor.

She took the cigarette and tossed it into the fireplace. Sleep, that's right, she thought. He'll go to sleep one day and not wake up. Large tears welled up in her eyes and she dashed out of the room into the kitchen, slamming the kettle on the stove, cups and saucers on a tray and, while the kettle was boiling, unwrapped the slab of rich fruit-cake purchased solely for Mrs Snow's enjoyment. When the tea was made she carried the heavy tray into the drawing-room and set it down on a side-table. Mrs Snow looked up warily. Mrs Bolter was towering over her, her fingers working furiously on the fringe of her apron.

'This has been a great success, hasn't it?' said Mrs Bolter. 'What a joke, you supposed to be helping me and this absolute disaster of an afternoon and you out with him and both of you drinking.'

'He don't need any encouraging,' said Mrs Snow. 'At least I got to know him pretty well in a short time.'

'And I suppose you'll spread it all over the Home that you and Mr Bolter got drunk, and about the lunch – and everything.'

'I'm never drunk,' said Mrs Snow indignantly. 'And anyway, mum's the word.' She tapped her nose gently. 'Soul of discretion, me. Rely on it. Not a word from me about it, I can promise you, dear.'

'I don't have much choice,' said Mrs Bolter, 'but you'd better be discreet or I'll have a few things to say myself, believe me.'

'Now, now, dear, don't fret yourself. Pour us a nice cup of tea and let's have a chat before your husband comes in.'

Mrs Bolter still felt uneasy as, with Mrs Snow strapped in the front seat beside her, she drove back to the Home later that afternoon. Mrs Snow had flatly refused to discuss any plan of action for the future with regard to Mr Bolter. 'All in good time,' she had said. 'I've got to think things out.' She'd swallowed three cups of tea, eaten two slices of the cake and had graciously accepted the remainder of it, wrapped in a doily, to take back with her to share with the Colonel. She'd visited the toilet twice; 'All that sherry wine, dear – the old kidneys aren't what they used to be. I'll get things buttoned up, don't you worry yourself, but meantime don't go around saying naughty things that someone might hear, like I did.'

'What things did you hear?'

'Things like,' Mrs Snow had paused, 'things like that

71

you're finished with him, and next time you'll get him with the cutlery.'

'You've been eavesdropping. How dare you listen to private conversations between me and my husband.'

'If that was private, you should have closed the door and lowered your voices,' said Mrs Snow. 'Take a tip from me, dear, either don't say it, which is best, because nobody knows what you're thinking if you don't say anything, or if you must, make sure you can't possibly be overheard and quoted afterwards. You can't be too careful, dear. I don't say anything to nobody these days.'

'You've said plenty to me about things. About your list, for instance.'

Mrs Snow tapped her nose again. 'That's different,' she said. 'I trust you. And anyway,' she added, almost to herself, 'no witnesses, and who'd believe her?'

Mrs Bolter drove as close to the front door as she could manage and they sat there for a few seconds without speaking. She fussed with the assorted debris in the glove-box and then in the side-door pocket before speaking. Her stomach seemed to be harbouring a large number of over-active butterflies.

'What do you really think?' she asked eventually.

Mrs Snow turned a beady eye in her direction.

'He's not such a bad old stick, is he? At least he wouldn't be if he was married to someone else. You can't stand the sight of him, can you? Any chance you could settle your differences? That would be the best way out of it.'

Mrs Bolter shook her head. 'There's been too many insults, too many words said, too many humiliations. It used to be different. I did try. At first, anyway.'

'You're what's known as incompatible,' said Mrs Snow. 'It's grounds for divorce in America.'

'It is here.'

'So why not divorce him, then?'

Mrs Bolter shook her head again. 'There's a lot of

reasons. Everything would come out in public. I couldn't face it.'

'And you couldn't make a go of it if you tried again?'

'There's just nothing there,' said Mrs Bolter. 'You've seen it. He won't divorce me and I can't divorce him.'

'Well then, let's sleep on it,' said Mrs Snow cheerfully. 'Meanwhile there's lots of other things to do. Would you help me out of this belt, please?'

As Mrs Bolter pushed open the front door of the Home she saw Matron in the corridor, hurrying past. The entrance lounge was empty of residents, which was unusual for the time of day. Matron saw them through the glass door, hesitated and then came over. How nice, thought Mrs Bolter, she's going to help me with Mrs Snow and get her settled. She smiled, but there was no answering smile from Matron.

'So glad you've come in, Mrs Bolter,' she said. 'Would you help Mrs Snow up to her room and then come down to my office for a few minutes please?'

'There's something wrong?' asked Mrs Bolter, who by then was standing behind Mrs Snow who was leaning on her frame.

'Yes. There's been an accident, I'm afraid. To Mr Patel.'

Mrs Bolter gasped.

'What kind of accident, poor man? How on earth . . .'

'When you come down I'll tell you all about it.' Matron held the door open and waved them in impatiently.

'You go along with Matron, Mrs Bolter,' said Mrs Snow. 'I can get myself upstairs without any help. And thank you for the visit out. Most enjoyable.' She heaved up her frame and set it down, one foot forward and then the other. 'Off you go,' she said. 'Regards and thanks to Mr Bolter.' Her progress was slow, deliberate, inexorable.

'Independent old woman,' said Matron, half to herself. Then to Mrs Bolter, 'If you could possibly spare an hour or so I would be so grateful. Sundays we're always short

73

staffed and it's most inconvenient when someone who should be on duty isn't.'

'Mr Patel should have been on duty tonight?'

Matron nodded. 'He was due back this evening from his weekend off. It's that car of his. I told him that it was a death-trap. You can't run a big car like that on a shoestring, doing all your own repairs and maintenance, unless you really know what you're doing. He thought he knew, but he never convinced me. The police telephoned this afternoon. It happened yesterday evening, apparently. He'd gone off the motorway somehow, down an embankment. No other car involved, they said. Must have skidded, or the brakes or steering failed. Or all three – or something. They don't really know. They're looking into it.'

'Is he . . . ?'

'I'm afraid so. The police say that he was dead on arrival at hospital.'

Mrs Bolter shuddered. It was awful. But at least Mrs Snow couldn't claim credit for that occurrence; she didn't even know if he was on Mrs Snow's list. But she was aware that Mr Patel was not one of Mrs Snow's favourite people. Perhaps she was a witch, able to harness dark powers and evil influences. Perhaps it was all a farrago of nonsense and she was rapidly heading for another sojourn in the happy farm – another of Mr Bolter's well-used synonyms.

'How can I help?' she asked, dismissing the vague thoughts briskly.

'Come with me,' said Matron. 'I'm so grateful.'

8

Mr Bolter, outwardly immaculate, took his usual Monday morning stroll down the garden path, lit a cigarette at the front gate, inspected some busy greenfly on the standard rose at the end of the row of rose trees in front of the low garden wall and, with a smug proprietorial smirk, crossed the pavement, got into his car and motored off into the morning.

It was without doubt a beautiful morning. Mrs Bolter, sleepless from the early hours, had watched dawn break over the red sloping roofs of her suburban environment and had seen, entranced, how a profligate sun had staggered over the horizon radiating a kind of liquid gold which poured generously through the thickly leaved ornamental trees in the next door garden. Such patterns! Such colours! An empty sky, clearing to bright blue, the world awakening around her, birds singing away for dear life and all kinds of summery sights, sounds and smells. Then he had got up and started clomping around, polluting the air with those foul cigarettes.

During the hours between dawn and his departure she had walked between her bedroom and that of her adopted daughter next to it, smoothing the counterpane, opening wardrobe doors, touching clothes, pottering about, anything rather than think about last night, about yesterday, about today. Stop thinking. It wasn't easy trying to halt or even divert the insistent train of thought, however hard one tried, and she wanted desperately, needed desperately, to avoid thinking about Mrs Snow. But despite her strenuous efforts, Mrs Snow's face insisted upon intruding itself between her and whatever she was looking at.

The deep-set eyes of the old woman haunted her from every angle.

Why not get a divorce? she had queried. Why not, indeed? Who could say that she hadn't tried bloody hard, even though it had been so difficult at times? She recalled, still with a shudder, her wedding over thirty years ago. The long, crazy, drunken drive from their wedding reception, her mother left crying helplessly on her father's shoulder, God rest their souls; him already on the way to maudlin, frightening stupidity, refusing to let her drive; the hotel bedroom, by herself, him in the bar drinking still and later the crude assault upon her and the weight of him and the grunting, heaving nothingness and lack of sensitivity, of preparation and even of sensation – except for the insupportable pressure of his unsupported weight crushing her, the day-long growth of beard against her face and the stale smell of alcohol – brandy – on his wet mouth. And then the abrupt momentary climax, the shamefaced rolling away from her, the grunted apologies and the almost immediate oblivion into which he had subsided. Marriage was a lottery all right, you never knew what you were getting until you'd got it, and then it was a case of putting up with it, making the best of it.

Even in the early days of their marriage, sex had never meant very much to him. He'd certainly made little attempt to make up for his physical deficiencies, and whilst she agreed that they were not his fault, he should have made her aware of them before tying her down in marriage. She'd tried dressing up in suspender belt and stockings and then undressing provocatively, had even sent off for some kinky underwear from a catalogue advertised in the personal columns of her favourite and staid Sunday newspaper in an effort to rouse his interest. She had purchased and read avidly manuals on technique with 101 different positions fully illustrated. But it just wasn't there, he just wasn't interested. His only comment on the illustrations was that he wasn't a gold medal

76

gymnast and he wasn't going to get ruptured for life just for the sake of a bit of upside-down how's-your-father.

She'd sworn at him, attacked him, her face distorted with rage, and had finally broken down, quite unable to cope with everyday affairs, constantly in tears and wracked with frustration and depression. The puggled period he'd called it, when she'd gone away and there were sedatives, tranquillisers and long talks with not very sympathetic doctors and counsellors. Perhaps she should have left him then, gone away for good, but she had her pride. Instead she'd tried to come to terms with it, turned more to Bob Roberts, who had assured her that she was fully, but not over-sexed, and if anybody should be in the funny farm it was her partner, not her. When she was better they'd adopted a two-year-old baby girl because it was quite clear that that was the only way they were going to have a family and there was the secret hope, long since extinguished, that a baby around the house might inspire him to want to father one of his own.

Poor baby Claire, she thought. Some of her own sexuality appeared to have rubbed off on her. The first indication was when she'd been brought home from a Wednesday afternoon meeting of the Brownies by Brown Owl herself in a distressed condition. She not only swears like a fish porter, Brown Owl had complained, but she is corrupting the pack. Please remove her, send her somewhere else, get treatment for her. Claire stood there, quite unabashed, a picture of innocence, a beautiful violet-eyed child, beautiful even at that age despite her ill-fitting uniform. Yes, said Claire, she'd talked about men and women, Mums and Dads, to some of her Brownie friends. Drawn some of the things she'd seen in the books left around the house, because she couldn't explain them in words and they didn't believe her when she had tried to tell them about it. And she'd told them that if a man wasn't any good at fucking he was no fucking good – just like you told Daddy last week. I woke up in the night and heard you.

Dear God, she thought. What else did she wake up to and hear and see? Had they really caused Claire's problems, as the men and women in white coats suggested later? She shook her head in distress. The things we do to children, and do they ever forgive us eventually? There wasn't much forgiveness yet from Claire. Perhaps it would come. It must come. At least she hadn't left home yet, not permanently anyway.

As soon as she was certain that Mr Bolter was safely out of the way she ran a bath and soaked herself. Her figure was still remarkably good, and as yet her skin was taut and smooth with no perceptible signs of ageing. Then she put on a dressing-gown. Bob like undressing her so she usually put on clothes with lots of buttons, especially down the front of her dress or blouse, and he crooned to himself as he unfastened them slowly and gently with his big fingers. And then she'd undo his buttons and zips and between them, when they were all undone and the clothes were piled together in an untidy heap on the floor, they'd both be more than ready. Then if it was her turn to choose she'd be flat on her back with her legs in the air and he'd plunge straight in, whoosh. But these preliminaries took time. And she wanted to talk. She needed to know what he, as the appropriate concerned Councillor, had learned about Mr Patel's accident.

She was still upstairs, on Claire's bed, when she heard him in the house. He had his own key to the back door, and he always walked purposefully from wherever he had parked the car to the house, carrying a brief case and a furled umbrella. He worked on the theory that the more formally he dressed the less likely he was to arouse suspicions in the minds of any casual observers amongst the neighbours, who he hoped would take him for a rather distinguished-looking insurance agent or tally-man, calling regularly for his dues. It had seemed a bit odd to him at first when she'd invited him back soon after her marriage and made it plain that she wanted him to screw her. Her husband was useless, according to her, so it was fair game, not really cheating. It was stranger still, though, when he'd married and found that he still wanted to go back. There was no doubt about it, she loved it and needed it, and if he didn't give it to her someone else would. So far he'd been able to keep it going, despite the waning of his youthful powers and the spread of his interests, but lately it was only because he'd been neglecting his wife in that direction. Not that she seemed to notice or mind. If she did, she hadn't mentioned it. Anyway after the birth of their second child she had never really recovered her former zest for it.

The all-clear sign, the corner of a duster hanging unobtrusively out of the side window of the front bedroom, was in place. He slipped round the path and into the back garden through the side door, which he left unbolted, across the back of the house and into the kitchen. What an unholy mess, he thought, it gets worse; each time he went through it he thought it couldn't possibly get worse, but it did. She must have been entertaining over the weekend, crockery and pots were piled high in the sink and the other stacks of rubbish had surely increased. He shut the door behind him, called her name softly and went on upstairs. They'd done it all over the house in the past, hardly a square foot missed, both upstairs and downstairs, except in that crazy kitchen, hardly a patch of carpet where they had not left an impression, he recalled complacently. They'd tried it once with her on the tea-trolley, he remembered inconsequentially, started in the dining-room by the French doors and ended up in the hall, stuff all over the place and both of them giggling fit to burst. But not to be recommended.

He went into the back bedroom and she motioned for him to come in and sit down beside her.

79

'What's all this, then?' he said, lifting the cord of her dressing-gown.

'I've got things to ask, saves time.'

'What sort of things? Before or after?'

'Both, I expect.'

She watched as he took off his jacket, then his shoes and socks, then loosened his tie. His hand went under her dressing gown and rested heavily between her thighs.

'I want to know all about Mr Patel's accident,' she said.

His eyebrows went up.

'What's your interest?'

She had thought he might ask something like that and was ready.

'He was such a mystery man to most of us. Nobody knew anything about him. Running that big old car on his salary. Driving on the motorway. Where was he going? Where had he been? Was there anyone with him? Had he got any family? Are the police certain it was an accident?'

'That's a lot of questions.' He leaned over and pulled open her dressing gown at the top. Her nipples were flat. He leaned over further and gently bit one of them and twirled the other between finger and thumb. To his chagrin there was no sharp intake of breath, the sound which showed that he was on the right track and which was usually his reward for such endeavours. He got up and began removing the rest of his clothes. With his shirt half-way over his head he heard her say impatiently, 'Well, which question are you going to answer first?'

His shirt fell to the ground, and he unbelted his trousers and let them fall.

'I don't know where he was going,' he said. 'The police didn't say. I assumed that he was coming from here. As far as I know, he was by himself. But I agree with you, he was a bit of a mystery, a loner, and he did have expensive tastes in cars – big old ones are expensive to run – and some expensive clothes. We're looking to see if there's any evidence that he's been swindling the old folk or getting money off them in some way.'

He took off his underpants. He was quite limp.

'Look what all these questions have done,' he complained.

'What about the last question?'

'What question was that?'

'Was it an accident, idiot.'

He sat on the bed beside her, feeling distinctly put out. All these questions about Patel and a soft member. What was the world coming to.

'You'll have to do something about this,' he said, pointing.

'Could it have been somebody tampering with the car?' she pressed on, ignoring his plight.

'How on earth do you expect me to know? The police will presumably look to see why the car ran off the road, and then at the road surface for skid marks and oil patches or whatever. And no doubt there'll be checks on the car itself for mechanical failures. But why on earth should anyone want to mess about with his car? I know garages do it all the time, but that's called servicing.'

'Please don't be flippant,' she said. 'One hears rumours. Perhaps he has been taking things from the olds. Perhaps one of them might have had it in for him.'

'I'd have it in for you if I could,' he said, 'but you're rapidly talking me out of it.'

'Oh, for goodness sake, come and lie down,' she said, and pulled him to her. 'Poor old Bob,' she went on softly, 'it's not the reception you usually get, is it?'

She struggled out of her dressing-gown and rolled on top of him. His hands came round and grasped her buttocks. She rubbed her fuzz on him and he began to feel happier.

'That's more like it,' he said appreciatively.

She stopped suddenly. 'But the police will look, won't they?'

81

'Look for what?'

'For evidence that the car ran off the road because of unnatural causes?'

He pushed her to one side and sat up.

'What on earth are you going on about?' he demanded. 'What's all this got to do with you? Why all this interest in Patel? Were you having it off with that bloody curry merchant?'

She giggled and pouted. 'You look like Bolter,' she said. 'Come here and I'll make it better for you.'

'The better for me the better for you,' he said. Then he added, 'Really, Phyll, are we here for a bit of mutual comfort or for a bloody inquest on Patel? The two aren't compatible.'

'You're quite right,' she said. 'But I'd just like to know. It's not just nosiness. All those olds, you feel responsible for them somehow. And if someone had discovered that he'd been robbing them in some way, they might have fixed his car to teach him a lesson.'

'You've been watching too many old movies,' he said. 'If it was fixed, who amongst those poor old sods would know how or have the equipment to do it, not to mention the time and the opportunity?'

She thought hard for a few seconds.

'Dear old Bob,' she said. 'You're quite right again. It's a ridiculous notion. Lie down and relax and let me do something nice for you.'

As she reached for him the telephone extension on the bedside table rang. They both froze. It kept ringing, insistently.

'You'd better answer it,' he said resignedly. 'You are supposed to be at home, aren't you?'

She lifted the receiver. He could hear pips and bangs and then the operator's voice. She covered the mouthpiece. 'It's a reversed charges call,' she said excitedly, 'from Exeter. It must be Claire.'

He got up, reluctantly, and began putting on his

clothes. He knew when to give up. He wasn't a local politician for nothing. Anyway, he thought philosophically, they'd got away with it for years. This was a sign that, like all good things, this was coming to an end. He should get out of it while the going was good, and whilst he had an excuse. He'd be Mayor next year, and what a scandal this little affair would make if some nosy reporter followed him around and found out. Or if she, as a woman abruptly scorned – he'd have to give up seeing her during his year of office anyway – spilled the beans to the local press. He could see the headlines, sure to be picked up nationally and perhaps by the weekend scandal sheets as well. By the time she'd finished talking on the telephone he'd dressed and talked himself into the conviction that it had been nothing less than a providential intervention. He stood there, holding his briefcase and umbrella.

'I've got to go,' he said. 'The time's gone, with all this jabber. How's Claire?'

She lay back, still stark naked.

'She's coming home, on Thursday, should be here by the evening. She's in some kind of trouble, I think. Bringing someone with her too. Wanted to make certain that we'd be here.'

'Nice of her to ring,' he said. 'What sort of trouble?'

'I'm not sure that it is trouble. She was a bit incoherent. It was just something she said. Could be anything. Isn't it lovely that she turns to me when she wants help?'

Nobody else would help the little cow, he thought.

'I've got to go,' he repeated. 'Meeting a client at eleven.'

'I'm sorry,' she said, 'but you'll be late, then, if you don't get a move on. You know when I see you all dressed up it's hard to believe that you and I have been making love for years. On the bed you're my sexy old Bob. Dressed and you're Councillor Roberts. Do you ever wonder what it would be like if you came home to me at night, instead of going to her?'

83

'Put some clothes on,' he said. Warning bells were ringing and lights were flashing. 'You know that's not possible,' he said non-committally.

'Oh, I don't know,' she said. 'I know you're an unfaithful swine, but you and I have remained friends for years, and we fit. That's not a bad basis to work from.'

He grunted. 'It's a bit too late for that,' he said gruffly. 'I must go.' At the bedroom door he paused. 'I'm not sure about Thursday afternoon. Anyway, Claire might be here by then. I'll give you a ring.'

He made his way downstairs, treading lightly from habit, uneasy until he was outside and striding along the pavement. It was true that he had an appointment with a client that morning, plus business at the Town Hall, but the doubt about his availability the next Thursday had been concocted on the spot. Things were getting out of hand. He liked to be in control. She seemed to be heading for another breakdown, unless he was very much mistaken. All this curiosity about an obscure Assistant Matron at the Home was very odd. All those ridiculous questions. Perhaps he'd call in at the Home this afternoon and have a talk with Matron. He might even learn something which would help him to achieve what now seemed to be a very desirable objective – bye-bye, Phyllis.

9

Matron paused in the act of putting the last few personal garments of the late Mr Patel neatly in his imitation-leather suitcase and sat heavily on his bed. The official from the Town Hall who had arrived importantly to supervise the task of seeing that all was duly accounted for coughed nervously. Mr Blake was a short plump man, prematurely bald, heavily married and mightily oppressed by Mrs Blake and their three daughters. Outside the house he was fussy and bossy but he meant well. Everyone said so.

'Must be very distressing for you, Matron,' he observed.

'It's not that I'm not used to this sort of thing, as you know,' she said, 'but we've lost a couple of residents lately as well, and now this. And going through his things – and you making lists – it makes you realise that it might be anyone's turn tomorrow, really underlines our mortality. And what is there to show for the years spent? What does one leave behind? For Mr Patel it's a battered suitcase half full of shirts, underwear, a couple of good suits, some books and a Post Office Savings book with a few hundred pounds in it. It gets you eventually; the sense of futility, wondering what the purpose of it all is.' She paused and put her hand to her forehead. 'I wonder if you would be good enough to slip down to the kitchen and ask cook to send me up a cup of tea? A pot for two would be very nice. I'm sure you could do with some refreshment.'

'Of course, of course,' he said. He looked nervously at the pile of books and papers and correspondence which still needed to be examined and listed. 'We're nearly finished, and I know you'll not touch anything until I get back.'

'Mr Blake,' she said icily, 'I'll go and tell cook myself if you prefer. You wait here.'

'No, no,' he said hurriedly. 'You stay put, wouldn't dream of it.'

He set down his clipboard and ball pen and edged out of the room. It was one of his more interesting tasks as a Social Services officer, to record in detail the possessions left by all who expired in any of the Council's homes for the elderly. Springtime was busiest; old people seemed to be able to cope with the rigours of winter weather and germs, but every year, for some of them, the effort was too much and come spring and the appearance of the tatty daffodils in the sour soil under the trees in the courtyard, and the first nasty cold germs of the season, they retired to their beds and gave up. But this was the first time he'd been called in for a staff death – at least it was something other than old age, makes a change. Some of the books and magazines the man had were a bit ripe, but you could never tell with these Asians, funny beggars, it was all part of their religion. Temple Maidens and Karma Sutra and all that stuff. It was a weird job without doubt, but fascinating in a kind of ghoulish way. And he was well aware that although he was called in to make the inventory as soon as the death was notified, and that Matron was supposed to put the deceased's effects under lock and key until he arrived, there were often several, sometimes a considerable number, of hours between death and his arrival. During that time the more valuable personal effects, jewellery, money, best clothes, etc., could disappear, and who would know? Most of the residents had few if any visitors or relatives to enquire about such matters, even if they cared to do so – and most didn't. Fellow residents were not informed until well after the event; if they had any suspicions nobody was likely to take any notice, and anyway it would be difficult to prove when the main complainant was six feet under or cremated and spread thinly over the rosebeds in the Council's Crematorium.

Burdened with uncomfortable thoughts, not least of which was the realisation that he of all people was well placed to do something to make sure that such things didn't happen, but hadn't lifted a finger, Mr Blake made his way down to the ground floor. Despite years of visiting such establishments he had never got used to the clammy odours in them. He blew his nose and kept his handkerchief to it. Good Lord preserve us from incontinence, he prayed every Sunday under his wife's approving eye as he knelt in church before the Service began, and when she thought he was giving thanks for her continued benevolence and forbearance.

The scene in the entrance lobby was distressingly familiar. Old folk in their high-back chairs, just as he'd seen them on the previous Saturday on Open Day, in what seemed to be in exactly the same positions, some asleep, some reading, some just open-mouthed, staring at nothing in particular. But as he drew near they all seemed to come awake and to stare at him. He smiled reassuringly, unaware that each of them had a very shrewd idea of what his duties were and that each of them was convinced, unjustly but immovably, that what was worth salvaging of their goods and chattels when they departed would find their way into his possession, or bank account, as appropriate, with perhaps a percentage split with Matron. Amongst themselves he was known as the Collector.

He went on through the dining-room and past the swing doors into the kitchen. It was all spotless, stainless steel, immaculate, utensils gleaming on the walls, not a thing out of place. It was the tidiest of all the kitchens of the Homes he visited but he had grave suspicions that the food was probably the worst. How could she possibly find time to cook properly and spend so much time cleaning up? Cook, fortunately, was elsewhere. One of the stewards, Sadie, made up the tray and produced a tin of iced cakes and in a few minutes he was on his way back to Matron. As he passed through the entrance lounge again he saw Councillor Roberts coming in.

'Ah, Blake,' he called, 'just the man.'

Mr Blake hurried across, ignoring the eyes which swivelled towards him and the tray he was carrying.

'Where's Matron?' Roberts went on. 'We've things to talk about.'

'She's upstairs,' said Mr Blake. 'Not feeling too bright. Mr Patel's accident has upset her.' He lifted the tray for inspection. 'A little refreshment,' he explained.

'Ask her to come down, there's a good chap. I'll wait in her office.'

A few minutes later the three of them were in Matron's office on the ground floor. Matron had apparently managed to shrug off her turn when she realised that the Chairman of the Social Services and Welfare Committee was on the premises and waiting for her. She had shot off Mr Patel's bed, leaving Mr Blake holding the tray. He had followed her, still clutching the tray until he was able to place it on Matron's desk.

'Dreadful tragedy,' said Councillor Roberts.

'Most upsetting,' said Matron. She poured out two cups of tea and handed one to him. She looked at the other cup and at Mr Blake, her eyebrows lifting. Mr Blake waved a self-denying hand. Old bitch, he thought. Typical.

'I've been thinking,' said the Councillor, 'about Mr Patel's accident. And about the two recent deaths amongst the residents. Could they be connected in some way, do you think?'

Matron choked over her teacup.

'What on earth do you mean?' she managed to splutter. 'What possible connection could there be between those events?'

Mr Blake leaned forward, his professional audit training showing in the foxy expression on his face.

'This is strictly entre-nous,' said the Councillor, straining to recall the notions put in his head by Mrs Bolter that morning. 'I'm probably being over-zealous, over-protective, what have you, but when it comes to the welfare of those old people out there, I'm prepared to stick my neck out.' He paused. That wouldn't look half bad as a theme for an inspired article in the local paper, he thought.

'Just supposing,' he went on, 'just supposing, mark you, that Mr Patel was cheating on the residents in some way. Now if you start with that premise, there's lots of possibilities. Supposing that the two old people who died recently, Mrs . . .' he snapped his fingers and looked at Matron.

'Mrs Southover and Miss Green.'

'That's right. They could have found out, and he could have done away with them to stop them reporting him. Women are nothing in his country. Two a day get burnt alive in Delhi alone when their families don't cough up enough dowry. Life is cheap out there.'

'But if that was so,' objected Mr Blake, 'are you saying that there is another murderer out there who knew about it and somehow engineered a fatal accident to get revenge? Or to prevent him doing it again?' His voice was high-pitched, incredulous.

Councillor Roberts silenced him with a look which boded ill for his promotion prospects.

'Not at all,' he said testily. 'On the evidence so far, I'm assuming that he had a highly fortuitous accident.'

Mr Blake and Matron exchanged glances.

'We're talking hypothetically,' said the Councillor. 'And if that scenario doesn't appeal to you, then supposing that the two old ladies popped off naturally. The Patel person helps himself to their personal effects – and someone here was promised a trinket or two and didn't get them, knows that Mr P. has done them in the eye, takes umbrage and has a go at his car. Or gets someone outside to fix it?'

'But that means surely that someone on the staff is implicated,' said Matron quietly. 'He would hardly be in league with a resident.'

'Why not? Patel could have been blackmailed by a resident who had found out what he was up to. And if Mr P. had failed to pay up, the blackmailer could have taken his revenge.' He was becoming acutely aware that his speculations were beginning to look flawed and completely ridiculous. 'But could we find out discreetly if anyone, resident or staff, is likely to have the kind of mechanical background necessary to fix the car in some way?'

'But do we know if the car was fixed?' asked Mr Blake.

Councillor Roberts shook his head. 'We may never

know,' he said. 'Depends on how badly it was wrecked and what the police are able to find out from the bits.'

'Shouldn't we wait then until we do know?' said Mr Blake. 'And if Mr Patel was cheating, as you suggest, surely there would be some evidence of it in his room, amongst his possessions? We've found nothing so far – Matron and I were making an inventory of his things just before you arrived.'

Matron put down her cup and very slowly, almost reluctantly, drew from the pocket of her navy blue uniform a small stiff-covered Building Society pass book.

'When you went down for the tea,' she said to Mr Blake, 'I found this amongst that pile of papers you've yet to go through. Councillor Roberts' unexpected call put it clean out of my head.' She put the book on the table.

Mr Blake picked it up and nodded to Councillor Roberts who nodded back. He opened the book, turned the pages over quickly. He whistled. '£7,000 plus,' he said, 'deposited in a half a dozen or so entries over eighteen months. Since he joined the staff here, in fact.'

'His pay was credited direct to his bank account, I do know that,' said Matron. 'But we haven't found any bank statements yet.'

Councillor Roberts stood up.

'I knew there was more in this than meets the eye,' he said triumphantly, 'whatever the truth of the matter is. What we need is some evidence. If we can show that the money in this book is in no way accounted for by his pay, but that the dates of the deposits are fairly soon after the dates of the deaths of residents – you can take that on, Blake – then we're on to something. Look at cheque stubs, paying-in slips, dates, amounts, balances and the like. We may well be on to something. And it may be that there are others involved. Could be a major scandal! I'm not suggesting that other staff are involved, mind you, but I'm determined to get to the bottom of it.'

'We should bring in the police,' said Mr Blake.

'You get your figures out first,' said Councillor Roberts. 'After all, there might be a perfectly innocent explanation for that pass book. The police don't work on inspired surmise, like us. We'll have to give them some hard evidence.'

'I agree,' said Matron. 'The last thing we want is the police in here questioning our residents and giving them heart attacks. All this is most unlikely, if you want my opinion, gentlemen. We don't even know that Mr Patel's accident was anything other than an accident. And what's more, if he was indulging in what you suspect, then he's got his punishment and there's not much we can do about righting past wrongs. Still, I would like to know if he was up to something, under my nose, too.'

'We'll keep you informed, Matron,' said the Councillor. 'And Blake, bring anything you find direct to me.'

'I'll get on to it right away.'

'You can show me his room first,' said the Councillor, and then to Matron, 'Let me take my leave of you now. Must get back to the Town Hall as soon as possible. Terrible business. You're bearing up well, my dear. I'll get on to the Department and see that you have a replacement for Mr Patel quickly.'

Matron watched them leave her office, their heads together, like a couple of conspirators themselves, she thought. She was right to have handed over Patel's pass book. The kind of enquiries that Blake would have made could have revealed the existence of it anyway, and only she or Blake could have taken it. Pair of fools, she thought. What a lot of rubbish they talked. Time for a drink. In their blundering idiotic way, like a couple of short-trousered boy scouts on a Treasure Trail hunt, banging about and thumping and theorising, who knows what they might turn up? It could be embarrassing, to put it at its mildest. I'll talk to Mrs Bolter tomorrow, she thought, with a sudden flash of inspiration. She's got influence with Councillor Roberts and if I can get her drawn into

91

this in some way . . . maybe . . . it was better than just
sitting and waiting, wondering if and when the axe would
fall, and on whom. Having Mrs Bolter around could be a
great help. She'd give her a ring in the morning, make
sure that she was coming in, and they'd have a chat. She
felt better already.

10

It was sing-song time in the Home for Ancients, as Mrs
Grimble, the entertainments organiser, liked to call the
establishment. A large puffy-faced woman with a florid
complexion, she arrived at the Home every Tuesday
afternoon without fail to entertain the residents with
community singing. The singing was followed by solo acts
of varying degrees of ineptitude; she herself sang, and
commanded a troupe of amateur artistes, all of whom had
volunteered their services to the Welfare Committee in
response to various appeals. This afternoon all that had
been available from the volunteers were a charming super-
annuated old gentleman who had no talent whatsoever
for monologues but who insisted on giving them, and a
female ex-ballet dancer who did aerobics, whatever they
might be. Mrs Grimble had a vague notion that it was
something to do with conjuring tricks performed to music,
since the woman looked like a witch and had brought
along her own cassette player and tapes.

Those of the residents who hadn't been able to move
away quickly enough had been rounded up and were
gathered in the lounge with the piano pushed away from
the wall by Sadie and Pearl into the centre of the L-shaped
space which remained. Sadie and Pearl now stood at the
back of the room, preparing to enjoy themselves, as usual.
It looked, thought Mrs Snow from her seat close to the

door, as if the pair were on duty to prevent anybody sneaking off. She was well aware that if nobody else enjoyed the entertainment. Sadie and Pearl did, and expected everyone to do so as well.

Mrs Grimble entered from the side with her usual grand gestures, acknowledged her audience, sat down at the piano with a theatrical flourish of her skirt and arranged her music in front of her. Then she stood up, adjusted her hat, peered all round with a jolly expression on her face and held up her hand for attention.

'Good afternoon,' she called, waving.

There were one or two mutters, more like veiled threats than happy responses, thought Mrs Snow. Most of her fellow-residents had already withdrawn behind either vacant stares or fixed, if somewhat apprehensive, smiles.

'Community singing first,' boomed Mrs Grimble, and struck the first twanging discord of the afternoon with both hands on the keyboard. 'Any requests?' A quick glance around. 'No? Rightyho, off we go then, what about Daisy, Daisy?'

It was the same every week, thought Mrs Snow; one of these afternoons I shall sit here and scream until she stops, and they can carry me out.

Mrs Grimble was in full swing with Daisy and her tandem when Mrs Bolter appeared at the door. She stopped briefly, winced at the sight and sound of some of the hardier residents puffing and grunting behind Mrs Grimble's lead, and was about to go off in the direction of Matron's office when she caught sight of Mrs Snow and the Colonel, side by side, apparently joining in the fun. She hesitated briefly, waved, and then went on her way again. What's her game, then? thought Mrs Snow; she knew that Mrs Bolter usually avoided Tuesday afternoons, for obvious reasons. What's up, I wonder?

The sound of Mrs Grimble's voice reached Matron as she poured tea for herself and Mrs Bolter in her office. Mrs Bolter's face had already registered pain and she nodded approvingly as Matron got up and shut her office door before handing Mrs Bolter a cup. Matron sat back, composed, her hands resting on her lap. Mrs Bolter lifted her spoon and gave her tea a few nervous stirs.

'Thank you for coming in,' said Matron.

Mrs Bolter made a fluttering movement with her hands. 'I'm very curious,' she said. 'You know I usually skip Tuesday afternoons.'

'I haven't thanked you properly for helping out on Sunday night. It was very good of you.'

'So pleased to be able to help,' said Mrs Bolter. 'It was nothing.'

'Indeed it was not nothing. I wonder how many people could and would have stood it in the way you did? And it set up a train of thought which I thought you and I might pursue. I hope to our mutual advantage. Hence my phone call.'

'Really?'

'Mr Patel's death leaves us sadly understaffed. Councillor Roberts has promised us a replacement quickly but I'm well aware that even given priority and the Councillor's influence, it could take weeks to get somebody satisfactory. I wondered – if I asked the Councillor to approve it – if you would be prepared to take the job on on a temporary basis? It would be of enormous assistance to me. We all need you.'

Mrs Bolter set down her cup.

'It's nice to be needed,' she said, 'but I'll have to think about it. Mr Bolter, you know.'

'I'm sure we could come to some arrangement about hours. You already come in at least once a day, sometimes twice; I'm sure Mr Bolter would understand, and of course it would only be a temporary arrangement until we got ourselves sorted out.'

Mrs Bolter shook her head doubtfully.

'My daughter is coming home unexpectedly on Thursday,' she said. 'I can't possibly commit myself until I know

94

how long she's staying. Besides, I must at least warn my husband.'

'I do understand,' said Matron. 'Perhaps you would think about it and let me know. Tomorrow if possible! You see how much we need you!'

She poured another cup of tea for her visitor.

'Did you know that Councillor Roberts has asked Mr Blake from the Town Hall to undertake a kind of unofficial investigation into Mr Patel's affairs?' she asked.

'What on earth does he think Mr Blake will find? Is there any information about how the accident happened yet?'

'We've no further advice from the police, and I'm sure that whatever is found in Mr Patel's personal effects there will be a perfectly logical explanation for it.'

'I'm sure you're right. I'm glad that the investigation is unofficial, though. Who knows what side effects it would have if the police were brought in, questioning the old people, upsetting everybody? It would be dreadful.'

Matron clasped her hands together.

'Almost my exact words to Councillor Roberts,' she said. 'What possible good could come of it?'

'It would be so nice if Mr Blake found nothing untoward,' said Mrs Bolter. 'Poor Mr Patel. He was so helpful on Open Day, on his weekend off, too.'

'So glad we understand each other,' said Matron. 'Do explain to Mr Bolter how essential it is for us to have you here. Bring him to see me – I'll put him in the picture – if you have any trouble persuading him.'

Mrs Bolter smiled. 'What a good idea,' she said. 'I'll certainly suggest that.'

Mrs Snow looked up as Mrs Bolter appeared at the end of the corridor from Matron's office. She observed her flushed cheeks and general air of excitement. What's bloody up now, she thought, as Mrs Bolter came towards them and stopped at the edge of the last row of olds. Mrs Snow caught her eye. Mrs Bolter hesitated and then

95

mouthed silently 'come to the visitors' room', and pointed in its direction. Mrs Snow nodded. There was one sure way of getting out of the serried ranks of the audience. She began to cough. Gently at first and then a great hawking rasp, cough cough, hawk hawk. She hauled herself up on her frame and, still hacking and wheezing, thumped her way around the outside of the row of seats.

Pearl looked at Sadie as Mrs Snow tottered past them.

'Some people got no manners,' she said loudly.

'Don't appreciate a bit of culture,' responded Sadie.

Fat black cows, thought Mrs Snow dispassionately. I'll have them too, one day. By this time the cough was not quite under control and she was still wheezing mightily when she reached the visitors' room, where Mrs Bolter was waiting, and collapsed into a chair.

'Give me a light, dear, will you,' she gasped, handing a box of matches to Mrs Bolter.

'Are you sure? You're having trouble enough now breathing.'

Mrs Snow extracted a cigarette from her bag, her eyes streaming. 'Just give me a light,' she said.

She took a deep drag on her cigarette when it was lit and then sat back, blinking wearily.

'These bloody sing-songs will be the death of me,' she said eventually.

'It's not the singing,' protested Mrs Bolter, 'it's those cigarettes.'

'Maybe,' said Mrs Snow, 'but it's funny how they stop me from coughing.'

'Well, I can't stay,' said Mrs Bolter. 'I just wanted to put you in the picture and to warn you to be careful. Matron has asked me to fill in here until a new Assistant Matron is appointed. Councillor Roberts has got Mr Blake from the Town Hall to investigate Mr Patel's affairs. If there's anything fishy, I expect they'll call in the police, and heaven knows where it will all end up.'

'Mr Blake? That'll be the Collector.'

96

'Is that all you have to say?' asked Mrs Bolter, and then she said, urgently, 'Was Mr Patel on your list, by any chance? Did you have anything to do with his accident?'

Mrs Snow smiled enigmatically.

'Me, dear? How could I make him have an accident? Don't be silly, dear. Put it out of your mind. Are you going to take the job?'

'I'm thinking about it.'

'It might be a good move,' said Mrs Snow. 'Keep your eye on Mr Collector Blake and Matron at the same time.'

'Matron?'

Mrs Snow nodded vigorously. 'If anyone wants watching,' she said, 'it's her.' She patted her nose. 'Mark my words,' she said. 'Just you mark my words.'

11

Mrs Bolter looked at her watch for the hundredth time that day and then went into the drawing-room to check by the carriage clock on the mantelshelf that neither clock nor watch had stopped. After Mr Bolter's departure to his office that morning she had rushed around the house, tidying and dusting; had changed the sheets on Claire's bed, made a rapid sortie to the supermarket and returned laden with packs of Claire's favourite foods – which she would have put in the refrigerator if there had been room, but which were still piled, accusingly she thought, on the draining-board in the kitchen. By midday she'd had enough. She sat down in the dining-room with a tumbler full of pseudo cold tea and gratefully took a large swig at it. That's better, she said to herself, and took another one.

She looked around the room. It was much the same as it had been on Sunday. Despite hours of work it still looked depressingly untidy, and it was useless doing anything more in the kitchen until some of the rubbish had been moved. But at least the beds were clean, with freshly laundered sheets. It was desperately worrying having Claire telephone like that out of the blue, saying that she was coming home, that someone would be giving her a lift, and it would be all right, wouldn't it, if that someone stayed the night?

It had been Claire's own idea to go down to Exeter well before the term was due to start, to look for digs. It was her idea too to move out of the accommodation provided for the students by the University, so handy for lectures and all the social and sporting activities that went on there. Not that she was terribly interested in that sort of thing. Mrs Bolter sighed and took some more refreshment. If only she had read something useful at University life might have been a lot different subsequently. She'd have met different people and acquired useful, marketable skills like . . . she paused. Her eyes were getting heavy. She wondered vaguely where Claire was right then. 'I'm getting a lift back home,' she'd said. 'Should be with you late afternoon. We'll be staying a few days if that's all right.' Comforted, her senses dulled with sherry on an empty stomach, Mrs Bolter nodded off.

Claire Bolter, the abandoned natural daughter of an Irish barmaid and her boss, the awkwardly individual result of a brief but passionate liaison, smiled at herself as reflected in the mirror of the ladies' room in a motorway service area on the M4. She saw violet eyes and dark hair shining, a pink and white skin and the kind of bloom which only the young possess and which, unfortunately, proves to be such a transient asset. At nearly twenty years of age she was an enigma, sexually experienced but with a kind of aura of innocence which positively invited enlightenment. It wasn't her fault, she had long ago concluded, if boys, and later, young men – and some not so young – declared

98

that they would die of unrequited love if she didn't allow them favours of a particular kind. And how one things leads to another, she thought. Not that she was at all averse to exploring to the limits the varieties of pleasure and experience which were on offer, but things tended to get complicated emotionally, at least as far as the men were concerned. They were so naive, so demandingly childish.

But Richard was different. In her first year at Exeter she'd known of him, and his reputation as a womaniser. A senior lecturer in political science, in his late thirties, tall, fair, good-looking, unmarried, he was reputed to have the pick each year of the first-year female undergraduates. Sometimes they lasted a term, sometimes two, but invariably by the end of the academic year he was unattached again and ready for the hunt at the beginning of the next. In the summer, in the long vacations, he gave his services to whatever overseas archaeological dig would have him, providing it was in a hot climate and that amongst his fellow volunteers there was a selection of nubile young women, preferably Scandinavian, with whom he could drink the local wine and make love in the evenings after the day's stint excavating old ruins. He'd return to the campus in the late summer, beautifully bronzed, hair bleached by the sun, a few more interesting wrinkles around his eyes and a few more words of Danish, Swedish or Norwegian to add to a basic vocabulary in those languages. He'd settle in his flat, check with the bursar for lists of female students registering, and make the rounds. It was as easy as falling off a log. Getting shot of his temporary partners was a different matter, but so far he'd managed without serious complications. Life wasn't at all bad. A job he liked, an entry to the real political scene whenever he got tired of lecturing about the subject, and an uninterrupted succession of girls, the envy of his peers.

And then he happened, quite by chance, to run into Claire in the last month of the first term of her first year. She was coming out of Professor Daly's room, talking animatedly, clutching what he assumed to be the work she had been discussing with him at a tutorial. The old man bent over her, clearly charmed out of his wits, his hand on her shoulder. He thought then that he had never seen anything so sensually innocent and attractive in his life and kicked himself for not having made a more thorough search of the available talent at the beginning of term. Who was she? By the next evening he had all the essential details. Claire Bolter, first-year student of politics, philosophy and economics. A bright young woman by all accounts. During the next few days he had arranged to transfer her to his list of students in exchange for the brightest female student on his list plus the loan of his sporty two-seater for a week. Since the female concerned was then his current sleeping partner, who was proving to be excessively difficult and demanding, and the weather was wet and cool and unsuitable for swanning about the countryside, he considered it to be a great bargain.

She'd turned up late for his next lecture and said nothing during it. She did stare at him though, and it was oddly disturbing to have so much concentrated attention and curiosity hanging on his every word, however much he tried to ignore her. She took no notes, but as he was shuffling his papers into his briefcase at the end of the session, having carefully avoided acknowledging her existence during it, she came to him, still staring, still silent.

He dropped a couple of papers and seemed to have difficulty in retrieving them.

'I suppose,' he said evasively, 'you're wondering why Dr Coleman and I have arranged your transfer between us?'

'Ah,' said Claire. 'It's nice to know that you think I'm capable of wondering why this great honour has been thrust upon me. Instead of being struck dumb.' She paused. 'Now let me think. You've swopped me for that

100

doll-faced Judy Hardy – who the whole world knows has been giving you a hard time – plus the loan of your notorious sex wagon. The reasons are pretty obvious, because even Judy has worked them out. Firstly, you want to remove her from the intimacy of day-to-day contact and the unrivalled opportunities for access which students have with their Senior Lecturers. This is preliminary to booting her out of your bed. Secondly, you don't want her to foul up the approaches you intend to make to her successor. The chosen one. Me. You expect moreover that I'll jump up and down at the prospect of replacing her between the sheets.'

He grinned. 'Your assumptions are remarkably spot on,' he said. 'I'll just scoot off and wring Dr Coleman's neck. I assume it was he who spilled the beans?'

'Which at least you have the good sense not to deny.' She smiled sweetly. 'No, it wasn't Dr Coleman, it was Professor Daly. Dr Coleman told him. Thought it was a great joke.'

'And what did Professor Daly think?'

She smiled again. 'We nearly fell out of bed laughing at the idea,' she said, 'but we decided to go along with it, get a bird's eye view of the technique employed by Exeter's prime stud. Prof said that it might come in handy.'

He managed to finish packing away his papers.

'I thought I was beyond being surprised . . .'

'Not shocked?' she interjected.

He shook his head. '*Chacun à son goût*,' he said. How on earth could she fancy that old goat, he thought. He was white-haired, what there was of it, the pink scalp showing slightly scrofulous. His beard and moustache were a dreadful gingery colour and he had a large nose, veined and open-pored and ranging in colour from deep purple to bright pink, and he drank like a fish, consuming vast quantities of bitter beer and real ale. In his mind's eye Richard roved over the known attributes of the head of his department with a new curiosity. He had a first-class brain, there was no denying that. But he also had uneven yellow teeth and a belly that hung over the belt of his trousers. Someone had once described him as a well-established sartorial disaster. She could hardly hope to ensnare the old boy, his wife was still very much in evidence. Perhaps she was hoping for better grades than she would otherwise have earned? How could she? He tried to banish the unsought vision of them in bed together which had suddenly intruded on his thoughts with garish clarity. He picked up his case.

She looked at him quizzically.

'Aren't you going to make a pass at me?'

'I don't think that we should continue this conversation,' he said. 'I'll arrange for your transfer back to Dr Coleman as soon as possible.'

'Don't bother. I can assure you that Professor Daly wouldn't endorse it, and I don't want it. You may be the most conceited prig on two legs but your lectures are far better than Dr Coleman's. Just so long as you assess my work fairly I promise not to embarrass you further.'

After Dr Richards's hurried retreat from the lecture-room she had skipped his tutorials and seen him only at lectures for the rest of term. She'd parted from Professor Daly, amicably and without regrets. He was a bit of an old bore, however charming. His wife had discovered that he'd been having a fling with an undergraduate, and, icy-faced and tight-lipped, she'd given him the option: give her up or get out, you silly old fool, will you never learn? They'd celebrated their parting with a bottle of champagne and a Chinese take-away in her room.

'If only I were twenty years younger,' he had said, wistfully.

'You mean forty years younger, surely,' said Claire. 'But perhaps it's for the best, you're a nice old professor.' She patted his paunch. 'Go home and have a couple of pints of old ale or whatever it is, you'll feel much better.'

It had been a successful year. Work had gone well, she had packed up early and left for home feeling that she had achieved a great deal and that next year was something to be looked forward to with pleasure and anticipation. Back home, she'd got a job as a waitress in a restaurant in town, sleeping most of the day, leaving the Bolters at about six o'clock each evening and arriving back in the early hours of the morning. It was sometimes as late as 3 a.m. that she got back, tired, but so tense with the strain of the night's work, waiting on a crowd of late night diners, some objectionably drunk, that she found it impossible to sleep. Sometimes she would put a tape on her player and in a few minutes there would be rappings on the wall and she would ignore them until Mrs Bolter came into the room, her face puffy with sleep, her dressing-gown wrapped tightly around her.

'Really, Claire,' she would say. 'Not again. It's so loud. People have to get up in the morning. It isn't fair.'

Sometimes Claire would turn off the player and face the wall, and Mrs Bolter would go out, thankfully. Sometimes she would just look at her adoptive mother and say nothing, or turn up the volume even louder, and Mr Bolter would come storming up from downstairs, his face flushed, and turn it off himself and they would all shout at each other until one or the other gave up. And while they were shouting there would be references to Claire's ancestry, to her wish that anyone, but anyone, other than the Bolters, had adopted her and, from the two of them, to her ingratitude for favours past, present and promised.

Much to Mrs Bolter's relief, Claire had announced that she was returning to college early to look for digs. She'd lived in one of the large dormitory blocks on the campus for her first year. Although the accommodation was comfortable, cheap and handy, she had decided that it wasn't what she wanted. The Bolters had agreed to underwrite her whim; her adoptive father had in fact not bothered to disguise his relief. Like her, he was exhausted,

103

and it was now his oft-repeated heartfelt wish that some randy young sod would get her in the family way and marry her tout de bloody suite. He could tolerate being a grandfather, he thought, for say about five or ten minutes a month, and there was something particularly linear and immortal about having a grandson.

Mrs Bolter had given her a lift to Victoria to catch the overnight coach service to Exeter and waved her goodbye with regretful tears. Claire had dozed fitfully on the coach. When she stepped off it in the early morning it was raining and she began to wonder if she had made the wisest of moves. Her shoulder bag was heavy and she was beginning to feel like a water-logged duck as she trudged towards the bus stop. Dr Richards saw her as he motored past in his open two-seater, did a double-take, turned at the next intersection and overtook her, banging cheerfully on the horn.

'Can I give you a lift?' he shouted.

Claire looked at the open car and a barely recognisable Dr Richards wrapped in a heavy raincoat buttoned up to the neck ad an old leather flying helmet on his head, and decided that it was better to get wetter motoring than walking.

'Please,' she called, and he reached over and unlocked the door so that she could slide in.

'Very civil of you in the circumstances,' she said, 'even if it is wetter in the car than it is outside.'

'Well, at least you'll get where you're going more quickly,' he said, 'which is where?'

'Let's try the bursar's office,' she said. 'I want some temporary accommodation on campus while I look for a flat in town for next term.'

'What's wrong with the dormitory blocks? As if I didn't know,' he added.

Out of the traffic he picked up speed and the rain continued to teem down. Claire shivered and turned up the collar of her thin raincoat. Her hair was soaking and water was dripping off the end of her nose. 'I'm cold,' she said. 'It's supposed to be summer, I think.'

'I suppose,' he said, 'if I took you to my flat, so that you could dry off and I could put the hood up on this thing, you'd assume that I was propositioning you.'

'And you wouldn't be?'

'You don't have to listen.'

'I can be very deaf when necessary,' she said. 'I'm also very wet, tired and hungry and I don't like it.'

'Let me make the offer formally. Allow me to drive you to my flat so that you can dry off. No strings.'

'Formally accepted.'

'Actually the place is in a bit of a mess. I came back early myself only a couple of days and there's still gear to be unpacked. But the shower's working and there's plenty of hot water.'

The flat was on the top of a small block built on a cross road but set back from the road itself, on the last hill before the University buildings.

Inside it Claire glanced around curiously. 'It's like home,' she said. 'My mother keeps open house for bundles and things waiting for collection for jumble sales. Trouble is, she gets attached to them and can't bear to part with them and they never leave the house. She's got a set of those in the garage' – she nodded in the direction of an array of spears and a zebra-skin-covered warrior's shield which adorned one wall – 'got it in a Salvation Army bring and buy, if memory serves me.'

'Sounds fascinating,' he said. 'I got mine in the Transvaal. The bathroom's through there.' He pointed.

When she emerged warm and dry from the shower in a change of clothing, he had cleared books and an assortment of clothes, jogging-shorts and shoes from the two chairs opposite the fireplace, which was fitted with an electric fire which he had switched on. She could hear him moving about in the kitchen. It was a compact pad, she decided, very handy, with lots of interesting things.

Pottery, whole pots and fragments, what looked like old bricks with patterns and cuneiform script scratched and baked on them. Some fearsome-looking masks, African she guessed, and rows of glassed-in shelves with smaller and, she surmised, more fragile and more valuable relics from his summer digs.

He came in with two mugs of coffee and handed her one.

'And what's in all these boxes and parcels?' she asked, pointing. 'And that crate? The place looks like a cross between an Oxfam shop and a small provincial museum.'

'Haven't had time to unpack,' he said. 'Come and sit down. While you've been making yourself more presentable, I've had an idea.'

'I knew it,' she said.' Forget it.'

'It's not what you fear,' he said and smiled at her. 'I've got to go up to London for a few days, leaving this afternoon. Why not stay here and do your flat-hunting from this base? The bus stops at the crossroads and goes into town six times a day, no less. What do you think?'

'If I thought about it I'd probably say no,' she said. 'What's the catch?'

'What a suspicious person you are,' he said. 'But if you have time and want to open those boxes and stash away what's in them and put the debris out near the rubbish bin, I'd be eternally grateful. But no obligation! Meanwhile I'll show you around, and demonstrate what keys fit where, and tell you which of my neighbours to avoid.'

When he'd gone – she had a suspicion that he was on his way earlier when he'd spotted her in town – and she'd waved goodbye to him from the balcony as he disappeared from sight in a rapidly forming mist, she sat down and hugged herself. There was no doubt about it, fortune was smiling on her. It was perfectly true that he had an appointment in London the following day. She'd suggested cynically that he'd made that up and was going to sneak back that night to force his evil attentions on her.

106

He'd sighed and shown her a letter forwarded to the site he'd been camping on, which conveyed an invitation to address a Committee of the Royal Geographical Society – the reason he'd returned early – on the finds of an expedition he'd been associated with the previous summer. It was a shipwreck, he'd explained, in the Mediterranean off Cape Ulu Burun, near Kaş on the Turkish coast. It happened about 3,500 years ago, at the time of the Trojan Wars, no less. The ship was made of wood, fir probably, and it was going to tell us more about the ships that sailed from Athens in those days, and what made that city such an important trading centre, than anything previously discovered. The ship had copper, tin and glass in its cargo, and no fewer than eight stone anchors, each weighing about 800 pounds; and how that lot got loaded without block and tackle was a mystery.

'Quite so,' said an unimpressed Claire. 'Anything to interest the romantic layman? Any jewels? Gold?'

'I'm disappointed in you,' he said. 'There was some gold, in fact – a Greek mug that is probably priceless, some beads, amphorae, and we may find other artefacts next year.'

'Well, good luck with your lecture,' she said. 'Hope you have a full house.'

'And good luck with your flat-hunting. Don't go too far away.'

When he had finally disappeared into the mist she explored the flat thoroughly. Firstly, it was ideally situated. Secondly, it also had two bedrooms. Dr Richards was good-looking, and despite her gibes, intelligent, eligible, etc., and whilst she had no intention of becoming the newest notch on his trouser-belt – and in any case he was an absolute bore with his jogging and keeping fit, and his little bits of broken pots and spears and masks – he might be prepared to rent her his spare room. If he wanted to bring in some buxom first-year female student to keep him warm at night, she wouldn't disturb them.

107

And she could make herself useful in other ways. Start unpacking those boxes for a start, tidy up the place a bit, the woman's touch. She smiled to herself. And if she didn't mind him bringing in a fancy piece full time, he couldn't very well object if she occasionally brought in a young stud if she so desired.

The next two days flew past, and when she went to bed late on the second night – he was due back the following morning – she felt extraordinarily self-righteous. While she had done no house-hunting, the boxes and parcels and the crate had all been unpacked, his scuba gear and wet suits were stowed away in his built-in wardrobe, his laundry had been washed and ironed and put away and the flat had been hoovered and generally tidied up. Looks quite liveable, she thought, weary with the unaccustomed labour. When she had eaten and bathed, she took some books to bed and fell fast asleep reading Thomas More's *Utopia*. What a gas, she thought, but as a sedative, highly effective.

She woke up suddenly at the sound of a key rattling in the door. The light was still on and she saw that it was 3.30 a.m.

She heard the front door open and close.

'Who's there?' she called, grasping the telephone by the bedside and rapidly dialling for the operator.

Dr Richards appeared at the bedroom door.

'Sorry,' he said. 'Didn't mean to wake you.'

She slammed down the receiver and glared at him.

'I'm sorry,' he said again.

'If I had a gun you'd be dead,' she said, sitting up. 'You're not expected until tomorrow.'

'Couldn't wait to get back,' he said. 'Fancy a drink?' He produced a bottle of champagne from behind his back. 'And you'd better put some clothes on if you say yes.'

She remembered suddenly that she'd gone to bed naked.

'If it upsets you, I'll put something on while you get a couple of glasses.'

When he returned she was still sitting up in bed but she had put on a tee shirt and had run a comb through her hair. He opened the champagne; the cork shot through the air and the wine whooshed out of the bottle. He poured out two glasses and handed her one before sitting on the edge of the bed.

'Cheers,' he said.

'Cheers,' she responded and sipped at the wine. It was a bit of a cissy drink, she thought, but this had a dry nutty flavour and did pleasant things to the back of her throat as it went down.

'I take it that you've had a successful trip,' she said.

He nodded. 'That's why I'm back sharpish. The Society have asked me to return to Turkey to represent them officially on the Greek cargo-ship exploration I was telling you about. It'll be for a year if I can get away. Starting as soon as possible.'

'And?'

'If I can get a year's sabbatical, there's nothing I'd like better.'

'More good luck,' she said. 'Does that mean you'll be looking for a tenant for your flat?'

'That's right,' he said. He took another drink. 'But I don't want you as a tenant. I want you to come with me.'

'Come with you,' she repeated. 'Are you off your rocker?'

'Don't say anything yet,' he pleaded. 'Hear me out. The trouble is I've fallen for you like the proverbial ton of bricks. Ever since you told me what a conceited prig I was, last year. I've tried my best to put you out of my mind, but the thought of leaving you here for another year, and all that you might get up to, just isn't bearable. I know that you'll miss out on your degree course, but you can take it up again when we return, and we'd have a whole year in the sun for our honeymoon.'

109

'Honeymoon? You have to be married to go on a honeymoon.'

He took another drink. 'Will you?'

'Will I what?'

'Will you marry me?'

She put down her glass. He looked quite pale and somehow very young and vulnerable. It must be this light, she thought. He was undeniably very good-looking.

'Let's have some more champagne,' she said, and when he had refilled her glass she lifted it to the light and watched the lines of bubbles blowing themselves to extinction in a never-ending procession. Life's but a something or other, she muttered to herself, and suddenly thought of her adoptive mother. Poor old Phyllis, she thought, what a life I've led her and wouldn't she be over the moon.

'Give me your hand,' she said. 'And now, truth and no lies.'

He nodded gravely.

'Have you ever proposed to anyone before?'

'Never.' He crossed his heart with his free hand.

'Not even hinted at it, as a long-term possibility, just to get some buxom blonde into bed?'

'Not the slightest hint of a hint.'

'Then how many girls have you slept with?'

He shook his head in mock dismay. 'I don't know. I don't keep records. What does it matter? I've never loved any one of them.'

'Do you love me?'

He nodded dumbly.

'You poor fish,' she said. 'What is to become of you?'

'Is that all you can say to the most eligible member of the faculty of this distinguished University?' he said indignantly. 'To a man who has just declared his love for you and made you an offer of marriage?'

'Where's my violin?' she asked. 'I have a strong urge to play Hearts and Flowers.'

He grinned and she felt herself warming to him. Or perhaps it was the champagne, cunning devil.

'Do I take it that you don't love me, could never love me and that I must suffer the pangs of unrequited passion to the end of my days?'

She laughed.

'You're right in the first part,' she said. 'But we can't have you suffer, can we? Come to bed and we'll talk about it in the morning.'

When she woke up she wasn't quite sure where she was. And then she saw the bedside lamp on the side table, the empty champagne bottle and glasses and his clothes in an untidy heap on the floor and her tee shirt on top of them. There was also a note on the bedside table. 'Gone for a run, back for your answer before breakfast'. She sunk back on to the pillows. He really was incredible. It's quite clear to me, she said to herself, that I've never done it properly before, and if it's like that again next time I'll be surprised. That was a one-off performance if ever I was involved in one.

She was still sleepy, relaxed, half-dozing, the events of the past few days since she left home remembered vaguely, as if they had not been quite real, when he returned. He had on his track-suit and had wound a clean towel around his neck. His face was beaded with perspiration and there was a healthy glow on the tanned skin. He sat down on the bed and smiled at her.

'Well,' he said.

'Well what?'

'I have a feeling we've done this scene before,' he said. 'Last night you said you'd tell me in the morning if you were going to accept my proposal. Remember?'

'So I did,' she said.

'And it's now morning.'

She pulled the sheets up to her neck.

'I don't believe what happened last night,' she said. 'It must have been the champagne. Can you do it again?'

111

'I'll go and shower.'

'Shower afterwards,' she said, 'together. Make love to me now – all sweaty and hot – if you can.'

'And if I can't?'

'You'll have to give up running, won't you.'

He stood up and stripped off.

'Come over here,' she said. 'Nearer,' and took hold of him.

'When you're certain you can get your year's sabbatical, and that I can come back afterwards and take up where I'm leaving off, I'd like to take you home to meet my parents. We can get married from there, if you like.'

'What are you doing?' he asked. 'Not that I'm complaining.'

'Did you hear what I said?' she demanded. 'I've said yes.'

'Why don't you telephone home now, before you change your mind?'

She let go of him, looked up at him and smiled.

'Let's have a few days together first,' she said. 'After all, I hardly know you.'

The few days, and more, had flown past so rapidly that she had hardly had time to draw breath. And here she was, on the way home, dabbing at her eyes in a motorway service-area lavatory mirror. Were there lavatories on site at Ulu Burun, she wondered? It's all happening so quickly it's hardly surprising I don't really know where I am or what I'm doing. Her mother had sounded a bit odd on the telephone a couple of days ago when she said that she was coming home. She wondered what sort of reception she would get. She wondered too why she was taking all this trouble to involve them. They could have got married much more easily at the University and gone on from there without any fuss. But she owed them something, she supposed, this at least. And there was a feeling, too, that she needed to prove something to them.

Richard looked tired. But that wasn't too surprising. All

112

that rushing about, meetings with senior people, telephoning administrators who were still on vacation, in outlandish places – Professor Daly had been marvellously helpful – and he'd got his year off and, in the very special circumstances, so had she, and they both had the old man's blessing. Funny how things had worked out, she mused. She emerged from the ladies' room grinning impishly to herself.

'Are you really ready?' he asked. 'Was there a queue or a blockage or something?'

'My poor old Senior Lecturer,' she said, 'you look so weary. You really should ease up. Would you like me to drive?'

And it was with eyes wide open with curiosity that Mrs Bolter, who had dashed into position behind the front-bedroom curtains, having been alerted by the full blooded roar of the car's exhaust, saw Claire execute a neat right-hand turn into the drive, brake violently to stop the car inches from the garage door, and leap out of it to the other side of the car where a tall fair-haired youngish man of ashen hue tumbled out as she pulled open the door with a victorious jerk. Claire looked down at Dr Richards prone in the driveway and then waved gaily at the upstairs window where, though unseen, she knew that her adoptive mother would be lurking.

'Look what I've brought home,' she called. 'Cooee!'

At precisely that moment Mr Bolter arrived back from his office. His car backed yet again into the long-suffering ornamental tree outside the front gate; it was a heavier than usual thump, since the car was a replacement and he wasn't quite attuned to its vagaries as yet. The tree shook in protest, but somehow remained upright as the back fender struck it. Mr Bolter got out, lit a cigarette and inspected the damage. He brushed away a few twigs and leaves from the roof and muttered under his breath. Bloody tree, he thought, downright dangerous, phone the Council and get them to remove it before it does some real

113

damage. Sod what the ratepayers' association think, getting lethal trees planted all over the place was not a service to the community.

Claire and Dr Richards, now standing together, watched in silence as he moved along the pathway to the door. He was clearly solemnly, majestically, drunk.

'Hallo, father,' called Claire.

Mr Bolter's eyes focused on the car, Claire and her companion, and he blinked. 'You're supposed to be in Exeter,' he said. 'Who's your friend?'

'This is no friend,' said Claire, 'this is my fiancé, Dr Richards.'

They shook hands. Mr Bolter winced and hitched up his trousers.

'A bit sudden, all this, what?' he said. Then he smiled benignly and blinked again as the realisation hit him that his beautiful but wayward daughter might be off his hands both physically and financially.

'Fiancé, eh?' he said. 'Well, well and well again! This calls for a drink or two and no mistake. Dr Richards, eh?' His face glistened as his smile broadened and he seemed to sway in the early evening air as he turned to Claire and took a deep drag on his cigarette. 'Well done, my dear,' he said, and as he stopped to kiss her cheek, 'well done indeed, you little minx!'

The front door opened and Mrs Bolter looked out anxiously.

'Phyllis,' called Mr Bolter, his arms and hands describing vague but generous gestures. 'It's champagne time. Claire's scooped the bloody pools and no mistake!'

12

Matron pulled to the sliding door of her wardrobe and stood looking at her reflection in the floor-to-ceiling mirror which showed not only her image but the whole of the room behind her and, in the mirror on the far wall, herself reflected back in a series of diminishing cameos along a tunnel which reached back for ever, beyond sight or touch or sound, an infinity of repetition. She smoothed the silky dark material of the skirt of her dress and then adjusted the SRN's badge which she wore on her left breast with a row of miniature medal ribbons.

Where had the years gone? she asked herself. What had happened to all those ambitions and high hopes she had once nurtured? And now, when she had her remaining years plotted with what she had thought was a fair degree of certainty, events were threatening to liquidate even those modest aspirations. Perhaps it was all the working of natural justice; the Hindus knew how to absorb the slings and arrows of outrageous fortune, and perhaps she too should accept things as Karma. But she wasn't a Hindu, and she wasn't going to lie down and let tinpot representatives of the juggernaut bureaucracy run all over her if she could help it. The slings and arrows could be deflected if you had the right equipment, and she had it, no doubt about it. Resilience, resourcefulness, a brain that ticked over like a well-oiled machine – even more efficiently under pressure – and experience. She would need all those attributes and qualities, she thought, and a fair measure of good fortune, in the immediate future.

Downstairs all appeared to be in order, breakfast was over and the last residents to leave the dining-room were following their individually erratic courses along the corridor to the entrance lounge. Mrs Snow brought up the rear, still chewing. A strange old woman, thought Matron. She ought to be dead, with that dreadful cough and that crippling arthritic hip, but her eyes were oddly bright and her medical records said that her heart was as sound as a bell. The Colonel was hovering about her, as usual, in his indeterminate way. They were an unlikely pair. She caught Mrs Snow's basilisk-like stare and nodded graciously in her direction.

She began walking towards her office. There was the time in the military hospital in Calcutta, she recalled, despite herself, when she had discovered one of the locally recruited female orderlies, half-naked, shinning up a drainpipe to their quarters, with a knife between her teeth. The girl, known as Susie, was obsessed with a new recruit who had already been claimed by a butch corporal orderly. Susie had planned, she explained under questioning later, to break into the corporal's room from the outside, kill her if she refused to give up the girl, and hopefully get away with it as an outside job! It was beyond belief. The questioning had taken place in Matron's room, the two of them together, alone, with the enormous fan overhead in the ceiling clicking and whirring softly and the perspiration still gleaming on the dark brown skin of the girl's beautiful body.

'How did you know that the new recruit preferred women to men?' she queried.

'When all new girls come, corporal she say, you no want any man here. They only want jig-jig with you, give you babies and you get put into detention hospital and the man he goes free and goes with some other girl and you get nothing. She say, you come to my room, much better than man, and I get you a nice soft job. That's how that woman got me into her room. But she a hard one to please, likes many girls. And I not like things done to me. I like to do things.'

'What kind of things?'

The girl was almost instantly at ease.

'You give me cigarette,' she said, 'and I tell.'

Matron shook herself back into the present with reluctance. What days they were! And nights! And from the balmy, exotic sweet-scented nights of the hospital's tropical gardens, from the even more exotic nights of the hill stations of Srinagar and Mussourrie – not to mention the unmentionable delights of Calcutta itself – to this. She shook herself again and went to her office. Tonight she'd have a few stiff gins, maybe just a couple anyway, as she'd not have Ranji Patel to patrol the Home or to answer any emergency calls, so she'd have to stay reasonably sober. But a couple of burra pegs would be sufficient to transport her, however temporarily, back to the next stage of Susie's questioning. She would relive again the pleasure-pain of humiliation, and the subsequent events which that episode had set in train.

Mr Blake was already in her room, pacing up and down.

'Good morning, Matron,' he said.

'Do sit down, Mr Blake, you make me nervous.'

'Thank you,' he said, 'but I must get on. I can only spare a couple of days for this job. We've got the auditors paying their annual visit to my department next week and I must be there for them. And I've no idea what it is I'm looking for here, where to look for it and what to expect.'

'You've been through Mr Patel's personal papers?'

'I was reading them at home last night.'

'And?'

'He must have been getting extra money from somewhere, that's for certain. He could just about afford to run that car on his pay, but he's been putting away more than he's been earning. So where did it come from? Could he have cheated the residents here out of their allowances in some way?'

'It's difficult to see how. As you know, what they are allowed to keep as pocket-money from their state pensions

117

is small. Whatever they take in cash is recorded and signed for. Some of them have savings, but it's never very much, and if there is a credit balance to their account when they die, it, and their personal possessions, are handed over to the next of kin, or to whoever pays the funeral expenses.'

'I know the system,' said Mr Blake, 'and I know that if I was a criminal I wouldn't consider robbing one of these places. The right stuff just isn't here in worthwhile quantities.' He paused. 'Could you let me have that list of dates of those residents who have died since Mr Patel was posted here, please? If he was stealing and then selling their personal effects, you'd expect to find the dates of the deposits in his Building-Society book to show some relationship to the dates on the list, wouldn't you?'

'I'll ask Mrs Bolter to make a list. I've arranged for her to work here full time until a new Assistant Matron arrives.'

'I'll press on, then,' said Mr Blake. 'I can't help feeling that we're not going to get very much further with this. It's so far-fetched, isn't it? Mr Patel doing the dirty on certain unidentified residents, and some geriatric taking revenge by sabotaging his car. It's ridiculous.'

Matron smiled wanly. 'Nobody is going to be surprised if all this brouhaha is quite unfounded. The sooner you establish the facts and wrap it up the better for all concerned.'

Mrs Bolter, put to work as soon as she arrived, finished typing the list and took it upstairs to give to Mr Blake. She found him sitting on the edge of Mr Patel's bed, gazing into space, papers stacked neatly each side of him and his clipboard on his lap. He had a distinctly ruminative look about him, she thought, perhaps like a short, sturdy beast of burden, with spaniel's eyes, a minor something on which to load things to be transported from place to place safely and without demur. A small, plodding ox in a yoke on a treadmill. He took the list from her and removed his

118

glasses. She was quite moved by the sight of his large brown eyes and – for a brief second – their vulnerability. Then the glasses were back on. He looked through the list briefly and then thanked her.

'I do hope that you're getting paid for your work here, Mrs Bolter,' he went on. 'Otherwise there'll be trouble with the unions, you know.'

'I expect it's all arranged,' she said. 'The last thing we want is union trouble on top of everything else.'

'You're a woman in a million, if I may say so, Mrs Bolter. To think that any one of us could end our days in one of these places. And this is a good Home compared with some.'

'Quite so, Mr Blake,' she managed to get out. 'Please forgive me, I must be off.'

She left him staring at the wash-hand basin, her beautifully typed list, unregarded, in his hand, the big brown eyes contemplating some inner vision which clearly was of more interest to him than his lists and papers and figures.

On the landing outside she almost bumped into Mrs Reynolds, the legless lady, who was being wheeled in the direction of the bathroom by Sadie. Mrs Reynolds liked to recount how she had smoked her legs away. By some capricious quirk of nature, the inhalation of the smoke from forty plus cigarettes a day, whilst leaving her heart and lungs in fine fettle, had cut off the blood supply to her feet, causing them to swell up and turn first puffy and then discoloured, first blue and then black, the skin shiny and taut. Not being one to complain, and not having much time for doctors, she 'managed', unwilling to suffer the embarrassment of showing her feet to anyone, unwilling too to inspect them carefully herself, until one morning, after a particularly uncomfortable night, which she had tried to get through with the aid of aspirin washed down with a succession of nips of neat whisky, she removed the bandages from her right foot and her little

119

toe, abused and blackened, came away from her foot with them. There was no pain, she related, just a bloody awful stink, and I got my friend to call in the doctor. Next thing I knew I was in hospital with both legs off right up near me fanny, and I haven't smoked nor touched a drop since. Gangrene, they said it was. Caused by the smoking. She remained extraordinarily cheerful, despite it all.

Mrs Bolter shied away instinctively from the gross torso and smooth pudding-face, heavily made up, which smiled toothily at her from the chair. It's remarkable how little I know about these olds, she thought. Mrs Reynolds was someone she had never liked. The woman had no right to be so offensively cheerful, so offensively misshapen. With a major part of her missing, through her own fault too, reliant upon others for the basic necessities of hygiene, she should have been suitably diminished. But no, there she was, with an enormous appetite, larger than life, loud-voiced, cracking dreadful jokes, staff running around her as if she was minor Royalty, actually enjoying her unique situation and greedy with it. It was quite intolerable. Mrs Bolter was not one who believed that one should be loved for one's disabilities alone, and found Mrs Reynolds particularly unlovable.

'Good morning,' grinned Mrs Reynolds.

'Good morning. Off for your bath, then?'

'My weekly dip. Want to watch? It's like having one of those rides at the fair. Better. It's free!' Mrs Reynolds laughed loudly.

Mrs Bolter took a step back. She knew what the special apparatus in the bathroom looked like, a stainless steel ducking-stool, no less, and the thought of seeing what there was of Mrs Reynolds strapped in it and lowered into the bath gave her the shivers.

'No, thank you,' she said hurriedly, 'I have things to do.'

With Mrs Reynolds' uninhibited laughter still ringing in her ears, she made her way downstairs again. Dreadful woman, she thought. Most of the residents had assembled in the lounge, seated in their usual chairs waiting for the morning coffee-break. The Colonel was having trouble opening the front door and she went over and helped him. He thanked her gravely, then went out into the tiny paved yard in front of the car park, and momentarily the sounds of the outside world intruded. Traffic, an engine accelerating, loud voices, a crash like the sound of crates falling, and then the door swung back again, shut. She turned away and saw eyes watching and heads turning towards her, some curious, some blank. Mrs Snow was in her chair knitting away like an old revolutionary by the side of the guillotine. Their eyes met, and Mrs Snow's lids effectively hid hers from any communication. Mrs Bolter felt strangely deflated. I'll find Matron, she thought, see what else I can do. I don't seem to be welcome here.

From somewhere along the corridor, faintly, she could hear acrimonious voices raised in dispute. Cookie in one of her moods, she guessed. She could see Pearl progressing along the corridor from the dining-room, wielding her odorous mop, and she caught the faint sickly smell of it before making her way quickly to the tiny group of rooms from which the Home was administered. Matron's room, which her assistant shared, the room set aside for the doctor which also served as a treatment centre, and a larger room where all the records were kept and where a full-time clerk maintained the books, paid the staff, handled the correspondence, kept close contact with the area hospital administration, the Town Hall and the Co-operative Society's local funeral director. Next to that office was a store-room in which were kept cleaning material and equipment, stacks of blankets and linen, a couple of spare beds and mattresses, a stretcher, bedpans and spare walking-frames.

There was a large handwritten notice pinned to the doctor's door which read 'Dr Jackson. Clinic Tuesdays and

121

Thursdays 10 – 12 a.m.' Taking her courage in both hands, she knocked and went in.

'I knew you were in, doctor,' she said, 'even though it's not Tuesday or Thursday.'

'Do come in, Mrs Bolter. Sit down. I'm just writing up some notes. We'll have a cup of coffee in a jiff.'

Mrs Bolter shut the door behind her and took the chair across the desk from the doctor. She was absurdly young, or so she seemed to be, after the sight and smell of so many old people. Her hair was a dark auburn colour, thick and cut short. She sported large reading-glasses and very little make-up. Her white cotton jacket was brilliantly white and the breast pocket carried a neat array of silvery objects: a thermometer in a case, a shiny pen, a slim torch. A stethoscope was slung around her neck. When she looked up and smiled, Mrs Bolter felt a wave of maternal feeling surging through her.

'Your baby must be due very soon now,' she said.

'Hm. I'm sure some of these old ladies will be almost as glad as I will. For some inexplicable reason it seems to embarrass them to be examined by a pregnant woman. Funny thing though, the old men don't seem to mind.' She got up and poured out two cups of coffee from a percolator which was plugged in by the side of the sink under the window. She brought the cups back to the desk and handed one to Mrs Bolter.

'Is this visit in the line of business, social, or what?' she asked.

'It's an impulse visit. You know that I'm acting as Assistant Matron for the time being?'

'Matron told me, yes.'

'I've been coming here for years, visiting, running errands for the residents, helping them with their corre-spondence, personal problems, anything I could, and it's been something to look forward to, could cope with and enjoy doing. It made me feel wanted. But this full-time business, however temporary, and I've only just started

122

doing it, is very worrying. I don't really know if I can cope now. I worry about it.'

Dr Jackson sat down and looked grave. With her hands folded across her stomach she could feel her unborn infant kicking, and she smiled to herself. All in good time, little one, she thought. Meanwhile Mrs Bolter needs some thought and attention. She had already caused eyebrows to be raised by asking persistent questions about Mrs Southover's death, and she had clearly been affected by Miss Green's not untimely end. And now there was Mr Patel's unfortunate accident. Mrs Bolter should by now have become, if not hardened, at least adjusted to the fact that familiar faces were liable to disappear literally over-night in this environment. Perhaps it was the three incidents occurring so quickly one after the other, and perhaps she also had personal problems. She also had some curious mannerisms. When she was excited words flowed from her in an unstoppable torrent. Verbal colitis was an apt description. There would be no waving of the arms or walking about, just sitting still with her face drained of colour and her lips mouthing a stream of words – almost as if she had no control over them. Very curious. Other times, when she was relaxed, she adopted, how-ever unconsciously, a kind of toffee-nosed accent and demonstrated a penchant for heavy-handed humour. For all the world as if she was acting the part of the Lady of the Manor, dispensing cold beef tea and gratuitous advice to the needy poor of the parish. She was obviously a good-hearted and sincere woman and, equally obviously, managed to get up more noses than most.

'All conscientious people worry,' said Dr Jackson. 'But there's nothing in this job you can't handle, I'm sure. What do your family think of it?'

'My husband complains anyway,' she said.

She sipped at her coffee.

'And there's another thing,' she went on. 'My daughter Claire has just got herself engaged. She's only just twenty, wants to marry this lecturer and go off into some far-flung wilderness with him, digging at some archaeological site. Taking time off from her University course, and she'll probably have babies and never finish it. We don't even know him; we've met him of course, and he's older than she is. What a waste.' Her face went a bright red as she recalled the sounds emanating from Claire's bedroom the night before, the house quiet apart from Bolter's drunken snortings below, the creaking and groaning and barely suppressed cries of ecstasy, Claire giggling and the man's voice growling and muttering. It was like the sound effects of some raunchy radio play, but it was Claire in there, not some bawdy actress who could be switched off, and it was insupportable. He slept through it all, of course, useless as usual, not disturbed in the slighest, whilst through the walls and the partly open doors she was assaulted by the noise of uninhibited sex which seemed to go on and on with precious little interval throughout most of the night. She had slept fitfully; in the morning she'd heard him get up and, incredibly, he'd gone for a run! Over breakfast they'd announced their intention of getting married as soon as it could be arranged. They'd gone off in his little car with Claire driving and the poor man – he'd be dead inside a year if he kept it up, she thought – slumped in the front passenger seat, to set the arrangements in train.

When they'd gone, she'd been disturbed, fidgety. In her mind's eye she could see the two of them at it in Claire's room and she went upstairs to tidy things, smoothing the sheets and patting the pillows. In addition to the lethargy and malaise which was the legacy of sleep deprivation she realised that there was something else affecting her, and she felt herself swelling up inside with frustration and anger. With a sudden shock she realised that she was seething with jealousy, and that she wished that she had been experiencing all the things they had been doing last night, with Bob, or – stifle the thought before it took shape – with Claire's Dr Richard Richards.

And there was a new feeling of hatred to be directed against that lazy good-for-nothing whey-faced pot-bellied nicotine-stained husband who was so utterly useless, shamefully useless, in bed.

She sat down on the bed, her legs shaky. I won't say it, she said. It's unladylike, undignified, but I want, I need, a man, but I won't say the word, the word that means I want him to do it to me, I won't say it. She picked up the telephone and dialled Bob Roberts's number and listened to it ringing. Supposing his wife answered? But she was lucky; she heard the receiver being lifted and Bob's voice say Hallo and give the number.

'Is it an emergency?' he asked after a second's hesitation.

She took a deep breath. 'I'm screaming out for it!' she yelled, and hung on, breathing deeply.

There was a silence of a few seconds which seemed to go on forever.

'In that case,' he said carefully, 'please ring the Good Neighbourhood Service at the Town Hall. The number's in the book.'

She slammed down the receiver in a fury. Downstairs the clock in the hall chimed, and she looked at her watch. Nine o'clock. She was due at the Home at eight-thirty. She pulled on her jacket and whirled out of the house. It is not surprising that I seem to be permanently out of breath these days, she thought.

Dr Jackson looked at her with renewed interest as colour flooded up again from some vermilion reservoir, staining her neck and face and forehead a deep red. Signs of menopause perhaps, she thought, but I'd like to know for certain what brought that on.

'Why do you say it's a waste?' she asked. 'You'll miss your daughter naturally, but she was living away from home anyway, and if she's marrying the right person, isn't that something to be glad about?'

'I suppose so,' said Mrs Bolter reluctantly. 'But it's all so

125

upsetting. What with her going off and this hastily arranged wedding – all our friends will swear it's a shotgun affair – and all the happenings here, and Mr Blake raking over Mr Patel's belongings, and everything. It's all very upsetting.'

'It's no use saying to you don't worry. People either worry or they don't, and you do. But if you like I can give you something to make you feel a bit better, help you to sleep so that you can cope better with all these problems.'

'You mean tranquillisers?' Mrs Bolter had had first-hand experience of them, and had also seen the piles of pills dispensed for the residents and seen the effect it had on them. 'I don't want to be turned into a vegetable,' she said.

'There's not much chance of that whilst you're in your present hyperactive state.' Dr Jackson unlocked a drawer of her desk and took out a plastic container filled with tablets.

'Take one of these now, swish it down with water, and lay off coffee. And a couple more tonight before you go to bed. No more than three a day. Try it for a couple of days, and when you're feeling better, more relaxed, let me have back whatever you haven't used.'

Mrs Bolter looked at the container doubtfully and inspected its contents, large white tablets like jumbo aspirins. She shook one out into her hand and then, making up her mind, put one on the back of her tongue and swallowed it, washing it down with the last of the coffee. Then she sat back in the chair and heaved a large sigh.

'I'm sure I wouldn't have all these problems if I could only talk to my husband,' she said. 'Discuss things with him; it isn't asking too much, is it? But he just isn't interested, isn't simpatico, you know; if he isn't talking shop about his work at the office he's out, entertaining clients. And he drinks too much.'

'I know the feeling,' sympathised Dr Jackson. 'My

husband is a Chief Inspector in the police and when he's out on a case I don't see him for days at a time. It can be very lonely.'

Mrs Bolter stood up. 'A Chief Inspector?' she repeated. 'How very interesting.'

'Yes. He's in the CID. A detective.' She smiled. 'His ambition is to be a Chief Constable before he's fifty. He's already picked out his manor, as he calls it. I expect he'll make it too, he's very good at his work.'

Mrs Bolter began backing out of the room clutching her container of pills.

'How very interesting,' she repeated. 'Thank you so much for these,' she waved the pills vigorously, 'but I must stop wasting your time and I must be off anyway. Duty calls, you know. The coffee was most welcome.'

Dr Jackson watched her agitated departure with some curiosity. It was much too soon for the pill to have had any effect, and if it had done so she would have expected it to have been the reverse of the reaction shown by Mrs Bolter. It was when she said 'Chief Inspector', 'CID', 'detective', that the reaction was most marked. Very odd indeed. Mrs Bolter really warranted more study, more attention. She would not be a bit surprised if her medical history included some kind of mental instability.

Matron was at her desk when Mrs Bolter entered unceremoniously. She looked up and reached for her note pad.

'Ah,' she said. 'Some news from the police concerned with Mr Patel's accident. They've been on the telephone.' She consulted her notes. 'They said that there is a possibility that the car had been interfered with, and they're still looking into that aspect. They've also found out a lot about his private life. They've been in touch with our local police and someone will be along to explain. What do you think of that?'

'I don't think anything of that or make anything of it,' protested Mrs Bolter. 'Why should I? It's all too much for

127

me.' Dear God, she thought, her worst suspicions were only too well justified. I must warn Mrs Snow. 'I've been talking to Dr Jackson. What a charming girl. I didn't know he was a policeman. Her husband, I mean. It seems odd somehow that a lady doctor should have a police officer husband. He must be a very unusual one.'

Matron nodded agreement. 'He was here on Open Day with her. Charming young man. Tall, slim, good-looking. Not a bit like Mr Plod.'

'Such a surprise,' said Mrs Bolter. 'And what would you like me to do next?'

Matron consulted her watch.

'Check all the rooms, if you would. Turf out anybody who has gone back in, we can't allow that, get them down to the day roms. Make sure that the cleaners are working, then pop along to the kitchen to see that cook is behaving herself and everything is in order.'

Mrs Bolter smiled thinly. 'I'm off, then,' she said. 'But I must say that I'll be glad when a replacement arrives. I'll get on to Councillor Roberts myself this afternoon. I'm afraid this place is getting me down just a little.'

Another problem looming up, thought Matron, as she watched Mrs Bolter dart for the door. She opened the bottom drawer of her desk and gave the square-shaped bottle of vodka there a reassuring pat. Not as palatable as gin, especially imbibed neat, but it imparted no telltale odour to the breath, and we must all make sacrifices in the line of duty. She poured herself a double measure into a medicine glass. Where would we be without modern medicines? she asked herself, and downed the spirit in one gulp. I'll ease up when all this is over, she thought, but right now I need it. There was a curious empty feeling, of panic almost, as she thought the words, and then the raw spirit began warming her stomach and the warmth spread around her body, up into her head and behind her eyes. That's better; she leaned against her chair and half closed her eyes. Perhaps I'll go back to India when I retire, she thought, rent a bungalow there, or perhaps in Ceylon, it can't have changed all that much even if its name has. Sri Lanka, where the sun shone brightly in the cobalt-blue sky and the beaches were pure silver lapped by the bluest of seas with the whitest of white caps and bordered with swaying palms. And where the girls were beautiful and round-faced and their skins were soft and dark and smooth as the velvet nights. And so understanding. She sighed, consulted her watch again. Perhaps I should telephone the good Councillor Roberts before Mrs Bolter contacts him, she thought. She really didn't want a new full-time assistant just yet, ferreting about. Most inconvenient. If I tell him what a good job she's doing already he won't hurry things along, whatever she says to the contrary. She reached for the telephone and smiled secretly to herself. In another hour or so she'd have another dose of medicine; mustn't overdo things. Too much was as bad as too little. The secret smile widened as she waited for the number to ring.

13

Mrs Snow clicked her teeth with the tip of her tongue and grimaced. Something small, hard and irritating had found its way behind the plate of her top set. They'd had a salad for their evening meal with a slice of corned beef, and then some rock cakes. It was some foreign body from the latter, she was certain, some evil little foreign body that had somehow lodged up there and, try as she might, clicking and sucking and poking, it wouldn't come out. She looked around the room. Already the blinds were down, although it was still only early evening and broad daylight outside. But the evening meal was over, it was TV time and most of the residents were positioned along

129

the three walls forming a U shape, with the large-screen TV set at the far end against the fourth wall. The early news was just finishing; there wasn't much difference between any of the editions of the news and it was always depressing whatever channel you looked at. All one wants, she thought despairingly, is a bit of a laugh, or some dancing, or a decent play. All those talk shows, and people shouting at you from the screen trying to make you buy stuff, and the bright flickering colours and loud noises and repetitious nonsense were not welcome at our time of life.

Surreptitiously she stuck two fingers in her mouth and tugged, cursing the manufacturers of the dental plate cement she used because it was doing its job properly. The adhesion broke down suddenly. Freed from its moorings, the top plate flew at speed from her mouth, landed on the polished floor and slid over the hard wax to end up with a genteel swish against the front wheel of Mrs Reynolds's chair. Mrs Reynolds looked down at the false teeth and then across to Mrs Snow who was holding a Kleenex to her face.

'I know you don't like the programmes, Mrs Snow,' she shouted, 'but don't chuck your teeth in this direction. The screen's over there!' She shrieked with laughter and pointed to the TV, where the weatherman was backing up his unconvincing forecast with a barrage of symbols and figures. Someone near her hooted, and one or two heads turned slowly in her direction.

Mrs Snow rose unsteadily to her feet, leaning heavily on her frame. You old cow, she thought, I'll have you. She gripped the frame tightly; making an exhibition of me in public is the last thing you'll ever do, she promised herself.

'Why don't you call them back? Whistle. They'll come back on their own. I bet they ache to be back!' Mrs Reynolds dissolved into an uncontrollable fit of heavings and gaspings, swaying from side to side on the axis of her foreshortened rump. 'Ache to be back, toothache!' She hammered home her feeble joke at the top of her voice, beating the arm rest of her chair.

Mrs Snow took another step forward, but one of Mrs Reynolds's companions, seated next to her, another round-faced greedy sow in Mrs Snow's considered opinion, poked at the dentures with her rubber-tipped walking stick and managed to flick them down the line of spectators. Someone else stuck out a foot, a purely reflex action on the part of its owner, and the teeth were kicked back into the centre of the room. There were titters and murmurs from all sides as Mrs Snow, scarlet-faced, the impedimenta on her frame swinging ominously, changed direction with a thump and set off in pursuit. The Colonel, who had been seated next to Mrs Snow, came to and in a rare moment of instant comprehension took in the scene. He got up, limped towards the plate, took out a handkerchief and picked it up and handed it to Mrs Snow.

There was a faint round of applause.

'Get him,' shrieked Mrs Reynolds. 'Sir Walter bleeding Raleigh,' and finally collapsed, snorting and grunting.

Mrs Snow stuffed the teeth, still wrapped in the Colonel's handkerchief, into her knitting-bag, turned the frame and stamped out of the room. The Colonel looked at her retreating figure and then went back to his own seat, smiling gently to himself.

Outside Mrs Snow continued on to the ground floor lavatories and manoeuvred her frame so that she could stand next to the wash-hand basin. That useless old fart, she thought, making fun of me, in that great loud voice, taking liberties with my dentures. I hate her. She turned on the tap and put the plate under the running water. Behind her she heard the lavatory door open and then felt it push against her frame.

'Careful,' she called, 'you'll have me over.'

The pressure continued and she managed to turn herself about. Matron's head appeared round the door, her face registering astonishment.

131

'Mrs Snow,' said Matron, 'what on earth do you think you're doing?'

'I'm cleaning my teeth, what do you think I'm doing?' Mrs Snow waved her teeth furiously at the disembodied head.

'There's no need to be facetious,' said Matron severely. 'And you're blocking the door with that frame. You know you're not supposed to do that. Someone might want to come in here in an emergency.'

'This is a bloody emergency,' grated Mrs Snow. 'They've been playing hockey with my dentures in the TV room and I've come in here to wash them.'

Matron's surprised expression intensified.

'Just come out of there at once,' she commanded, 'you're getting to be a real pest.' The door swung to behind her.

Mrs Snow finished washing her teeth, dried them and fitted them back in her mouth. The foreign body which had caused her to remove her plate had vanished. Not surprising, considering where it had been and what it had been through, and the plate seemed to be no more uncomfortable than it had been before. She took out her compact, powdered her nose, pinched her cheeks and sucked in her lips a few times. Refurbished and feeling more or less herself she backed against the door, opened it and got her frame round it. Matron was standing waiting for her at the end of the corridor. She had her legs slightly apart, her hands flat against her stomach.

Mrs Snow lifted her frame with a determined jerk and continued on her way to within a couple of feet of the statue-like figure of Matron. She looked up at Matron's tight-lipped face.

'If I didn't know you better, Matron,' she said, 'I'd say that you were cross about something.'

'I just want you to know,' Matron's voice was oddly thick, 'that I've been watching you for some time now. You don't really belong here, don't fit. You stick out like a

132

sore thumb.' She swayed slightly. 'A disruptive influence. If you don't conform I'm going to have you transferred to another Home.'

'You're not cross,' observed Mrs Snow, 'you're just plain drunk. And if you move a finger to get me transferred I'll have my friends Mr and Mrs Bolter down on you like a ton of bricks.'

Matron said nothing. In her mind's eye she could see quite plainly the angles of the vodka bottle glinting in the light of the reading-lamp on her desk. She'd been punishing it most of the day, and this dreadful disreputable old woman was being hateful and challenging her authority and littering up the place. Blocking the downstairs toilets with her frame indeed – and what an excuse she offered!.

'I'll ignore your insulting remarks this time,' she said, 'but whoever your friends are, Mrs Snow,' and despite herself she heard her voice slurring and rising in pitch and volume, 'I'm in charge here and what I say goes.'

'You don't own this bloody place,' shouted Mrs Snow, stung into retaliation. 'You work for the bloody Council. Don't give me your airs and graces. We all know what you are.'

Matron's eyes focused on Mrs Snow's.

'And just exactly what do you mean by that?' she asked icily.

Mrs Snow held herself in check. 'You're the Matron in charge,' she said. 'You tell us often enough.'

'And while I'm in charge you'll do as I say.'

'This is my home.' Mrs Snow changed tactics. 'Nobody, least of all a drunken old biddy like you, tells me what to do in my own home.'

'You'll do as I say,' repeated Matron. 'You can go straight up to your room now and when you come down in the morning I trust that you'll be suitably apologetic.'

'Oh, sod off,' said Mrs Snow bitterly. 'I'm eighty-five years old, not eight. I'll go to my room when I feel like it.' She lifted her frame and brought it down heavily on

Matron's highly polished shoe. Matron gasped, staggered and reached for the wall for support. Mrs Snow, surprisingly agile, lifted the frame again and passed Matron whose face was distorted with pain.

'Take more water with it next time,' hissed Mrs Snow as she went past her.

Several of the more active residents had gathered round the door of the TV room, staring in their direction, aroused by the sound of raised voices. Mrs Snow brushed by them unceremoniously and made for her chair. The Colonel looked up as she sat down and fussed about, making herself comfortable.

Mrs Reynolds opposite smiled broadly. 'All right, dear?' she called.

Mrs Snow smiled in return. 'No harm done,' she said. 'Just a bit of fun.'

'Haven't laughed so much in years,' said Mrs Reynolds. 'You're a good sport.'

'You'll laugh the other side of your fat face when I've done with you,' Mrs Snow promised, half to herself.

The Colonel smiled. 'Anything I can do for you, dear lady?' he asked.

Mrs Snow's grin was wolfish. 'There's plenty more you can do, dear, but all in good time,' she said, 'all in good time.'

Matron had recovered her equilibrium and had half started after Mrs Snow as she made her way up the corridor, when she decided that she was going to break off hostilities and retire for refreshments. The vodka was calling and the spirit was strong. The next engagement with Mrs Snow would be carried out at a time and place of her choosing. Mrs Bolter, returning for a brief tidy-up session, found her in her office, empty medicine glass in her hand, gazing vacantly into the middle distance.

'Are you all right, Matron?' she asked. 'You look a bit under the weather.'

'Nothing I can't handle,' said Matron, then she smiled.

134

'Funny, nobody asks how Matron is. We're supposed to be indestructible. I didn't expect you back here this evening.'

'I've brought a couple of errands,' explained Mrs Bolter. 'I can't stay.'

'I understand. Thank you for coming anyway. It's going to be a long night on call.'

Mrs Bolter delivered her errands, boxes of Kleenex and packets of biscuits, to the TV room. It was exceptionally quiet, she thought, most of them enjoyed muttering away whilst the programmes were on but tonight there was hardly any of that, she thought, as she counted out change for a five pound note into the last claw-like hand. Her task completed, she went over to Mrs Snow. Even she looked a bit strange too, she thought, her eyes bright and her movements jerky.

Mrs Snow smiled as she approached.

Mrs Bolter smiled in return. 'Good evening, Mrs Snow,' she said. 'I've brought you some chocolates. Specials. They're very rich, and you're not to eat more than one a day.'

Mrs Snow's face cracked open wider. 'Thank you, dear,' she said. 'Would you slip them into my bag? That's it. You are kind.' Then she sighed. 'I've had a bit of a set-to with Matron,' she went on wearily.

'What on earth about?'

'She ordered me upstairs as if I was a baby. Simply because I was using the downstairs lavatory.'

'How extraordinary.'

'I soon saw her off, I can tell you. She's been drinking. Not the first time.' Mrs Snow leaned forward. 'You'll be in tomorrow, won't you?'

'Of course,' said Mrs Bolter. She too leaned forward so that their heads were nearly touching. 'I wanted to tell you to be careful. The police are coming in about Mr Patel's accident, so-called, and Dr Jackson's husband is a detective,' she whispered.

135

'Don't worry.' The finger rested on the nose in a familiar gesture. 'Just make sure you come in tomorrow. We'll have a visit.'

Mrs Bolter got up. 'I must be off,' she said, 'so many things to do and think of. My daughter's getting married next weekend. Would you like to come to the reception?'

'I like weddings,' said Mrs Snow. 'I'd like that very much.'

'We'll talk about it tomorrow, then.'

Mrs Snow leaned forward conspiratorially. 'I've got a raging headache with all these commotions and aggravations,' she said. 'You couldn't possibly get hold of a few tablets for me to calm me down before you go, could you? I'm not asking Matron, that's certain, and I could do with a good night's sleep.'

Mrs Bolter felt in her pocket for the container which Dr Jackson had given her that morning.

'I'm not sure what these are, tranquillisers of some kind. I've no intention of taking any more and you're welcome to them. Not more than three a day.'

Mrs Snow opened one of her plastic bags hanging on her frame.

'Drop them in there, dear, will you? You're very kind.'

Mrs Snow's smile was a positive benison. Wasn't it fortunate that she was able to help, it made her feel so much better. Everybody needs to be needed, thought Mrs Bolter as she hurried out of the Home. Bob Roberts had telephoned her from the Town Hall during the day to explain and reassure her that he wasn't really suggesting that the Good Neighbourhood Service should be allowed to help with her particular problem. It was just that Mrs Roberts was standing next to him, listening to what he was saying. My word, you made my hair stand on end, I can tell you. And that's not all!

Somewhat mollified, Mrs Bolter had swallowed the remnants of her anger and invited him to drop in 'for a drink' that evening. Mr Bolter had promised to be out working late, Claire and her Dr Richards had gone into town for theatre and dinner. We'll have hours to ourselves, she thought, time for his pleasure and time for mine. And then, who knows what? She shivered a little in anticipation. She hadn't mentioned how she felt about working at the Home, but there would probably be time and opportunity to do so later that evening. She drove back quickly from the Home after talking to Mrs Snow, ran herself a bath, was in and out of it inside five minutes. She sprayed herself with his favourite perfume, put on a light robe and then went downstairs into the drawing-room.

It was still daylight when he arrived with a large bunch of flowers. She pulled him in quickly.

'For you,' he said, and thrust the flowers at her.

'I'll find a vase for them,' she said. 'Later. Afterwards.'

'Where are we going, upstairs?'

'That's a waste of time,' she said. She led him into the drawing-room, kissed him briefly and then knelt down and untied his shoelaces.

'We can be seen in here, for Chrissake,' he muttered, at the same time discarding his jacket and then fumbling for his tie.

'Down on the rug,' she said, 'we'll be fine. Nobody can see us down there.'

He began unbuttoning his shirt and she unfastened the belt of his trousers and began pulling them down.

'Steady on,' he grunted and, with one hand still on his shirt buttons, reached down and tried to speed up the process. At the same time he lifted one leg, hopped unsteadily, lost his balance and collapsed untidily into an armchair, his back to the window. She flung herself on him, her robe flapping open. The chair keeled over slowly and for a few seconds they lay in an untidy heap, legs up in the air.

'Oh dear,' he said eventually.

137

He rolled across Mrs Bolter's unresisting body, managed to get to his feet and, while she was picking herself up, got rid of the rest of his clothes. Her robe was now off and they clung to each other briefly before somehow sliding to the floor. She felt his hands over her, roughly, and bit her lip as he went into her without preliminaries or warning, like some randy old boar. It was all over in seconds. Bob Roberts, astonished at this unusual and unlooked-for display of premature ejaculation, remained heavily and impassively on her. She opened her eyes.

'Is that all?' she demanded. 'Is that all there is, then?'

He nodded shamefacedly. 'You get me all worked up,' he said apologetically. 'I've been thinking about it all day, ever since you rang.'

'And what am I supposed to do?' she asked, almost beside herself. 'Claire and that man were at it literally for hours last night, and you're not all that much older than him. It isn't fair. It just isn't fair.'

'You got me all worked up,' he repeated. 'And I haven't had the pleasure for some time. Let's have a cup of tea or something and perhaps we could try again.'

'Get off me, you great useless oaf,' she snapped. 'You're crushing me. I've been looking forward to this ever since you rang back, and all you can say is let's have a cup of tea or something.'

She managed to push him to one side, slide away from under him and sit up, her face red and her expression one of bewildered fury. He sat up and put one large hand on her knees and then reached across clumsily to begin kneading her breast with the other. She looked at him and her upper lip curled.

'Big Bob Roberts,' she sneered. 'What a laugh!'

He stopped abruptly and stood up, looking down at her. She still looked good, especially in the half-light with soft shadows emphasising her considerable assets. Full breasts, the nipples hard and dark and protuberant, a well-defined waist, rounded hips and good legs. He felt

138

himself stirring again. But he'd had enough; he'd had enough since last time. It was the urgency in her voice, the way she had said 'I'm screaming out for it' when she telephoned, that had persuaded him to come over despite all his recent misgivings. Ever since that time in the park when they were school kids she'd used him, and whilst it suited him and flattered him and excited him, there were some things he couldn't overlook. Being taunted about his performance was high on the list.

'If I'm not in your league,' he said unkindly, 'I suggest that you make other arrangements. You may find the local football team more satisfactory in that direction, one after the other of course, not all at once, and not before they have a match. They're doing badly enough without that to contend with.' He picked up his clothes and began dressing. She watched, not quite believing that the evening was ending so disastrously. And then some vestige of her shattered pride reasserted itself. She reached for her robe and put it on.

'You're not the man you were, Bob Roberts,' she said. And then, 'Perhaps I shouldn't have been so forward. I know that men like to make the running. I suppose it's a compliment in a way that you couldn't control yourself.'

'I've never let you down before,' he said pompously, 'and if there's one thing I don't like it's bloody women being bloody unfair. First you turn me on, and then you turn on me when I react quite normally. Then you put me off. Right off, I can tell you! Remember last time? Was that my fault? It's upsetting. And bad for me. My balls ache. They feel like they've been in a crusher.'

She watched miserably and in silence as he finished dressing.

'When will I see you again?'

'I'll give you a ring,' he said, his head averted.

Something in the tone of his voice caused her to look at him sharply.

'You'll give me a ring?' she repeated. 'After all these

139

years, is that all you can say, the best you can come up with?'

'Right now it's the best I can do,' he said. 'I'll let myself out.'

She followed him into the hall and picked up the flowers he had brought with him.

'Here,' she said, 'take them. I don't want them. Give them to your wife.'

He took the flowers, looked at them and then at her, and let himself out without speaking.

She went back into her drawing-room. The bastard, she thought, didn't even pick up the armchair for me. She went behind it and pushed it upright. Then she went round it, looked at the rug and suddenly all the anger and tension disappeared. She felt as if she had been drained of all energy, drained of life itself indeed, and she felt her shoulders droop and her legs become heavy and flaccid. Dear God, she thought, what is to become of me?

Bob Roberts seated himself more comfortably in his car before starting up and driving away. She was acting very strangely, he thought, confirming the suspicions he had had the last time they'd been together. All these goings-on and the extra hours at the Home, and Claire arriving back with her problems, were obviously having a bad effect upon her. And with her previous history of dottiness . . . Two things wanted doing. First he must talk to that part-time doctor at the Home, get her to keep an eye open for any obvious signs of eccentricity. And he must get an official replacement for Patel as quickly as possible, despite Matron's glowing report over the telephone of the way in which she was coping. Perhaps he should also talk confidentially to Matron, put her in the picture. She already knew that the local police were going to visit on behalf of the Midlands police. He would have thought that if the latter had come up with any hard evidence of something fishy about the car or Patel or both, they'd be sending one of their own men along. Funny people, police, he mused. It was a good job he had a clear conscience, just thinking about the police made one feel uneasy.

His thoughts changed direction.

He'd see Phyllis right. She was going through a bad patch. They'd been good friends. What times they'd had! He pushed the lever into Drive and moved off, a warm righteous glow suffusing his whole being. He'd see her right. He wasn't one to forget old friends.

The warm glow was still there, fuelled by several stiff snorters downed in quick succession when he got home. His wife was out and the place was deserted. Where the hell does she get to? he asked himself. And what does she do all day during the long hours when he was either at work or in the Town Hall, doing his best to earn an honest crust and to discharge his civic duties? He chuckled to himself like an old warrior warming himself with the memories of battles fought and won and lost, as he poured himself another drink. Still smiling, he reached for the telephone and dialled the number of the Home. It picked up and began ringing immediately. He heard the receiver being lifted and then there was an ear-shattering noise as it was dropped. He switched the receiver to his other ear.

'For Chrissake!' he shouted. 'What's going on?'

Matron's voice was clear and restrained.

'I beg your pardon,' she said. 'Who is this?'

'It's Councillor Roberts,' he shouted. 'Are you all right?'

'Of course I'm all right, Mr Roberts. The telephone just slipped out of my hand, that's all.'

'My eardrum's just slipped its moorings,' he said. 'I just want a quick word. I've seen Mrs Bolter since we spoke this morning. I want you to keep an eye on her for me. She's very strung up about everything and I think it may have been a mistake to get her so closely involved. Anyway, I'll be doing what I can to get you a replacement quickly, and if that isn't soon, we'll talk about drafting in

141

some help from one of the other Homes. But will you watch her for me? Send her home if she looks off colour?'

'Mrs Bolter and I were chatting this afternoon. She's doing a remarkably good job, as I told you earlier. I was hoping that she would stay on for a while, we really don't want any more strange faces about. But she'd be glad to resume her voluntary association, I know, and I believe that she was going to have a word with you to see when that might be.'

'Ha! I knew it. She's stretched and it shows. Can't have that, Matron, even if the residents will get a bit upset when someone new comes in. After all, she'll still be visiting when she can.'

'What do you suggest, then?'

'I'd like to see the doctor at the Home about her. Can you arrange that for me?'

'Of course. She'll be in on Saturday morning, if you could come along then.'

'Splendid, Matron, splendid.' He reached for the bottle of Scotch and topped up his glass. 'I'll try and get in then. I do hope I didn't disturb you. Is everything quiet?'

'Quite and peaceful, Councillor. No problems.'

'Goodnight then, Matron.'

'Goodnight, Mr Roberts.'

He put down the telephone. Desiccated old bag, he thought. He suspected that she was a drinker, but if she was she hid it well. There was no detectable slur in her voice and he might be doing her an injustice. But he'd watch her a bit more closely from now on. Meanwhile, down the hatch and sod 'em all.

Matron put down the telephone and stood up, swaying gently. Quiet it was, peaceful, quiet as the grave indeed. The amount of drink she'd taken during the day added up to a considerable quantity. If I was unused to taking a glass or two, she thought solemnly, I would be dead drunk by now, dead drunk and as quiet as the grave, how impossibly appropriate. The sole person on night duty

142

had already completed her first round of inspection and had looked in to report that all was well. With an effort she had focused her eyes on the shape of that ample personage and when she spoke her voice was clear, each word enunciated precisely, perfectly under control. But when she stood up the room seemed to be contracting and expanding, the walls retreating and advancing in accord with some silent rhythm emanating from an unseen source. She knew from experience that if she went upstairs and stretched herself out on her bed the light fixture in the ceiling would revolve slowly about her. She would go cold, the colour would drain from her face and perspiration would bead her forehead. If she was lucky she would pass out. She didn't want any of those things to happen. She wanted another drink. There were bottles upstairs in her room. Not spirits though, wine. Her tongue tipped out of her mouth and explored the thin dry lips. She made her way out of her office, locking the door at the third attempt, and then proceeded deliberately along the corridor to the stairs leading to her flat. To her quarters, where the wine is. I shall get there safely and set out the glass and the bottle on the tray and pour myself a drink. Then I will go to sleep and dream of a tropical sun and warm nights and fireflies. And in the morning I'll be back in this grey place with all these dreadful grey people and I'll go and get another bottle of vodka and face up to the day.

Mrs Snow, one of the last residents left in the entrance lounge, looked up from the book she was reading, her spectacles perched uneasily on her sharp nose. Night nurse had left her there undisturbed and she wasn't due to make another round for hours yet. Mrs Snow's sharp eyes could see clearly the glazed expression on Matron's face as she walked carefully towards the stairs, noted how her hand reached for the guide rail and how her knees buckled slightly as she took the first step up. If she's not drunk, I'll eat my hat, she thought, and hers as well.

When they'd had that row earlier she was dead certain that Matron had been drinking, and she'd probably had a few more since then. But she carried it well, like a former employer of hers, she recalled, who had the same problem, at least a bottle a day, of the hard stuff to. She went off her rocker, though. Matron looked as if she was made of leather and her insides were pickled. But she's drunk all right and in a very short time she'd be out to the wide and impossible to rouse for hours.

She turned down the corner of the page she was reading and put the book in one of her plastic bags. Time to get upstairs, she thought. It's all very interesting, very interesting indeed.

14

Mrs Bolter awoke the next morning to the sound of birds greeting the first light of dawn. It was impossibly early. She shut her eyes and tried to recapture sleep.

He'd come in reasonably early, having said he was going to work late, only slightly drunk too, wanting to discuss the arrangements he was making for the wedding. It was something she would dearly have liked to have got involved in herself, but she was busy at the Home and he and Claire had discussed it in detail while she was out. He was going ahead, booking a reception in the better of the two local hotels, and all the invitations had been or were being made by telephone. Richard had contacted his parents and bachelor brother and Claire had been busy ringing her friends. Between them they'd had a score of acceptances. And who have I got on my side to ask? she thought bitterly. Councillor Bob Roberts and his wife and family, Mrs Snow from the Home, perhaps Dr Jackson and her husband, a few neighbours, and that was that.

Not that they'd asked her who she was inviting, all they wanted to know was numbers. They'd arranged for a special licence, the Registrar had been notified and a wedding-dress was to be hired. It was quite clear that Claire couldn't get away from home quickly enough for her liking.

And how long will that marriage last? she thought gloomily. How long would the good doctor be able to keep up his award-winning performances in bed? She was entitled to ask herself that, and to ask what they would have in common after the first year of not being able to get enough of it tailed off, inevitably, into the period of routine activity and ritual. As far as she could see the only interest they shared was a mutual delight in love-making, and the long-term prospects of their remaining together were hardly encouraging.

The young lovers had returned from their theatre excursion just before midnight, the taxi's diesel engine knocking for six the peace and tranquillity of the suburban night. They were ready to talk – providing it didn't take too long, said Claire with a sideways look at her fiancé; we really must get some sleep if we're to cope with all these excitements. Sleep was the last thing she had in mind, thought Mrs Bolter, even though he looked as if he could do with an uninterrupted seventy-two hours or so.

Mr Bolter had gone over the arrangements again. Champagne, wine, etc., laid on by the crate, on sale or return. An informal affair, sit-down lunch, a minimum of speeches and the happy pair could bugger off back to Exeter as soon as they liked. The bride and groom were superfluous at wedding receptions anyway, and as soon as they'd cut the cake and had their pictures taken, they could disappear.

'You've ordered the cake, then?' Mrs Bolter asked.

Mr Bolter looked slightly discomfited.

'That's something you can do,' he said. 'I forgot all about it.'

'You can't get wedding-cakes at a moment's notice,' she protested. 'They have to be ordered well in advance like everything else.'

'Well, I bloody forgot, that's all.' He stood up, immediately resentful, his face flushed and his eyes beginning to bulge. 'I would have thought that you could at least have done that for your daughter,' he went on. 'You've left everything to me and Claire to do. You should take an interest.'

Mrs Bolter looked at him, speechless. Claire kicked Richard's ankle under the table, as it looked as if he was going to say something.

'You can do that little thing for me, Mummy, can't you?' she pleaded. 'It needn't be a big one.' She described a large circle on the table. 'Just about that big. And a couple of tiers. Maybe three would be nice. And a pair of little figures, made of sugar, on the top, a bride and groom, for us to keep.'

Mrs Bolter managed a smile. 'I'll get on to it tomorrow,' she said. 'I'll get something.'

'Not something,' said Claire sweetly. 'A super big three-tiered cake with masses of icing and a big silver stand. I'm sure you can get one easily with your contacts.'

'That's right,' said Mr Bolter. 'Don't want to spoil things. It's going to be an expensive do, and if you have a stupid little cake it'll show us all up.'

'I'll do my best,' said Mrs Bolter.

Dr Richards smiled at her encouragingly. 'I'm sure you will,' he said, 'and if you can't get a monster it won't be the end of the world either.' During the few days he'd been with his future in-laws he had become acutely aware of her. Not a bad-looking woman, still. Must have been really attractive in her younger days. But one of nature's victims; someone who existed to be put on, to be put down, despite her own obvious attempts at manipulation, her attempts to take charge, which almost invariably went wrong. Like when they'd suggested to Claire when they'd

146

first arrived that he should sleep in the spare room, father wouldn't like any other arrangement.

'Don't tell me that you didn't sleep with Daddy before you were married,' Claire had said, 'because I won't believe it.' And, unconsciously arousing old memories, 'You wouldn't want us to go and make love on a bench in the park, would you? Because that's the alternative.'

If I'd slept with him before we were married I'd never have married him, thought Mrs Bolter, and that unfortunately was a potent argument for pre-marital sex.

'I'll speak to your father when he's eaten,' said Mrs Bolter.

'That'll be a change,' quipped Claire.

Mrs Bolter had retired defeated from that particular exchange. Mr Bolter was undoubtedly a pig, and all in all there was a distinct feeling of relief in the knowledge that neither of them was Claire's natural parent.

In their room later, when they were undressing, Dr Richards paused, shoe in hand, as the thought struck him.

'Why don't you like your mother?' he asked.

'She's not my mother. I'm adopted.'

'Is that why you dislike her?'

Claire finished the task of sliding out of her clothes.

'I don't like her,' she said, 'and I despise her too. Do you know that she's been having it away with Councillor Roberts – Uncle Bob – for as long as I can remember? I've seen and heard them at it so many times. They didn't even seem to care. And I don't suppose that either of them confined their extra-marital activities to each other.'

'Does your father know? Or mind?'

'You can see how things are. Daddy sleeps downstairs now. They have nothing to do with each other these days. One of my earliest memories is of them arguing and shouting about it. I didn't understand then. I don't know what came first, him neglecting her or her sleeping with

147

Bob Roberts, and I don't care. She disgusts me.' She went over to him and took his hand.

'You wouldn't cheat on me like that, would you?'

'That's a question I should be asking you,' he said.

'What would you do if I did?'

'Honestly, I don't know.'

'Well, I know what I'd do,' she said. 'I'd make sure you couldn't do it again, ever.'

He took off his other shoe and smiled at her.

'That's an out-of-character remark if ever I heard one,' he said.

She began unbuttoning his shirt.

'Do I sense that we're about to have our first quarrel? Why out of character?'

'You've led such a liberated existence, that's why. We both have. How could you want to do something so devastating as castration to anyone, let alone me, for such a trivial offence as sleeping with Councillor Roberts?'

She finished undressing him in silence, then pressed herself against him.

'You know bloody well what I mean,' she said. 'What's done is done and doesn't matter. What happens from now on is important. Now let's get to bed.'

He picked her up and dropped her lightly on the bed.

'There's hope for you yet,' he said.

In the next room Mrs Bolter had heard the initial sounds of pleasure and then, after what she assumed was a pause for breath, the more muted sounds as Claire and Richard began to demonstrate yet again their affection for each other, to what was clearly their mutual satisfaction. It sounded at times more like grievous bodily harm than a friendly act, she thought, and harked back wistfully to the days when she and Bob Roberts, in the full flower of their sexual development, would spend an afternoon exploring the range of intimate experience. She too was given to much vocalising at such times, and it was surprising that there had been no complaints from the neighbours. She smiled to herself.

She had dropped off to sleep, dreaming fitfully of wedding-cakes and an enormous bright-bladed sword which chopped and cut through the cake by itself without a sound. It was terrifying. By the morning the lack of sleep had left her feeling flattened and drained, her eyes smarting and her lids heavy. When the dawn chorus, having awakened her, began to fade away, she fell asleep again, only this time it was a deep, dreamless unawareness. Incredibly, it seemed that she had no sooner gone off when sharp noises began sounding insistently. However hard she tried to shut them out, they were dragging her back out of the warm dark comfortable womb where no hands could touch and all identity was lost. She fought the sounds, but they were both constant and demanding. Finally she gave up the struggle, floundered into semi-consciousness, swore, and reached, still half asleep, for the telephone which was ringing by the side of the bed. She picked it up with her eyes still shut. It was Matron's voice she heard.

'Good morning, Mrs Bolter. Sorry to disturb you. I hope I didn't wake you.'

Mrs Bolter grunted. 'No, you didn't,' she said. 'I'm still asleep, I think.'

'It is early, I know, but I wanted to make certain that you were coming in, and I wondered if you could possibly come in promptly. There's been another incident.'

Mrs Bolter jerked awake, upright.

'Who is it this time?'

'It's Mrs Reynolds. You'll remember her, the resident in the wheel chair. The double amputee. No legs and a cheerful disposition. Passed away in the night, poor thing. We're not sure of the cause just yet, but Dr Jackson will be round. There's so much to do; I was hoping that you could come in early if it's at all possible.'

'I'll be in as soon as I can. Give me half an hour or so.'

'So grateful.'

Mrs Bolter replaced the receiver, staring at the wall opposite. She had half expected that something would happen to Matron after her row the day before with Mrs Snow. But Matron was still in the land of the living, and it was Mrs Reynolds who had been incidented. It wasn't altogether surprising that someone of Mrs Reynolds's age, and with her handicap, should pass away peacefully in the night, and there probably wouldn't even be an inquest. She got up and washed her hands and face in the wash-basin in her room. While she was dressing she tried to banish the guilty feeling which memory of her dislike of the departed brought on. I must be more charitable in future, she chided herself. At least there was one good thing; Mrs Reynolds, as far as she knew, had not been on Mrs Snow's list.

Downstairs there were sounds as if he had fallen out of his chair, with subsequent bangings and mutterings. Then she heard him open the dining-room door, and almost immediately detected the acrid smell of his first cigarette of the day. She listened as he went into the cloakroom, hawking and spitting, and then went downstairs. She had the kettle on when he emerged, struggling out of the shirt he had slept in, the cigarette in his mouth, and watched without speaking as he grunted his way around the obstacle course of the kitchen and got his shaving gear from under the sink and plonked it on the draining-board.

'There's no point in me asking you to shave in the bathroom, I suppose,' she said resignedly, 'not even just for the time Claire and Richard are here?'

'I don't keep my stuff down here to shave up there,' he said. 'And what are you doing up so early? Have you planned to get the week-end off to a lousy start for me, or are you about to be constructive and start looking for a wedding-cake?'

'Neither,' she said. 'I'm wanted at the Home.'

He grunted inaudibly.

'What did you say?' she demanded.

'I said it's nice to be wanted.' He smoothed shaving-cream on his face and grinned at the world-weary expression of his reflection in the mirror he had propped up on the tap. The sophisticated, well-used look, utterly devastating! Who could resist it! And the wit!

'I've made some tea,' she said. 'One of the residents died last night. It always means extra work.'

'I didn't think that they were allowed to snuff it at weekends,' he said. 'Can't spare the staff to cope with the extra work.' He laughed and then cursed as he cut himself with a carelessly directed sweep of his razor.

'Oh, shit,' he said. 'It's you putting me off. I can shave myself forever without nicking myself if you're not around. Directly you're in the room I slice myself to ribbons.'

'Don't talk such utter rubbish. You bleed easily anyway. My father always said you were an old-fashioned bleeder. If you see Claire tell her that I should be in early this evening, meanwhile you'll all have to fend for yourselves today. And ask her to ring around about a cake, if she's so anxious to have one to her specifications.'

'You really are the end,' he protested. 'I suppose you will be there next Saturday? At the reception at least, if not for the ceremony? It's only your daughter's wedding, you know, if you can spare the time from all your important good works.'

She ignored his barbs. 'I've made out my list of guests for the reception,' she said. 'Just make sure they're catered for, that's all. It's on the table in the dining-room. I'm off.'

He finished shaving, patted his face with the expensive aftershave lotion he favoured currently and shook a generous measure of it under his armpits. The aroma that's guaranteed to drive them mad, he thought complacently. He got her list and went over it quickly. Mostly neighbours, Bob Roberts and family, of course, Dr and Mr Jackson, Mrs Snow and what looked like 'the Colonel'. It

151

was surprising she hadn't invited all of the staff at the Home, and the bloody residents as well. One had to be thankful for small mercies, he supposed.

Upstairs Claire opened her eyes, immediately awake. Right next to her, back to back, she could feel and hear Richard breathing lightly and regularly. She heard the sound of voices, but was unable to make out any words. A few seconds later the front door banged to, and in a few minutes she heard her mother's car start up and move off. She looked at her watch. Not yet eight o'clock. Perhaps she had started out early on the great cake-hunt. She grinned slyly to herself. Let her chase around for me for a bit, she thought, do something for me instead of those wretched old people who took up so much of her time. Get her priorities right for a change. She rolled over on to her side and then sat up.

'Wake up,' she said urgently, and poked his shoulder.

He turned round sleepily and she leaned over and kissed him.

'Say you love me?' she demanded.

'I love you,' he mumbled.

She slid on top of him under the bedclothes and his arms went round her.

'What's all this about?' he asked, and began stroking the smooth flat skin at the base of her spine.

'I'm scared,' she said. 'So many things happening at once. Things I don't understand.'

'Tell me about them,' he said, and his arms tightened around her protectively as, without warning, her body was wracked with uncontrollable sobs.

Mr Bolter finished his tea, lit another cigarette, went to the kitchen door and listened for a few seconds. Not up yet. He had to hand it to her, he thought, probably been at it all night. There was a time when he'd got pleasure from a torrid session. When he was first married he was as keen on it as she had been, but she was so bloody demanding it wasn't true. A man liked to make the

152

running, and a woman should be a damned sight more modest than she'd ever been. She'd been absolutely insatiable, and the more she wanted it the less inclined he had felt like giving it to her. Especially when they were told that she was infertile.

It had been her idea to adopt an infant, and when they'd brought Claire home something else happened. She'd shut up shop, told him to get out of her bed, clumsy unfeeling idiot. He'd sought solace in the bottle, and after a few admittedly half-hearted attempts to reclaim his conjugal rights, had decided that she could do what she liked with her assets. She was still a remarkably good-looking woman. But he'd sooner have a couple of stiff gins or a bottle of wine any day. But even that didn't please her. Occasionally he would wake up in his chair downstairs to find her standing over him, taunting him, shouting at him. He'd tell her to lower her voice, the child would wake up, and she'd go on and bloody on until at times he felt he could strangle her. But he'd never laid a finger on her, despite the provocation. Perhaps that was what she wanted. He'd never understand women, not if he lived to be a million years old.

He went out the back door and looked at the garden. A few sacks of peat on the rose-beds, a couple of cartons of fertiliser on the lawn, maybe a spot of watering, and that would be his lot for the weekend. Something very satisfying about a garden, he thought. Might be worth while investing in a summer-house next year. Put a couple of loungers in it, and in the really warm weather he could sleep there in peace, at one with nature and the great call of the wild. He drew deeply on his cigarette. Nothing like a bit of nature, a plot of your own, reap and sow, put a bloody fence around it and the rest of the world could get stuffed. He turned back indoors, coughing vigorously. Must remind myself to pick up another carton of cigarettes from the cut-price shop in the High Road, he thought, on my way back from the Garden Centre. Can't risk running short of the only pleasure – apart from wine, which was more a food than an indulgence – he had left in life.

15

Matron and Mrs Bolter sat opposite each other across the desk in Matron's room. Mrs Bolter had sipped a cup of indifferent, barely warm, coffee and was beginning to be in need of a visit to the ladies' room, but she was fascinated, held rooted to her chair, by Matron's odd appearance. Overnight she seemed to have aged ten, maybe twenty years. The whites of her eyes were yellow, tinged with red in the corners. Lines and wrinkles could be detected under the hitherto mask-like smoothness of her skin. Her body seemed to have shrunk, and she looked frail, bent over and used. Her hands shook as she poured the coffee and when she lifted the cup to her mouth. Of course it must have been a shock, finding Mrs Reynolds dead, but she also looked as if she had had no sleep for ever, or had been aroused from a drunken stupor after a binge of monumental proportions. The two possibilities were not irreconcilable. She continued to stare at the poor thing with concentration and concern, hoping that by some mystic means a shaft of light from on high would strike down on them both, illuminating and revealing all things.

Matron sat, her eyes unseeing, her hands holding the cup on the desk in front of her, the fingers pushing and poking and smoothing the china, revolving it ceaselessly. Since she had been called in by the night nurse, who had discovered the body, she had finished off the bottle of vodka – a litre well inside twenty-four hours – and if she'd had another she would have started on that as well.

The night nurse had been quite calm and matter-of-fact

about it and didn't seem surprised when, after prolonged knocking on Matron's door in the early hours of the morning, it was opened by Matron fully dressed, and looking simply ghastly. The Home was still quiet and the familiar stuffy atmosphere strangely comforting, as they went into Mrs Reynolds's room together, closing the door behind them. Her bed was fitted with an overhead steel gantry, with a dangling chain and a bar attached to it, so that from a prone position in bed she could reach up for the bar and pull herself into a sitting position. She must have done that during the night, thought Matron. The bedside light was still on, and the bedside locker was overturned, with toiletries, a bottle of orange squash and a vase of flowers littering the floor. Mrs Reynolds was out of bed, up-ended, her head between the locker and the side of the bed. A box of chocolates, open, the contents partially spilled out, was just outside the reach of her outstretched hand. She must have woken in the night, fancied a chocolate, switched on the light, reached for the box and overbalanced, and the strain of it all, and the shock, had been too much for her.

'It must have happened after my second round,' said the night nurse defensively. 'She was in bed at midnight, sleeping.'

'She had a very suspect heart,' said Matron. 'And she was a very greedy woman. It was astonishing the amount of food she could put away.'

Between them they had managed to heave and push Mrs Reynolds's body back into bed and cover it with a sheet. Then they tidied up the room, set up the bedside locker and its spilled contents, replaced the chocolates in the box and put it away. Apart from a dark damp stain on the carpet caused by the water spilled from the flower vase, the room looked normal, that is, if one didn't look at the anonymous shape in the bed. And that was not particularly corpse-like. Matron shivered. The Angel of Death certainly knew the way to the Home, she thought.

155

She shivered again. Who would be next? When would his dark wings cast their shadow on her door?

'We'll send for the doctor as soon as it's morning,' she said, 'and I'll get Mrs Bolter over early. There's nothing more we can do here. You might as well go as soon as the day people arrive. I'll take care of things.'

'Poor Mrs Reynolds,' said night nurse. 'She didn't even have the pleasure of a last chocolate.'

Matron's eyes refocused on Mrs Bolter opposite.

'Ah, Mrs Bolter,' she said. She sounded surprised and spoke as if she were having trouble in finding the words. 'How nice of you to respond so promptly once again. These crises are really becoming so very tiresome. The doctor's in Mrs Reynolds' room now. Meanwhile we must get on with the business of running the Home. We have a duty to the living. Could I ask you to supervise things for me while I carry out the necessary formalities? Poor Mrs Reynolds, she will be missed. Such a cheerful person.'

'Of course,' said Mrs Bolter. 'You do look as if you could do with a rest, if I may say so, Matron.'

'Mr Blake still poking about,' murmured Matron, half to herself, 'and the police asking for information about Mr Patel.'

'Everything happens at once,' said Mrs Bolter sympathetically. 'I know the feeling. All this going on here and so many things to do for my daughter's wedding next weekend. I saw Mrs Reynolds yesterday. She looked the picture of health – as far as anyone in her condition could look healthy, that is. How did she go?'

'How did she go?' repeated Matron.

The door opened and Dr Jackson came in, her white jacket emphasising rather than diminishing the very obvious signs of her near full-time pregnancy, followed by a tall sharp-featured young man. She nodded at Matron and smiled at Mrs Bolter.

'Good morning, Mrs Bolter,' she said. 'Let me introduce my husband.'

Chief Inspector Jackson took Mrs Bolter's outstretched hand and shook it warmly.

'Nice to see you again, Mrs Bolter,' he said. 'I've seen you at Open Days, dashing about, but we've not been formally introduced.' He looked around quickly.

'I'll get another couple of chairs,' he said, and went out.

Mrs Bolter watched him go, warily.

'Thank you for letting us both into Mrs Reynolds' room,' said Dr Jackson. 'I've not seen my husband at work before, and I must say that I found it very interesting.'

Matron looked at her, her head turning slowly.

'At work?' she said. 'I thought he was helping you with Mrs Reynolds, not conducting an investigation.'

'You know what policemen are. Specially detectives. Always on duty.' Dr Jackson smiled fondly.

The Chief Inspector reappeared, backing into the room, carrying two chairs, one stacked on the other.

'There you are,' he said triumphantly. 'Now we can all be comfortable.'

Matron watched them settle down, looking as though she was peering through the wrong end of a telescope. She ignored him and concentrated on Dr Jackson, who was smiling affectionately at her husband.

'I've no doubt that there's nothing mysterious to report,' said Matron frostily, as if daring Dr Jackson to contradict her.

'All old people are susceptible to myocarditis,' said Dr Jackson. 'The heart is a very efficient muscle, but in some circumstances it can degenerate into fatty material or fibrous tissue; a combination of old age, lack of exercise and overweight can be fatal – as it proved, indeed, for Mrs Reynolds. Her heart just stopped, and that's all there is to it.'

'Poor Mrs Reynolds,' said Mrs Bolter. 'Still, I suppose that's the way most people would choose to go, peacefully and in their sleep.'

'The body was neatly arranged in bed when we saw it.'
Mr Jackson's voice made it plain that he was intrigued.

They all turned to face him.

'And a very curious thing,' he went on. 'She was
clutching a chocolate in her left hand. Did she usually go
to sleep holding chocolates? And that damp patch on the
carpet by the locker? And no water in the vase on it?'

Dr Jackson's face expressed her deep admiration as she
turned and looked first at Matron and then at Mrs Bolter.

'I'd never have noticed that,' she said. 'Would you?'

'It's quite simple,' said Matron. 'When we found Mrs
Reynolds she was out of her bed, the locker was over and
we assumed that she'd been reaching for the chocolates,
and had a heart attack. The water came out of the vase of
course. It was simply routine to get her back into bed off
the floor, a respect for the dead, you know.'

'I thought that was what happened,' said Mr Jackson,
'at first. But thinking about it, that scenario doesn't quite
fit, does it? If she'd over-reached and overbalanced, is it
likely that she'd still be clutching the sweetie? She'd
obviously managed to grab one, it was in her hand. But
why didn't she let it go, when she slipped out of bed, to
try and save herself? On the other hand, if she'd slipped
out of bed before she'd grabbed one, it wouldn't be in her
hand, would it?'

Mrs Bolter's deep intake of breath could be heard quite
plainly.

'Oh dear,' she said. 'What make of chocolates were
they?'

Mr Jackson made exasperated noises. 'I can assure you,
Mrs Bolter,' he said irritably, 'that the brand name, and
whether they were soft or hard centres, plain or milk, is
not relevant.'

'Quite so,' said Mrs Bolter. 'Quite so, quite irrelevant.
So silly of me.' She got up and looked around her like a
trapped animal.

158

'You will excuse me,' she said, 'I must get on. Breakfast to supervise.'

All three of them watched her hurry from the room.

'Really, Mr Jackson,' said Matron, 'your imagination runs away with you. The facts are quite plain. Mrs Reynolds had a fatal heart attack last night, and it was brought on when she fell out of bed. What more do you want?'

'Is it imagination?' he asked. 'Was her emergency bell, that one on the flex hanging over the back of her bed, always tucked behind the bed rail, or was that something else you just tidied away?'

'The night bell, the emergency bell, as you call it,' said Matron indignantly, 'is always over the head rail with the push-button itself resting on the pillow beside her. I can't recall where it was this morning, but if you found it behind the bed rail then I or night nurse put it there, out of the way. I don't remember. I will repeat, Mr Jackson, that what happened is as plain as pikestaff.'

'I agree that the facts are plain enough,' he said softly, 'but there are several valid interpretations of them. That's all I'm saying, for the time being.'

'I'm more worried about Mrs Bolter,' said Dr Jackson. 'She isn't used to this sort of thing.'

'It's a great strain for all of us,' commented Matron.

'But she hasn't been trained to cope with it,' went on Dr Jackson. 'She's been showing signs of strain lately. Fancy asking what make of chocolates they were. I ask you!'

'Councillor Roberts rang me about her last night,' said Matron. 'He wants both you and I to keep an eye on her, so we're not the only ones to notice that she's not herself. He wants to talk to you about her particularly.'

'How interesting,' said Mr Jackson. He turned to his wife. 'I believe that we're invited to her daughter's wedding reception next Saturday. Is it still on?'

'As far as I know,' Dr Jackson said. 'It'll make a change

159

from all this. I'll drive so you can have your share of whatever's flowing without worrying.'

'I shall be on duty,' said Matron primly.

'And now I must put on my official hat,' said Mr Jackson. 'I've been asked to make enquiries on behalf of the Police Authority where Mr Patel had his fatal accident. An interesting late gentleman, our Mr Patel.' He looked at his wife. 'There isn't any need for you to hang about,' he said gently. 'Why don't you go home and put your feet up?'

Dr Jackson got up and stretched and yawned gently. 'I'll hang on here in my office. I was coming in today anyway, and I can use the time to write up my report. I may have a word with Mrs Bolter later.' As she passed him to get to the door her husband patted her stomach.

'Mind how you both go,' he said.

Matron winced. He shut the door and then came back into the room and sat opposite her.

'We know all about it,' he said softly. 'Why don't you tell me everything?'

'I beg your pardon,' she said icily.

He laughed. 'I often open conversations like that,' he said. 'You'd be surprised how some people react. Especially those with guilty consciences.'

'My conscience is perfectly clear, and I don't like your attitude, Chief Inspector, or your methods. And I was not aware that I was to be interrogated.'

'Easy on, Matron. I'm only trying to be sociable.' He took a notebook from an inner pocket. 'On behalf of the Midlands Police Force,' he began, 'I am enquiring into the circumstances surrounding the death of Mr Ranji Patel on the M1 motorway on the evening of . . .'

Matron stood up, interrupting him.

'I've had an appalling night,' she said, 'and an unforgettably unpleasant experience this morning. An experience made many times worse by your unfortunate presence here. There's nothing I can tell you about Mr

Patel that Mr Blake from the Town Hall doesn't know, and I suggest that you direct your questions to him here this morning. I intend to fill in the necessary forms about Mrs Reynolds and then I'm going to my quarters for a rest.'

'I'm sorry that you feel unable to co-operate,' he said smoothly. He closed his notebook with an ominous snap. 'I note your remarks, and we'll talk later. It will be necessary, I'm afraid.'

'Mr Blake goes straight to Mr Patel's room,' Matron said. 'He keeps normal Town-Hall hours and should be here about nine o'clock. You can see him then. And don't threaten me, young man, not even obliquely.'

He stood up as she went out. There goes someone with all their marbles, he thought. But there was something odd about her too. She was much older than she had appeared to be on the few occasions he had seen her with his wife at the Home. It was almost as if she had been drained of energy-giving lubricants, leaving her without vitality, stiff, wrinkled, bent. And all since last Open Day! He would quiz his wife that evening as to what medical reasons there might be for such a dramatic change in someone's appearance, which would produce such edginess. The hairs on the back of his neck began to bristle. Was he on to something here, he wondered? He sat down at the desk and took from his jacket pocket the letter which the Superintendent of the Midlands Police Authority had written to his opposite number at the local station. In the circumstances it deserved to be read rather more carefully, he thought.

Matron paused outside the doctor's room. Of all the infernal luck, she thought, to have one of the staff married to a busybody senior police officer. And even more disconcerting that he should have been provided with an opportunity to come into the Home and start poking and prying when another resident had died. Even in the case of Mrs Reynolds, which was clearly the natural result of an accident, he was casting doubts and fabricating unpleasant theories. Fortunately Dr Jackson seemed to be satisfied that the death was from natural causes, and presumably that would be that. But he was clearly one of those dog-with-a-bone men, and in the matter of Mr Patel, what theories would he formulate and where would his theories take him? And what construction could he erect around the earlier deaths, all fortunately certified by his wife? She shook her head. She was feeling desperately old and tired and in need of a drink. There was nothing left in her room and it was too early to get out and replenish her stock. Some of the residents had bottles in their lockers. Then there was the bar stock which she had never touched previously, but there was always a first time for everything. But the residents would be coming downstairs soon for breakfast and it would be far easier, and less suspicious, to go into a resident's room and take whatever liquor she could find, than to open up the cupboard in the lounge where the bar stock was kept. How could she explain that if observed? Yet who would question her right to go in and out of any room in the Home at any time of the night or day?

She turned over in her mind a list of residents likely to have a bottle or two. Mrs Snow was a likely prospect, and she owed her a lesson for the insubordination she had shown last night. Nasty old woman, she thought. There was also the point that she moved slowly and noisily, so that once she was downstairs there wasn't a chance that she could get back quickly or without being noticed. That decided her. Whatever drink Mrs Snow had in her locker she would take. She would walk into her room with an empty bottle on a tray covered with a cloth, as if it were some kind of medication. Pour Mrs Snow's drink into the bottle on the tray, replace the empty bottle in the locker and then get away sharply. If she felt like it, and there was time, she could replace the drink later, after she'd been shopping for her vodka, during the evening meal.

162

Mrs Snow would be unlikely to discover her loss during the day, but she would undoubtedly make a fuss when she did so later, if it hadn't been made good. Even so, there would be nothing to point the finger of suspicion at Matron. Who would suspect her? It wouldn't be the first time that persons unknown had siphoned away the contents of a resident's bottle, and once consumed, where was the evidence?

She nodded approvingly to herself. That's what she would do. And if Mrs Snow was out of stock, she would search about until she found a bottle in some other locker.

Mrs Snow opened her bedroom door and swung her walking-frame out into the corridor. She was invariably first up on her floor. It was an increasingly difficult task, getting about, and at times she wondered if it was worth the candle. For two pins, she thought . . . but immediately cut the thought off in its prime before it had time to mature. Life still had some interest, even if life itself was proving to be so hard to sustain. Two steps along she saw Mrs Bolter almost running up the stairs, her face white and strained. She's a bit off; perhaps she's sampled breakfast, thought Mrs Snow. Serve her right. Another two steps forward and Mrs Bolter was right in front of her, blocking her path.

'Good morning, Mrs Bolter, you're in a rush.'

'We must talk. Have you heard the news?'

Mrs Snow's head lifted, scenting the air.

'What news?'

'The chocolates I gave you last night, what did you do with them?'

Mrs Snow's face was expressionless. 'You're talking riddles, my dear,' she said. 'Riddles.'

Mrs Bolter stared at her. I'll kill her, she thought desperately. She shook herself to get rid of the tension which had built up around her shoulders and neck. Then

163

she smiled, came round the side of Mrs Snow and put her hand underneath her arm. 'Come along,' she said lightly, 'there's nobody about and we can talk on our way down.'

Mrs Snow, her pace hindered rather than speeded up as a result of Mrs Bolter's assistance, nodded acquiescence.

Mrs Bolter's voice sank to a conspiratorial whisper.

'Mrs Reynolds died last night. Heart attack. She fell out of bed reaching for a box of chocolates in her locker. The heart attack was a direct result, so they say.'

'She made fun of me last night,' said Mrs Snow. 'Had a good laugh at my expense.'

'And now she's dead.'

Mrs Snow smiled. 'Seems like it don't pay to cross me, nor to make fun of me, eh? Someone should tell Matron that!'

'Did you give Mrs Reynolds the chocolates I gave you last night?'

Mrs Snow took another two steps. 'I'm not saying I did. But supposing I did? Supposing I wanted to make it up with her?'

'Quite so,' said Mrs Bolter. 'Very admirable, indeed. The trouble is Dr Jackson's husband came in with her this morning. He's the detective, you know. He's asking all kinds of questions, Making up all kinds of theories.'

'Really,' said Mrs Snow. They had reached the lift, and Mrs Bolter pressed the bell. The stairs were just behind them and Mrs Bolter felt goose pimples on her back; it was just here that Mrs Snow claimed to have knocked Mrs Southover's stick and sent her rolling down the stairs. Somewhere below, the lift motor clicked smoothly into life and the lift began purring its way to their floor. When it appeared Mrs Bolter stepped forward and pulled the lattice gates to one side. They ran smoothly in their rails.

'This place really is beginning to get the better of me,' she said.

'It would do if you lived in it,' said Mrs Snow. 'Unless

you did something to liven it up!' She turned and faced Mrs Bolter, who was still holding back the lift gates.

'Why are you telling me all this stuff about Mrs Reynolds?' she said slowly. 'It's all very interesting, and I suppose that policemen are always asking questions and making up stories, so why should it bother you? Or me? It's one thing to say what might have happened, or what could have happened, but it's another thing to be able to prove it. Isn't it?' She fixed Mrs Bolter with an unwinking stare.

Mrs Bolter beckoned her into the lift, then pulled the gate to and pressed the down button. The lift began to descend at a leisurely pace.

'Suppose,' she said, 'just suppose, that the box of chocolates is an important clue. Not that I think it is. But just suppose. The police will want to know where she got them, right?'

'I still don't know what you're driving at,' said Mrs Snow. 'You just told me that she had a heart attack. But if you want to play games, let's suppose that the chocolates were the ones you gave me. They're expensive and I'll bet you won't find them in any local shop, will you? Can't be many shops that sell them, and the police would be able to trace them back quite easily.' She paused and then added, 'And find out who bought them.'

The lift stopped and they moved out into the corridor. One or two of the more sprightly residents were making their way down the stairs, and others were already in the entrance lounge.

'But I gave them to you,' protested Mrs Bolter.

'Nobody saw you. You put them straight into my bag here on my frame. Remember? And they've got your finger prints on them, not mine!'

Mrs Bolter drew breath sharply and a grin cracked across Mrs Snow's face.

'So if I did give her the box you gave me, and it means

165

something, and the police are suspicious and make enquiries, they could be asking you questions, not me.'

'That's ridiculous,' spluttered Mrs Bolter, but her stomach churned over angrily and she tasted again the morning's coffee in her mouth. 'Never heard anything more ridiculous.'

'Of course it is,' cackled Mrs Snow. 'But it just goes to show, doesn't it? You can make a meal out of anything if you've got the imagination for it.'

'But did you give them to her?' insisted Mrs Bolter. 'And did you give her anything else with them? Tablets?'

Mrs Snow's grin faded.

'What tablets?' she said. 'You ought to be ashamed of yourself, suggesting things like that to me. You must take me for a pretty fool indeed.'

Mrs Bolter's grip on her elbow eased. If she was anything, Mrs Snow wasn't a fool, and when you thought about it calmly, how could she have had anything to do with it, even if she had passed on that stupid box of chocolates? And she wasn't even sure that she'd done that! It was only that nasty policeman's insinuations that there was more to the event than met the eye that had caused her to go off in a blind panic. Mrs Reynolds had in effect killed herself, the victim of her own gluttony. There wasn't even a suggestion that she'd been given a box of large expensive truffles as part of a diabolical plot to pay her out for making fun of Mrs Snow. And if she had, Mrs Snow would have had to have made certain that Mrs Reynolds reacted in the right way, that is, would have had to have woken in the night, to have reached for the irresistible truffles, fallen out of bed and had her attack. And that was clearly absurd.

She gathered her thoughts. Chief Inspector Jackson could be right, though; there could be other plausible and sinister explanations for what appeared to be a simple over-reaching in the night. Someone could have gone into Mrs Reynolds's room and put a pillow over her head and then tipped her out of bed. She shuddered. That someone would have had to have made certain that the emergency bell on Mrs Reynolds's pillow was safely tucked away, and would have to know about the timing of the movements of the night staff. Then a chocolate would be pressed into Mrs Reynolds's hand, the rest of the box scattered over the floor and the bedside locker overturned. What absolute rubbish, she thought, to think that Mrs Snow could have done all that. Looking at Mrs Snow beside her, it was clear that she had just about enough strength to lift up her frame sufficiently to progress along the corridors at a near zero rate of knots. What absurdities that Chief Inspector has inspired in me, what grisly flights of imagination!

'You're no fool, Mrs Snow,' she said. Suddenly she felt light-hearted, almost her old self again. 'You've got scrambled egg for breakfast,' she said. 'Off you go and enjoy it.'

Mrs Snow snorted. 'By the time we get it, it's all cold and rubbery.'

By now ambulatory residents were moving purposefully towards the dining room.

'Another few yards to go,' said Mrs Bolter.

A tall, spare figure brushed past them, listing slightly to one side. The Colonel went on and paused by the entrance, his pale blue eyes vacant, his thoughts turned inwards. As Mrs Bolter glanced at him his eyes focused on Mrs Snow and he straightened up and smiled. His shoulders went on for ever, she thought, he must have been a fine figure of a man in his prime. Such a pity that his wits were scattered by the onset of premature senility. Even now, when he was erect, back on earth at it were, he looked a strong vigorous old gentleman, and he was obviously very aware of, and perhaps in some inexplicable way even fond of, Mrs Snow. How odd, she thought. What a contrast!

Mrs Snow caught the Colonel's smile. Momentarily her face softened and lit up. Then, as she turned sharply to intercept Mrs Bolter's slowly spreading look of comprehension and disbelief, her own expression changed as if shutters had slammed down, obliterating all traces of warmth. What remained was hard, her eyes hooded and the nose and chin carved in stone, the lips straight and thin. The Colonel lifted his stick in a half salute and went on into the dining-room.

'Thanks for the chat,' Mrs Snow muttered, 'and if the invitation still stands, we'll see you at the wedding, if not sooner.'

Before Mrs Bolter could answer, Mrs Snow, with a sudden swing of her frame, had reached the dining-room entrance at the same time as two other residents. There was a momentary hiatus in the flow of people eagerly seeking the first meal of the day. Mrs Snow, in the middle, must have managed to get in first, the two ladies either side of her colliding as she moved forward.

She wouldn't, thought Mrs Bolter, she couldn't have got that nice, harmless old gentleman involved; she couldn't have used him. I won't even think about it, I'll put it out of my mind. But as she stood there, staring in the direction of the dining-room, with olds pushing past her on either side, her mind's eye filled with a succession of tableaux. Mrs Snow in deep head-to-head conversation with the Colonel. The Colonel emerging from underneath Mr Patel's car with a hacksaw in his hand. Mrs Snow inviting Mrs Reynolds to take the chocolates from the bag on her frame. Mrs Reynolds in bed, asleep, the box, sampled and enjoyed, safely stowed away in her locker. The night nurse looking in, smiling serenely and then on her way. Then the tiny bent figure hunched over her walking-frame at Mrs Reynolds's door. Then the tall male figure, listing slightly to one side, inside the room, moving to where Mrs Reynolds was sleeping and breathing heavily, blocking her view as he bent over the bed, leaning over the shape in it.

She could stand it no longer. She put her hands to her

head and ran back down the almost empty corridor. The pictures came in and out of her head one after the other.

Chief Inspector Jackson emerged from Matron's room feeling very pleased with himself. Next step, to see the Town Hall man Blake, and then he'd be back on the trail of Matron, snooty old hag with her chest full of ribbons. Like some old martial dowager. What a joke, lording it in these circumstances. He could do with some coffee, might even be able to charm a slice of toast from cook if he laid it on thickly enough. He knew where the dining-room was; nothing venture, nothing gain. As he turned the corner Mrs Bolter ran into him blindly and he staggered and almost fell.

'What the – ' he began. Mrs Bolter recoiled, shaken, and stretched out a hand as if warding off the devil.

'No,' she said. 'No, it's not true, it isn't. Don't come near me.'

'If I'd been one of the old people I'd have been sent flying,' he said severely. 'What's the matter, Mrs Bolter? What isn't true?'

Mrs Bolter put both hands over her face, her shoulders hunched. Those dreadful endless nightmarish pictures, like an amateur movie gone wrong. It couldn't be true, not true.

She felt an arm around her shoulders.

'Come along with me,' he said. 'You need my wife's attentions.' Then, insistently, 'What isn't true, Mrs Bolter? You can tell me.'

She shook her head. The pictures were fading now. In a little while all would be fine again. There were more voices and then she was sitting down and Dr Jackson was holding something under her nose.

'Oh dear,' she said faintly. 'I am a nuisance, aren't I?' She looked around. Somehow she was in Dr Jackson's room. The Chief Inspector was there too, watching her, in the corner. Matron was there and Mr Blake, and as she looked at them they looked at each other and smiled in a relieved way.

'I'm sending you home, and no argument,' said Matron. 'And I don't want to see you for the rest of the week. Understand?'

Mrs Bolter smiled weakly. 'I'm sorry,' she said, 'so sorry.'

'No need for that,' said Matron. 'I'll drive you home in your car and get a cab back. And don't argue.'

If I take her home, she thought, I can get myself a bottle on the way back without raising any comment, which is very desirable, especially if it's vodka 90° proof. All that trouble getting Mrs Snow's whisky out of her room. Needn't have bothered. But it would come in handy and she'd hang on to it.

'I'll be all right,' said Mrs Bolter. 'There's so much to do here.'

She tried to stand up, but her legs seemed to have no strength in them.

'We can manage,' said Matron firmly. 'Mr Blake can hold the reins while I'm out, and I won't be long anyway. Come along, Mrs Bolter.' She turned to Mr Blake. 'And perhaps you'd telephone Councillor Roberts. He said he would try to get along here this morning in any event.'

'Go to bed when you get home,' said Dr Jackson. 'And go and see your GP.'

Mrs Bolter nodded. She was feeling infinitely better already, and the prospect of getting away from the Home and Mr Jackson, now that it was in view, was tempting. Once home she could forget about the nightmares, forget about Mrs Reynolds and Mrs Snow and the Colonel, the chocolates, everything, and plunge into the wedding arrangements, track down a many-tiered cake on a silver stand, buy a new outfit for the occasion, get back to reality, see Claire and her husband off to a good start. The wedding-present was no problem; she had already

170

decided that since they were taking off almost immediately for far distant parts the most practical thing she could do was to write out a cheque. I'm behaving like a normal conscientious Mum, she thought, and that's what I am, normal and conscientious. She stood up and smiled, and Matron picked up her handbag and took her arm.

'Goodbye, everybody,' she said. 'I promise not to be a nuisance any more.' She smiled brightly, but as she turned towards the door it was as if an enormous black pit opened up in front of her, there was darkness all round and the world was full of shattering screams and demented voices. Just as suddenly, as she almost stumbled into the mind-bending terror within her, the room reappeared and Matron was beside her still, gripping her arm. Nobody seemed to have noticed anything. Perhaps I will go to bed when I get home, she thought, I can't take too much of this kind of thing.

Chief Inspector Jackson watched them go out and turned to his wife. 'And what do you make of that?' he asked.

'The giddiness and fainting, I suspect, are due to all that dashing about on an empty stomach,' she said. 'The hallucinations I'm not so sure about. It's pretty obvious that she has a lot on her mind right now.'

He turned to Mr Blake. 'And after that diversion,' he said, 'let us go upstairs to Mr Patel's room.'

'Is this an official visit?'

'It is.'

'I thought the police would be called in some time. I'll lead the way.'

In Mr Patel's room Mr Blake handed over the folder in which he had filed all the personal papers he could find. Beside it was the ledger he had requisitioned from the administration office.

'Such as it is,' he said, 'it's all there.'

Chief Inspector Jackson went over to the fitted wardrobe and opened the doors wide, looking briefly at what he

171

judged to be expensive suits and shirts hanging in a neat row. He bent down and picked up a pair of shoes, turned them over and then threw them back into the wardrobe.

'Not a lot,' he said, 'but what there is must have cost a packet. What's in the folder, and what have you got to tell me.'

Mr Blake produced his pipe and began stuffing it.

'There's really nothing conclusive,' he said. 'It's quite clear that Patel had more money than can be accounted for by his official salary. But there's no indication where it came from. One might however make certain deductions.' He paused. 'Looking at the ledger – that's the one you're turning over now – the residents' income is on the face of it all accounted for. There's what they get from their state pensions. They're entitled to draw a nominal sum weekly and it's all recorded in and out. That pile of paper on the spike there is the individual receipts they sign when the money is handed over to them. They all check out as far as I've gone back, which is for this financial year.'

'So?'

'It's when you learn of the circumstances in which the receipts are signed that bells start ringing. About half the residents don't know A from a bull's foot. They're old and confused and alone. I'm told that Patel used to get them to sign the receipts, then the clerk would enter up the ledger in her office and he'd collect the money which he was supposed to take to them. But who knows if they know what they're signing for, or how much they're supposed to get? And if they've got no relatives, or only the kind that don't ask questions, they're not going to complain. They might have been told that if they make a nuisance of themselves they'll get transferred somewhere else where they'll be much worse off. Or sent back to their relatives, if they've got any. Old people frighten easily and they don't like change.'

'What kind of figures are we talking about?'

'If you assume that the trick could be worked on about

172

half the old people here, and he wasn't too greedy, he could possibly have been getting away with about £500 a month.'

'But he couldn't have done it if his senior was doing her job properly, or unless she was in on it.'

'That's been worrying me too,' said Mr Blake. 'I can't prove any of this. If you tried to get corroboration from the affected old people you'd have a job, and it would be hearsay only. But if it was going on, she must have known about it.'

'Perhaps we should ask to see her bank statements,' said Chief Inspector Jackson. 'I wonder what she knows about off-shore deposit accounts? Any other fiddles likely or possible?'

Mr Blake looked uncomfortable. He twisted his pipe nervously before answering.

'Possible,' he said. 'I've often thought about it. One of my official jobs is to take into safe custody the belongings of the residents who die in the Council's homes. I lock them up until either the next of kin claims them or the Council disposes of them. I've never known a family to query the "estates", as they're called, but some of them are ridiculously small. A couple of dresses, maybe, a worn top coat or a couple of pairs of crummy shoes and a plastic bag full of underwear. But thinking back I would say that invariably, where there was nothing or next to nothing left, the deceased was someone who had few visitors, no close family to take an interest in them or what they had to leave. The Home's staff know who those people are. When they pass away it would be a simple matter to gather up the bulk of whatever had any value, any good clothes, rings, jewellery and so on, before I could get here, and then dispose of it at leisure.'

'And you've never voiced your suspicions?'

'Never had any proof. What was the point?'

'Well,' said Chief Inspector Jackson, 'you will be interested to learn that Mr Patel had a wife in Bradford

173

and that she is a proprietor of a crummy shop which sells second-hand clothes, bric-à-brac and jewellery, and that trade appears to be excellent. Patel kept her existence very quiet, but we assume that he was on his way to her when he had his accident.'

'Profits would be pretty good if she was getting half her stock for nothing!'

'Or if it fell off the back of a hearse, as it were.' Mr Jackson paused. 'But if Matron and Assistant Matron were really fiddling the pension income,' he mused, 'it would be in their interest to keep the residents alive and well, would it not?'

'Unless either of them could expect a legacy or something of value as the result of a death. I don't think that any of the recently deceased were in a position to make handsome bequests.'

'Hm. My colleagues in the Midlands police think that Patel's car could have been tampered with. But the car was a complete wreck, and they've had a job trying to figure out what really happened. The brake fluid pipe could have been partially severed, but it's not certain.'

'A method much employed in the movies,' commented Mr Blake. 'Off goes the victim, happy until he starts to go downhill. Then he puts his foot on the brake, and bingo! nothing happens.'

'It's not the kind of thing that happens too often in real life, though.'

'Do you think that he might have fallen out with Matron over something, you know, thieves falling out? Could she have done it? Or had it done?'

'She's seen service in the Far East,' said Mr Jackson. 'That is, if she's entitled to wear those medal ribbons she sports. She might even speak Hindu or Urdu or Bengali or whatever, and the two of them could have been in cahoots. But fiddling the books and stealing from the dead is an entirely different game from either committing or arranging a murder. They're different leagues.'

He sat down on the late Mr Patel's bed, looking out of the open window. The sun was shining and the sounds of the traffic on the main road could be heard distinctly. What a dump of a Home, he thought, and what a pair of ghouls running it. From what he had learned from Blake it would be difficult to pin anything on Matron. But that shouldn't deter him from trying to get to the truth; he might dig up enough to get the scheming old sow the sack, and that would be something. He couldn't imagine Matron, even if she had quarrelled bitterly with Patel, climbing under his car and sawing through a vital bit of it – always assuming that she knew which bit was vital. It was difficult to believe, too, that she could have arranged with a third party to have it done. And if Patel's death was a legitimate accident, well, OK, that still left a question mark over the other recent deaths. His wife had certified two of them as being due to natural causes, and it seemed that she was minded to do so in the case of Mrs Reynolds. Clearly he had to tread carefully here. Perhaps they were all legit. He got up and looked through the ledger again. Was there a connection between all or some of these events? If there was, it was one that was not readily discernible. At the present it was a conundrum which his empty stomach was certainly not helping to solve. A sudden vision of eggs and bacon flashed before his eyes.

'I'm going to scrounge some breakfast,' he said. 'Coming?'

Mr Blake shook his head vigorously.

'I've eaten, thanks,' he said, 'and I should be downstairs in Matron's room, seeing to things. I hope she's not going to be too long. I'm not too well qualified for the job.'

'Well, would you write up briefly what you've told me? I'll see that it stays confidential. Let me have it on Monday?'

'I'll have it ready for you,' said Mr Blake. 'There's nothing more I can do here.'

175

'Good man. And not a word to Matron, there's a good chap.'

16

Mr Bolter slipped into the hired long-tailed morning coat he had brought home to wear at the wedding. He patted on his topper and preened himself in front of the hall mirror. Not bad, he thought complacently, he'd make a fine figure of a man walking down the aisle with Claire on his arm, all tiny and white-veiled. And the wedding photographs would be great! He'd organised the best photographer in the district, and it was lucky that Claire had managed to get a special licence to get married in the Parish Church; the entrance was very impressive, stone pillars and a pointed arch, great wooden doors with strap hinges, and the whole place kept very nicely indeed. Much more suitable than that dreary Registry Office building as a background for wedding photographs.

He'd had a good night. Richard had left a couple of days ago for his parents' home and had promised to turn up at the church on time complete with them and his best man. All of their gear was in suitcases and bundles in Claire's room, and Claire herself had spent the last night she had as a free agent on the tiles with some of her girl friends. Phyllis, who should have been basking in the glory of her achievement in having found a three-tiered cake and arranged for its delivery – guaranteed – direct to the reception, was moping about and looking very odd and fraught. She had sensibly arranged time off from that bloody Home to help cope with it all, though at times she looked as if she was a refugee from it; she must be a bit upset at the thought of Claire taking herself off, he thought, women got very broody and peculiar when their offspring flew the coop, instead of counting their blessings.

He'd had the best part of two bottles of a very reasonable claret with his evening meal – and that after a few celebratory drinks at lunch time and a few more on his way home – and had felt no pain as he dozed and snorted in front of the television in the evening. Phyllis had fussed and clucked about aimlessly, though to be fair she'd done a remarkable job in clearing up the place, removing completely the more sordid bits of rubbish, and the house looked more or less normal for the great occasion. He'd finally gone off into a deep dreamless sleep and had awoken fresh and vigorous, if somewhat furry-tongued, and ready for the fray. He looked at his watch. Half past eight. He smiled again at his reflection in the mirror. It was going to be a great day.

'Phyllis,' he called up the stairs. 'Come and see. What do you think?'

Mrs Bolter straightened out from the foetal position which she had assumed during the night, sleeping fitfully, hugging herself when she wasn't asleep, dreaming disturbing dreams when she was, dreaming the kind of dream where nothing happened but in the empty menacing stillness there was an overwhelming sense of fear; the kind of dream which she so dreaded and which disorientated her so badly that it was difficult to decide whether she was awake or dreaming, or dreaming that she was awake, whilst the fear mounting up inside her met and joined forces with the silent horror surrounding her outside. She had tried to put out of her mind the thoughts and pictures which had caused her to break down in the Home, but the sense of it was never very far away. It was a relief to hear the birds once more greeting the dawn and to watch how the light from the window in her room changed almost imperceptibly from dark to lighter shades of grey, and to see how the humped-back monster lurking on the end of the bed resumed once more its mundane existence as the cardigan discarded the night before and then forgotten. She heard him calling. I won't answer him, she thought, I'll not get up. Not yet. I'm not ready to get up and be in the same room with him. Not yet.

She'd been particularly busy the evening before. She planned, after the reception, to entertain Richard's parents and his immediate family at the house before they departed on their respective journeys home. She had no idea whether they were coming by car or train or what. It would have been better to have met them socially before the wedding to discuss the arrangements, but the least she could do for them was to ask them back to the house for a bite to eat and drink, to chat and learn something about each other. She'd tried talking to him, but he'd been in a particularly stupid mood. He'd arrived home drunk, had more wine with his meal, muttering away in that infuriatingly aimlessly stupid way he had, talking to himself, giggling, drinking more wine and finally ending up sprawled in his chair, his head on one side, snoring, the empty bottles by his side, the television on, the coloured images flickering and posturing unnoticed.

She'd made what she called finger snacks for the post-reception get-together. Filled tiny pastry cases with various savoury mixtures and, with the aid of an assortment of packs of frozen goodies, had turned out sausage rolls, a set of pizzas, scotch eggs and a couple of quiches; defrosted a stack of ready-cooked fresh frozen chicken drumsticks. Tomorrow she would split the bridge rolls and stuff them with pâté or whatever, make a salad, slice the enormous egg and ham pie and arrange it on a silver serving-dish. He could look after the liquid refreshments. It didn't matter if they didn't eat much, the thing was to have a good show, not to let Claire down. When she'd finished, all the available space in her newly reorganised kitchen was filled with plates laden with food and covered loosely with greaseproof paper or clean linen towels, and for once she felt agreeably tired. Perhaps I'll sleep tonight, she thought.

She had just finished washing up the last of the preparation dishes when Claire came in from her night out. She had heard her key in the lock and the sound of a cab moving off down the road as the front door opened. It was nearly midnight by the kitchen clock. She had opened the kitchen door and stood in the doorway, holding her apron.

'Claire,' she called softly.

Claire, in the hall, finished putting her key in her handbag.

'Yes,' she said.

'I heard you coming in,' said Mrs Bolter apologetically. 'Thought I'd come and see if you'd like a cup of tea, or coffee, or perhaps something stronger as a nightcap.'

'Did I disturb you, then?' said Claire. She fumbled in her bag and extracted the keys she had only just put away. 'Well, you won't need to worry about me making a noise at night or coming in late after tomorrow.' She held out the keys. 'I won't be using these again.'

Mrs Bolter looked askance at the keys, shocked.

'Keep them,' she said. 'Put them back, please. Keep them. This is your home for as long as you want it. You're not leaving us for ever. You'll be back. Won't you?'

Claire remained stony-faced. 'Just as you wish,' she said. 'I've had an excruciatingly boring evening and I'm tired. I think I'll go to bed. Big day tomorrow.'

Mrs Bolter's hands wrestled frantically with each other and her apron.

'Come and see what I've prepared for tomorrow, for after the reception. For Richard's people,' she pleaded. 'Tell me if it's all right.'

'Shouldn't bother too much,' said Claire. 'Spoke to Richard on the phone this evening. His parents will be wanting to get back quickly after the reception. It's a long drive. They might not want to come back here.'

179

'Come and see, anyway.'

Claire pulled her light coat about her more tightly and took a few reluctant steps towards the kitchen. Mrs Bolter moved to her, put her arms around her and hugged her tightly.

'Oh, Claire,' she said.

Claire froze. She'd spent the evening in the company of three of her former school friends. They'd seen a show, had a meal and talked. They had talked, after some naive questions about Dr Richards, almost exclusively about themselves, each of them seemingly determined to press upon the others the brilliance of their prospective careers, the unique nature of their respective experiences and personalities. Claire had found herself becoming more and more depressed as the evening wore on. Was she really a contemporary of these giggling, chattering bird-brains? she asked herself. What am I doing here? Where are the dreams I dreamed of my own career? What am I giving up tomorrow and for what reason? She'd telephoned Richard from the restaurant. He'd just returned home with his younger brother from a bachelor pub crawl, but sounded remarkably coherent. We just went to my local, he explained, had a few pints. We'll be at the church on time, and sober, he had reassured her.

'I love you,' she said. 'Why don't you motor up tonight? I miss you.'

He laughed. 'You know that's not on,' he said. 'I miss you too. See you tomorrow. Sleep well.'

When she returned to the table it seemed to her that in her absence her friends had been talking about her, bitchifying as usual, they had that look about them. She sat down and looked hard at each of them in turn. There was an awkward silence.

'Well,' she said, 'it's been an evening to remember. Dead boring, but memorable in a queasy sort of way. Thank you all for coming.'

180

Janice, her best and closest friend, put her hand over Claire's.

'We've a little something for you,' she said. 'You sprung all this on us at such short notice. In a couple of weeks or so we'll all be back in our respective colleges and you'd have been friendless on your big day. We haven't had much time for shopping, I'm afraid. Anyway, if you don't like it you can change it, no bother. It comes with much love from the three of us. We'll miss you, Claire. We really do hope that you'll be tremendously happy.' She handed over a small parcel.

Claire took the package, looking down at it. When she raised her head there were tears in her eyes.

'Thank you all,' she said. 'I'm sorry. And I won't change it, whatever it is.'

She'd got up and barged her way out into the street and flagged down a passing taxi. On the ride home she'd hugged the parcel tightly, her eyes brimming over with unsought and unexpected tears. I must be tipsy, she thought, which was not possible on the amount she'd imbibed. What should have been a lively night out had proved to be the pits. The show had been awful, the meal abysmal and the conversation trivial beyond belief. And just when she had decided that the most sensible thing to do was to put as much distance as possible between her and these silly simpering females, the whole world turns topsy-turvy. 'This comes with much love from the three of us', and with the words the strange choking emotion which welled up in the throat and overflowed and filled her with the oddest feeling of embarrassment.

Her adoptive mother's arms were now warm and strong about her, and again there was that uncomfortable feeling of embarrassment. I don't want this, she thought desperately. Not now. I've grown up and I'm going away. It's come too late. I can't be doing with all this. I can't handle it.

Mrs Bolter released her and stepped back.

181

'All I've ever wanted, dear,' she said quietly, 'is your happiness.'

'Really?' said Claire. 'I must say you could have fooled me. And what did you want for him?' She pointed to the open door of the dining-room through which Mr Bolter could be seen and heard, despite the crackling of the late-night movie which blurred away on the television screen in the corner.

'What do you mean?'

'Councillor bloody Bob Roberts, that's what I mean, the original long-term fornicator!'

Mrs Bolter stared.

'I suppose that you thought you'd got away with it after all these years?' Claire went on. 'I can't tell you the number of times I've been in the house with the pair of you upstairs and you moaning and groaning and the bed creaking. What about father? And what about me? If I hadn't had your example of promiscuity thrust in front of me, under my nose, up it, from an early age, I wouldn't have behaved the way I did, would I? Do you have any idea what knowing about you did to me? Have you any idea how dirty I felt, how angry I was at you, at myself?'

'It isn't the way you think it is,' said Mrs Bolter desperately. 'I mean, it's all over now. And as for him,' she gestured towards her husband, 'he just isn't interested. Hasn't been for years. It isn't my fault that I have these needs, desires. It's perfectly normal – you know that.'

'Does he know about Uncle Bob?'

'I don't know. I've never told him. But he's not bothered, truly. Just as long as I don't bother him.'

'Well then, let's wake him up and tell him now.'

Mrs Bolter turned away and went back into the kitchen. She heard Claire going upstairs, slowly, as if she was carrying something unbearably weighty. Dear God, she thought, she's known for years. She felt humiliated, diminished. It explained an awful lot of things, though. Claire's hostility towards her, which she had attributed to

182

the normal adolescent rebellion, but which had not abated. And Claire's early experimentation and apparent obsession with boys and sex. It might also explain why she was so insistent on knowing who her natural parents were; she was clearly more than critical of the mores and standards of her adoptive family.

Mrs Bolter sat down at the table and looked despairingly around her. The fruits of her labours, of hours of work, finger food in all its dreadful variety, surrounded her. None of it would get eaten, she despaired, no one would come back after the reception; or if they did, Claire would tell them all about her and Bob Roberts and there would be rows and scenes and utter disgrace and it would be unbearable. She got up and retrieved from the broom-cupboard the half-consumed bottle of sherry which had fuelled her earlier efforts, poured herself a large glassful and swallowed half of it in one gulp. Mrs Snow would be able to cope with all this, she thought. Maybe if she had another drink everything would go away and she could start tomorrow with only remembered nightmares and a hangover, not real-life confrontations to cope with . . . Mrs Snow was tough . . . she'd arrange anything. She hadn't liked Mrs Southover, so, tap her stick and she falls down dead. And the others. It was all dreadfully compli-cated, but she had to think of something so that she had no need to think of Claire, could banish the memory of her white, unhappy, accusing face. She took another drink. I'm a useless, wicked, unloved and unlovable woman, she thought, as tears welled up in her eyes and rolled slowly down her cheeks. A useless, unwanted article. Not even a person. I'm nothing. Nobody will miss me when I'm gone. Nothing matters now.

Upstairs Claire unwrapped her parcel. Inside there was a small fragile piece of beautifully decorated china; a bowl with a lid crowned with a tiny but ornate bunch of delicately worked flowers. She had no idea what to put in it, but she held it up to the light, turning it slowly, and

183

then held it to her. It was the first furnishing for a new life, she thought. How incongruous, how useless, how beautiful! She giggled. Of all the things one might need when setting up home in a tent or a caravan on the site of a dig in the Middle East, a bone china trinket bowl for a dressing-table had to be well down on the list. But I love it, she said out loud, and wherever we go it will come with us. She replaced the tissue paper round it and put it back in its box. I must go back down to her, she thought. Who am I to judge? Perhaps it was at least partly my fault. I gave her a hard time when I was growing up. And then perhaps it was all meant to be. She didn't have to adopt me. She loves me. Do I want to go away remembering her the way I've just left her? She really doesn't deserve to be hurt like that. I'll show her my gift from the girls and we'll talk. She took the small box and went downstairs quietly.

The TV was still on in the dining-room and the savoury smells of her mother's preparations, which could now be acknowledged, perhaps even sampled, were reminiscent of party times when she had been at school. There had been some good times. There had been a lot of good times, in fact. She pushed open the kitchen door and went in smiling, the trinket bowl in its box held in front of her like a charm carried to attract and to give out good vibrations.

Mrs Bolter was seated at the kitchen table. She looked up, her face flushed, bleary-eyed and tearful. In one hand she held a glass full of sherry and in the other a tattered and clearly much pawed-over, unframed photograph of Bob Roberts. She looked inexpressibly guilty.

Claire dropped the gift box on the tiled floor and there was a dull sound from it. For a few brief seconds which seemed to go on for ever her eyes travelled from her stepmother's tormented face to the well-fingered photograph of her lover. Mrs Bolter was incapable of movement. I'll die she thought. I want to die. Without saying anything Claire turned on her heel and went out of the room. Mrs

Bolter stared after her until a grunt from the dining-room reminded her that he was still there and could have been awakened by the sound of footsteps running upstairs. In a couple of lost, dejected movements, she put her arms on the table and her head on her arms and the tears streamed uncontrollably down her cheeks.

And now, after that, on the morning of the wedding, he was calling her. There was no sound from Claire's room. She got up and looked over the banisters to the hall below where he was prancing about in the morning coat he'd hired. His hair was all over the place, uncombed since he'd got up, and he had on an open-neck shirt and the baggy trousers he'd slept in. And this absurdity is what I have to comfort me, she thought; Claire on his arm, walking to the altar, and me in the side pews, unwanted, despised. She went back into her bedroom. Dear God, she said out loud this time. What is to become of me? But there was no sign that anyone had heard her.

17

Mrs Snow creaked slowly and painfully out of bed, struggled into her thin housecoat and, sitting on the bed, lit the first cigarette of the day. She bent over, almost doubled, coughing, the veins in her scrawny neck bulging, holding on to her walking-frame for support as she hawked and spluttered, shifting what she called the night's poisonous deposits from her lungs. She smiled with satisfaction as she felt the stuff moving. It's cigarettes that keep me alive, she said to herself. If I couldn't have a good old cough and a spit in the mornings I'd be dead of accumulated muck in my tubes within a week. Whisky helps too. That reminded her. She got up and rummaged

185

painfully in her locker and took out the bottle of whisky which Mrs Bolter had given her. It felt curiously light. She held it up to the light, moving it from side to side. She could see that at the most it contained about a spoonful. The last time she'd looked at it, it had been almost full.

She took another deep inhalation and felt the tobacco smoke penetrating and narcotic inside her. It wasn't the first time that someone had stolen from her whilst she had been in the Home, and the fact of the theft itself was not surprising. But she had been foolish, very foolish indeed, to have left such a tempting article in her locker. She should have carried it around with her, in her knitting-bag. It wasn't the whisky so much, although that was loss enough, but she had carefully crushed up the dozen or so sleeping-pills or tranquillisers which Mrs Bolter had given her and poured them into the bottle, shaking it well to make sure that they were dissolved. If someone only took a tot at a time out of it, they'd have a good night's sleep, without doubt. But there was no telling what the effects would be if they decided to get rid of the evidence by drinking the lot in one fell swoop, as it were. It was a bloody nuisance being deprived of her knock-out drops. You never knew when they might come in handy, and she'd have to replace them pretty smartish.

Her eyes glinted and she smiled grimly. Well, she said to herself, whoever took it is going to have a mighty fat headache. She looked out of the window. Although it was early, what she could see of the morning suggested that it was going to be a fine day. A fine day for a wedding. Mrs Bolter had promised to send a car for her and the Colonel, to take them to the church and then on to the reception. Mrs Bolter was a stupid woman, but she was a good soul and she could still be useful. When things had settled down a bit she would spend some more time talking to her, reassuring her and trying to solve her little problem. Right now the most pressing thing was to get herself ready, to get some breakfast down her, mustn't drink

186

champagne on an empty stomach, and to make sure that the Colonel was spruced up and presentable. She removed her teeth and began scrubbing them under the hot tap in her wash-hand basin, humming to herself. Nothing quite like a wedding, hymns and orange blossom, champagne and a sit-down reception. Who could ask for more on such a beautiful day as this promised to be? She was looking forward to seeing Mrs Bolter again after her week's absence; even that sharp-nosed policeman husband of Dr Jackson's might be feeling at peace with the world today. And if he was there with his wife she'd give them both a wide berth. She grinned at her reflection in the mirror and popped in her teeth. Not bad, she thought, considering.

Chief Inspector Jackson finished the routine exercises which he performed every morning. Running on the spot, pedalling on his exercise bike, doing press-ups and finishing with a series of postures which he had seen in a book on Yoga. They were painful, sinew-stretching contortions which, according to the book, not only took care of his external self, but also did beneficial things to his internal organs, which would otherwise function inefficiently in some kind of torpid limbo. His wife remained unconvinced of their benefit. She was not an exercise buff and was well aware of the serious nature of the injuries which sporting types, unsupervised, could sustain. Take up swimming, she urged him, keep your mouth closed and don't swallow any of the bath water unless you want some obscure kidney infection. In the summer, when the kids are on holiday, I've read that an analysis of the stuff swilling about in some public swimming baths – I won't call it water – shows that it is about 99% urine. But at least you'll not get a hernia or dislocate one of your joints trying to emulate the feats of some double-jointed Indian Fakir.

He went into the bathroom breathing heavily. His legs and ankles ached abominably. His wife, in the bath, her distended belly and full breasts appearing to float independently of the rest of her body in the soapy water, looked up with concern written on her face.

'I'll sabotage that stupid bike of yours,' she said. 'You look dreadful.'

'I'm OK,' he said.

'You don't look it.' She patted her stomach. 'You don't want junior here to be brought up fatherless, do you? Take it easy.'

He reached for the soap and gently rubbed the taut skin around her navel.

'No chance,' he said. 'How's it all going?'

'We're still on schedule,' she said, 'but with a first child there's no guarantee. Could be any day between now and the end of the month. Probably sooner than later.'

'You'll be well out of that Home for a while,' he said. 'You should have left it weeks if not months ago, even if it is only part-time. There's all kinds of things going on there, very dodgy things indeed. I've spent far too much time thinking about them. It's an aggravation we can both do without. If that Patel person's accident was caused by someone tampering with his car – and the local boys seem to think that there is a good chance that it was – then it was murder. Manslaughter at the very least. You're best out of the way until we can clear it up.'

'You're not seriously suggesting that someone in the Home did that, are you? Here, help me up.'

Out of the bath she wrapped herself in a towel and he put his arms around her protectively.

'It's a worry,' he said. 'If the car was got at, the most likely place for it is the grounds of the Home where it was parked. But for the life of me I can't think of a single person in the Home capable of doing it, or of a strong enough motive.'

'Perhaps it was a team of them.' She laughed. 'And it still could have been nothing more than fair wear and tear, or sub-standard maintenance. The car wasn't exactly this year's model, was it?'

'Maybe,' he said. 'Anyway, that's enough uninformed speculation. I need a shower.'

'Cook could have done it,' she persisted. 'She's got a terrible temper and drawers full of knives and saws and things.'

'So could Matron.'

'How about Mrs Bolter? She's been acting very strangely lately.'

'Go and get dressed,' he said, 'before we swear out warrants to arrest the lot of them.

He drew the plug out of the bath and watched the water gurgle away before pulling the shower curtains across. Under the hot spray he relaxed. From the brief exchange with his wife he had had a germ of an idea, a theory trying to sprout, but the harder he tried to put a shape around it, to pin it down, the more it eluded him. I'll start with Matron, the most likely one, he thought. His mind began ticking over the facts, name, age, background, relationship with the deceased. There was no doubt that she could be a prime suspect, she could even have had a motive. But what evidence was there? Perhaps he should ask her a few more questions, let her see the way his thoughts were shaping, see what developed. It was time he resumed his official conversation with her. He'd do that, he decided, right after the weekend.

Matron's body lay stretched out on her bed in her flat.

The night before she had seen the night nurse on the first of her rounds at about ten o'clock. I'm going to bed, she had told her. I just don't know how I've got through this week without even the Bolter woman to help. I'm dead tired and I don't want to be disturbed or woken up whatever the emergency until morning. Understand?

She'd got on the bed fully dressed. The chintz curtains on her windows were drawn together and the lamp on

189

her bedside table was switched on. On the table itself were a glass and the bottle into which earlier that week she had poured the whisky borrowed from Mrs Snow. Since then she had survived on replenished stocks of vodka, but it seemed to be losing its effect; she was full to the gills with it and still dead sober. Over the previous seven days she had consumed a vast amount of alcohol even by her standards, and had got away with it. Proof that she was still functioning properly lay in the fact that she was able to say to herself that it would be a good thing to drink the whisky, which she had managed to keep in reserve untouched, not only because she fancied a change and it might work better than the vodka and help her to sleep, but also because by the morning there would be no smell on her breath as there would be if she drank the vodka now and the whisky in the morning.

She needed a drink now. Really needed it. The ghosts of sights and sounds of all her yesterdays were materialising in waves to haunt her and conspiring to rob her of sleep. And she needed sleep too. God, how she needed to sleep. She half-filled the glass with neat whisky, swallowed most of it, grimaced and then finished off the rest of it. It was even more foul than she remembered. She refilled her glass. How anyone could drink it for pleasure was beyond her. There were so many more acceptable ways of coming to terms with reality. She poured herself another glassful and drained that. She watched herself, projected somehow beyond her supine body, from between heavy-lidded eyes as the room moved and pulsed around her, pour yet more whisky into her glass, set down the bottle carefully on the bedside table, lift the glass equally carefully to her lips and drain it. What a foul taste. Perhaps it was one of those Japanese brands one heard about, an Oriental rice-water distillation with faint Gaelic connections.

Dear God, she thought, I feel dreadful. Please let me

190

sleep. Her eyes turned up under her lids, her breathing became faster, then slowed and became shallower as the room swirled in a nauseating vortex around her and she felt herself being eased mercifully into the deeper darkness. And then, quite suddenly, there was nothing.

In the morning, in the early hours of the morning of the wedding, before the brief night had run its course and whilst the noise of the traffic outside was still an intermittent, rather than a continual, assault upon the ears, Matron had given a small child-like sigh, not moving, and had died.

Chief Inspector Jackson finished his shower and was in the process of dabbing himself with spots of Eau Sauvage when the extension telephone on the bedside table began to ring. His wife was downstairs.

'I'll get it,' he called, and picked up the receiver.

He heard a breathless, troubled voice. 'Dr Jackson?'

'Who wants her?'

'It's Mrs Dennison, at the Old People's Home. I'm the night nurse.'

'Yes?'

'It's about Matron.' The voice faltered and then came on with a rush. 'I didn't want to disturb Mrs Bolter by ringing her because she's away ill, and I know it's her daughter's wedding today, and I couldn't think of anyone else. I keep knocking on Matron's door and there's no answer. I know she's in there because the light's still on. I saw her go in last night and she looked dreadful. But I can't get her to hear.'

'You were right not to ring Mrs Bolter, but ring that fellow who runs the social services – Councillor Roberts – and put him in the picture. Suggest that he rings Mr Blake, who works in the Town Hall, to give you some assistance. I'll bring Dr Jackson over. We'll be with you as soon as we can.'

He put on his clothes and went downstairs. There was a good smell of coffee and toast.

'Good job we're up early,' he said. 'That call was from the night nurse at the Home. She can't rouse Matron, and it sounds as if it might be another crisis. She wants you to go there and see what you can do!'

'Why me? What am I supposed to do?'

'Why not? I suppose everyone knows that Matron's a not-so-secret lush. She's probably in a stupor, still dead drunk or suffering from a colossal hangover, out to the wide. So put your most powerful antidote in your little black bag and when you're ready I'll run you there.'

'I think you're right about this job,' she said. 'It's getting to be just a bit too much.'

Councillor Roberts was not amused at being awakened by the nerve-taunting peep-peep of his bedside telephone. He looked at the clock and swore. His wife, next to him, grunted and rolled further away.

'Hallo,' he said resignedly.

Mrs Dennison, calmer now since her conversation with Chief Inspector Jackson – such a nice man, you'd never believe that he was a policeman – spoke up confidently.

'Am I speaking to Councillor Roberts?' she asked.

'The very same,' he said.

'I'm Mrs Dennison, night nurse at the Home. We can't rouse Matron and I've been in touch with Dr Jackson and she's coming round straightaway. Her husband said that I was to telephone you and that you were to telephone Mr Blake at the Town Hall and get him to give me some assistance.'

'What the hell has it got to do with Chief Inspector Jackson?' he shouted.

'He answered the telephone, when I rang Dr Jackson.'

Bob Roberts spluttered, at a loss for words.

'Do me a favour,' he said at last. 'Go and thump hard on Matron's door, tell her that Councillor Roberts wants to speak to her. If she doesn't answer to that, get on the internal telephone and give it a good hard ring. I'll hang on.'

'Yes, Mr Roberts. I'll do that. Hang on, please.'

'I said I'd hang on,' he shouted. He put his hand over the mouthpiece. 'Stupid cow,' he said.

Mrs Roberts woke up, immediately resentful.

'What is it now?' she demanded. 'Can't you tell your women to ring you at the office?'

'Go to sleep,' he said testily. 'I've got enough on my plate without your stupid comments.' He swung his legs over the bed. 'Bloody incompetents,' he went on, 'and that policeman Jackson telling me what to do. Saucy young sod.'

'Speak to the Chief Constable, will you? You couldn't even get a parking ticket fixed.'

'Oh, shut up,' he said, still holding the telephone.

'I'll shut up,' she promised. 'And you can take yourself off by yourself to the Bolters' wedding. I wouldn't lower myself to get in the same car as you.'

The telephone in his hand crackled.

'Councillor Roberts?'

'Any luck?' he asked.

'Not a sound, I'm afraid.'

There was a silence for a few seconds.

'All right, Mrs Dennison. Tell Dr Jackson when she gets there not to go before I see her. I'll be around in about an hour. Can you stay and cope with things until we can sort this out? OK?'

'I'll stay on,' said Mrs Dennison. 'We'll manage between us.'

'That's the ticket,' he said. 'I'll see you later.' He turned to his wife. 'I've got to go out,' he said. 'An emergency call from the Home. Matron can't be roused.'

'Why do you have to go out? What's wrong with all those highly paid staff at the Town Hall? When you get to be Mayor, I can tell you, there's going to be a few changes up there.'

193

'Well, I'd better get ready,' he said despondently. 'Do you think I should contact Phyllis Bolter?'

'You've had enough contact with that woman to last a lifetime,' she said bitterly.

'Perhaps you're right,' he said. 'I'll go and make some tea.'

18

Mr Bolter surveyed the crowded reception rooms of the hotel with satisfaction. They were all there, friends, relatives, neighbours, the bridegroom's family as well, all with glasses in their hands drinking his wine at his daughter's wedding. He had to hand it to Claire, never thought she'd do so well so quickly. Not a bad-looking fellow either, a bit older than her and with very tired-looking eyes, but otherwise most suitable. He smiled and dragged at his umpteenth cigarette; if you can't indulge yourself on your daughter's wedding day he'd like to know when you could.

The morning had all been a bit of a blur. He recalled trying on his tail coat and calling her down to see it – without success – bloody disgrace she was, eyes all swollen and looking as if she was going to a funeral after a week of disturbed nights. Talk about the spectre at the feast. And Claire didn't look all that much better either when she finally emerged, all dressed up, and before she'd put on her little hat thing with the veil.

He'd had a couple of drinks whilst Mrs Bolter pottered about dolefully, tidying up and putting out food and generally spreading depression. She'd been acting very strangely of late, even for her. Mothers were traditionally upset on these occasions, but she really was the limit. It wasn't as if the two of them had been all that close either.

Claire had obviously avoided her too. In the car to the church she held his arm and he could feel the tension in her body, even through the induced euphoria of his own mood.

'Cheer up,' he said. 'It'll soon be over and you can enjoy yourself.'

'I wish it were over,' she said. 'Oh, how I wish it were over.'

Most unlike Claire, he thought, but then as one of the principal performers in the day's show, she was entitled to some display of nerves. They'd been photographed getting out of the car, walking up the steps to the path leading to the church entrance, on the path itself, and outside the church door. Made a lovely background. They'd walked down the aisle and heads had turned and faces had beamed at them. The service was mercifully short, flowers everywhere – who paid for them? bloody me of course, he thought ruefully – and then the happy couple were in the vestry signing the register, flash bulbs popping and much kissing, and then more photographs, singles, groups, hundreds of them, and finally, praise be, they were away to the reception.

In the car, driving to the hotel, he beamed fatuously to Mrs Bolter.

'Good job you're driving,' he said graciously. 'I'm not quite drunk you know, but I've had a few and I intend to have a few more; good job you don't indulge, my dear.' He patted her knee. She had her uses. Not a bad old stick.

Mrs Bolter drove on in silence. She too had managed to down several glasses of sherry, secretly, before driving to the church, and was aware that she was not quite herself.

'I must say, though,' he went on, 'the wedding pictures would be a lot more festive-looking if you weren't in them. You've got a face like a wet weekend.'

She turned to look at him, and momentarily he was appalled by the look of abject misery he saw.

'For Chrissake,' he said, passionately, 'it's not the end

195

of the world. They'll be back in a year. And you can go and visit them if you want!' Bloody good riddance too he thought. 'But for Chrissake cheer up, if not for my sake, for hers.'

'You don't understand,' she said wearily. 'And if I told you it wouldn't make any difference. You never have understood.'

She had not told him that Bob Roberts had rung from the Home, earlier, to say that he might be late at the church, and that the main purpose of the call was to tell her about Matron's death, and that Chief Inspector Jackson had taken away bottles and glasses from her bedside for forensic tests and that there was going to be a post-mortem not only on Matron but on Mrs Reynolds as well.

'Can't think what Jackson is up to,' he had said. 'With Matron it's a plain case of alcoholic poisoning. The place stank of booze – and as for the empty bottles! I've got Blake coming in to give a hand, but if you could see your way to coming in tomorrow?'

She had managed to murmur assent, but, Matron gone now as well! Amidst all those geriatric half-functioning olds, it was hard to grasp that someone like her would go first. It was of course a coincidence that she'd quarrelled with Mrs Snow publicly such a short time ago. Of course it was a coincidence. But there was a nasty nagging uncanny feeling about it all, very nasty. The feeling had begun when Bob Roberts had said in passing that Matron appeared to have been drinking Scotch, and it looked as if it were a combination of Scotch and sleeping pills that had proved to be fatal. She'd given Mrs Snow Scotch, and, God forgive her, she had also given her the tranquilliser tablets she'd got from Dr Jackson. And although she dismissed the thought as a tortuous unlikelihood, taken with her other earlier nightmares about the way Mrs Reynolds could have gone, the feeling of involvement persisted and would not be dismissed.

He relapsed into silence and then brightened up.

'That old biddy from the Home,' he said. 'She was enjoying herself. She and that nut-case Colonel with her, nodding and smiling, like a couple of old Chinese idols. Marvellous.'

She agreed. Even through her private and profound misery in the church she had been aware of Mrs Snow and the Colonel in the back pews. In Mrs Snow's own words, she had done herself up sensationally, with a red splodge of rouge on each cheek, brilliant red lipstick, pencilled-over eyebrows and a thick dusting of face powder. She sported a shiny blue suit with a blouse printed with mauve roses the size of cabbages, a necklace of black chunky beads, a blue straw hat with a pink silk flower on its brim. She'd even tied a length of white ribbon on her walking-frame, the long ends fluttering festively as she stomped her way from the cab, hired for her by Mrs Bolter, to the church. Well, at least she'd got some pleasure from it all. The Colonel looked magnificent in a dark blazer and a fresh white shirt and a striped tie. Perhaps he really had been a Colonel. He certainly looked the part. What an odd pair they made, oddly complementary.

'What you want,' he said, breaking into her thoughts, 'is a couple of quick snorts. Liven you up a bit!' He chuckled to himself and then laughed out loud at the thought of a lively Phyllis.

She turned again and looked at him. How I detest and despise him, she thought. If he had been different, everything else would have been different. There would have been none of those ridiculous conversations and meeting and comic plottings with Mrs Snow. What an incredible liar that old woman was. She would not have had to seek comfort and sex with Bob Roberts if he'd done his duty by her, and there would have been nothing for Claire to have found out, and she wouldn't have been caught mooning over Bob's old photograph. The look of disgust on Claire's face was something she would have to live with the rest of her days. I hate you, she said to herself. I hate you. She turned violently into the car park.

'Steady on!' he exclaimed. And then, 'For Chrissake, stop looking at me as if you could nail me to the ground. If you want to do me in, wait until after my speech, eh!' He slapped his thigh and laughed again.

Do you in, she thought. I wish it were true about Mrs Snow. You'd be in your box before Claire's honeymoon was over.

She parked and he climbed out of the car, swaying slightly, carrying his topper and wearing a fixed benign expression as he walked carefully between the cars, parked and parking, and went into the reception foyer. Claire and Richard were by the door already and behind them was a waiter with a tray of assorted sherries, offering drinks to the guests as they arrived.

'Marvellous,' he said. 'Great!' He gave Claire a bear-hug and shook her new husband's hand vigorously. 'Well done,' he went on, waving aside the proffered sherry. 'And now let's get the champagne flowing, eh?'

He went on inside, still beaming. Friends, relatives, restaurant staff beginning to fill up the place, flowers everywhere, the top table particularly splendid, all crisp linen and silver and the bloody great cake in front. Where's the Maître Dee? he thought. Let the bloody champagne corks start popping. It was going to be a great party. Sod the expense.

Mrs Bolter negotiated the hurdle of the newly weds, took two glasses of sherry from the waiter, downed one quickly and then went on into the main reception-room holding the other. She ought to go and say welcoming things to Richard's family, but Bolter was in there already with them, with a bottle, pouring champagne into their glasses. They all seemed set for a large ingestion of liquid refreshment and the kind of tipsy good humour which, if she had to endure it, she knew would quite literally make her vomit. Mrs Snow hobbled in, with the Colonel, and

198

she went over to help her, guiding her to a seat by the window. The Colonel followed, holding two glasses of sherry. Mrs Snow took one of them and lifted it in salute.

'Cheers,' she said, 'here's to the bride.'

'And the groom,' added the Colonel.

'I know who I drink to,' said Mrs Snow.

Mrs Bolter finished her second glass and handed it to the Colonel, who seemed to be very much in possession of his faculties.

'Would you mind getting me a refill?' she asked, 'please?'

She watched him shoulder his way to the wine waiter, and bent to talk urgently to Mrs Snow.

'Did you know that Matron was found dead this morning?'

Mrs Snow shook her head. 'What a turn up!' she said. 'I thought that something was up when night nurse was still around at breakfast time this morning. How did it happen?'

'She was found dead in bed. There'll be an inquest, without doubt.'

'Can't say I'm sorry she's gone,' said Mrs Snow. She paused. 'Does that mean that you'll be taking over as Matron?'

'God, no,' said Mrs Bolter. She leaned over further until her face was almost on Mrs Snow's. 'Are you sure you know nothing about it?'

'Me?' Mrs Snow was indignant. She thought for a few seconds and then smiled enigmatically. Was it Matron that had stolen her whisky, then? And not drunk it until last night? Serves her right. She got what was coming to her, just like Mrs Southover.

'She probably had a heart attack,' she said eventually. 'Anyway, I can't say I'm going to lose any sleep over it. She wasn't a nice woman. And here's your other sherry coming up.'

'I'll see you later, then,' said Mrs Bolter. She took the

199

drink from the Colonel. Mrs Snow watched her move towards Councillor Roberts and his wife, who were talking together with Chief Inspector and Dr Jackson. As she watched she saw the Chief Inspector raise his head and look in her direction. For a couple of long, long seconds he caught and held her gaze, then he looked at the Colonel and smiled. But it was a smile without a vestige of humour about it. It was as if when he looked at her and the Colonel together something had clicked into place and what had been confused was now plain, and the clear vision was not welcome. Mrs Snow sipped at her sherry and returned his gaze, unwinking, when he looked back at her, his expression unchanged. She did not even allow herself the luxury of wondering what he was thinking. He knew nothing! There was no way he could pin anything on her or the Colonel, and she'd had enough of the game anyway. She'd get rid of her list, tell Mrs Bolter that it had all been in her mind, maybe get a transfer to another Home. The only reason the police had become interested was because of Assistant Matron Patel's death. Getting the Colonel to do his stuff on the car had been her only mistake, her one regret. Not that that Nosy Parker could prove anything anyway. She smiled to herself, it had been great while it lasted, but all good things must come to an end. She treated herself to a half sigh, and the Chief Inspector looked away.

It was strange, thought Claire, seated at the top table with Richard and his parents on one side and her parents on the other, how drink affects different people differently. Her adoptive father was hail-fellow well-met, expansive, back-slapping. Having toyed with salmon mousse and the chicken salad and the pêche Melba, all washed down with an endless supply of champagne, he was reaching for happy oblivion with a large balloon of cognac and a fat cigar. Her adoptive mother, on the other hand, whom, she was beginning to realise, she had treated less than generously and completely without compassion, and who too had been soaking up the liquor indiscriminately and earnestly, was looking thinner, paler and paradoxically more sober as the festivities progressed.

The best man, Richard's brother, with his hair slightly awry and his collar and grey tie doing their best to part company, was very dishy indeed. She guessed that he had taken very little in the way of drink; probably staying sober and fit so that he could service later any or perhaps all of her friends who looked as if they might welcome such attention. And there were one or two, without doubt. But it was her new husband who was the enigma. He'd had a fair amount of drink and she knew that he wasn't used to large amounts of alcohol. But it had no apparent effect on his behaviour. And it was odd how when they were apart he seemed not to be. It was as if, she thought, his existence was dependent upon her own and that he took form and shape only in her physical proximity. And although that perhaps was not altogether surprising, there were other people, people one cared for, who left something of themselves with you when they went out of the room, who could be with you in an almost overpowering way, instantly recalled by a sound or a scent or a trick of the light, even though they were literally miles away. Apart from being fantastic in bed, what did she really know about him? She shivered, earlier doubts that she had experienced about the wisdom of getting married returning in strength. She caught her mother's eye, briefly, shivered again involuntarily and reached for her glass. Why am I sitting up here dressed in this ridiculous fashion, with everybody looking at me and nudging each other? Out of the corner of her eye she saw her mother push away from the table and walk towards one of the doors leading to the restaurant garden. I must talk to her, she thought. She made a move to follow her, bu found a restraining hand on her wrist.

'Speech time,' her husband said, and swivelled his chair

round to face his best man, who had risen to his feet and was banging on the table for quiet and attention.

Mrs Bolter hardly knew how she got outside, but she was convinced that she neither hesitated nor staggered. That look Claire had given her, and the shudder that followed it, had been the last straw. I can't stand it or him any longer, she thought. And at any time at all he'd be up on his feet, drunker even than usual, making speeches, and God alone knows what he might say. It was suddenly necessary to step outside just for a few minutes, get a bit of fresh air, walk around for a while and try and shrug off this terrible black cloud of mounting depression which had settled on her. Here she was, a not unhandsome woman, physically in good shape, creeping about on her daughter's wedding-day, bowed down by an almost insupportable sense of guilt, of failure, of self-disgust and foreboding.

And it isn't enough to say that I can't help the way God made me, that I have no control over my thoughts and actions and feelings; I am what I have made myself and I don't like it. Tears welled up in her eyes. That wicked, wicked Mrs Snow, how can she live with herself, killing or planning to kill or pretending to kill, and corrupting without even a twinge of conscience? And Matron, the leader at the helm, now lying dead and alone and the police taking an active interest. Suppose that Mrs Snow had had a hand in it, and a connection between her and Mrs Snow could be established? There would be even less hope of a reconciliation with Claire. What would Claire say when she knew that she had not only been friendly with but had actually incited that old witch to do something to her father, of whom, despite his complete failure as a parent, she was clearly still very fond?

She wished that she had never met Bob Roberts or Mrs Snow; never been in the Old People's Home. I must go to Matron she thought, I must see her, ask her forgiveness, even though she is beyond reach in this world.

202

She walked on through the paved gardens into the car park and got into her car. I'll just run myself to the Home, she thought vaguely. I'll be back inside ten minutes, a quarter of an hour, no one will miss me, or if they do, they'll think I'm in the loo. She pressed the starter and moved off, just grazing Bob Roberts' big Peugeot parked untidily at the end of a row. She fumbled with the seat belt, but had trouble pressing it home with one hand as she steered an erratic course with the other. It won't matter for that short journey, she thought, she'd often run up to the shops with the belt just draped around her instead of being securely fastened, and it was marvellous how intuitive driving was and how much better one drove after a few drinks. She turned the car sharply into the main road and headed down the hill. Must get a move on, she thought, must be back quickly before I'm missed.

The best man finished reading the few telegrams of good wishes and Mrs Snow sipped at her wine appreciatively. The Colonel next to her had fared well and, much to the consternation of Mrs Roberts, who was sitting opposite him, was muttering and chanting away to himself, his eyes rolling and his clenched fists occasionally banging on the table. Mrs Snow had observed Mrs Bolter's exit from her vantage point near the window and a few minutes later had seen her car weave out of the car park, turn and accelerate at the same time. She could almost hear the tyres slamming. She took another sip of her drink. The best man was still yammering away.

'And I now call upon the father of the bride to say a few words,' he concluded, at last.

Mr Bolter felt his new son-in-law prod him gently and heard him whisper, 'Speech time'. He stood up with a jerk and his chair fell over behind him. A waiter put it back into position and he smiled his thanks, leaning forward and still clutching his cigar, holding on to the table for support. His face was now a brick red in colour and beaded with perspiration, his features split with a benevolent smile.

'Ladies and gentlemen and friends,' he began, mock solemnly. 'It gives me great pleasure to see you here on this auspicious occasion.' His speech was slurred and he was having difficulty in keeping upright, swaying gently. 'My wife and I,' he waved in the direction of Mrs Bolter's empty chair without appearing to notice that it was unoccupied, 'are delighted to welcome Dr Richards into our family.' He paused. 'And we hope that he can keep Claire in order, because it's more than we could do.' His smile became even wider as his audience laughed in response. He's going to make a bloody fool of himself, thought Bob Roberts, exchanging significant glances with his wife, who looked like a cat which had been offered an unexpected bowl of cream. They both settled back to enjoy what they were about to receive.

'My good wife and I,' he went on expansively, 'don't agree about much these days. Well, it's no secret.' His cigar-end waved in the air. 'You want different things, take a different view of life, as you get on a bit.' He paused yet again. 'Nothing stands still. Everything changes. You're lucky if you both change in the same direction, but if you don't you have to be tolerant.' He looked up and caught Bob Roberts' eye. 'Friends help,' he went on. 'Isn't that right, Bob? He's been helping us out for years.' He ignored Claire's audible intake of breath, took another drink of brandy and wiped his lips.

'One of the family is Bob, good luck to him,' he said softly, almost to himself. And then more strongly, his voice rising, 'And if there's one thing I have to say to my beautiful Claire and her husband, it is – give and bloody take – that's the secret. Be tolerant. Live and let live. Make the most of life whilst you've got it. Phyllis won't mind me saying that, will you, Phyllis?' He turned to his wife's empty place. 'Where's Phyllis?' he asked plaintively. 'Phyllis?'

204

The best man stood up and started clapping. Mr Bolter, still swaying, looked anxiously around him as his guests showed their appreciation.

'Sit down, please.' Dr Richards tugged at Mr Bolter's coat tails. Mr Bolter sat down, heavily.

'She's not been well,' he said lugubriously to no one in particular. 'Silly cow. Great strain working all hours in that mucky place. No need for it at all. It's going to stop.' He slid the ashtray towards him and ground the remains of his cigar in it.

'Where's Phyllis?' he demanded again, loudly.

'I'll go and find her,' said Claire.

The best man, still on his feet, launched into another speech.

Dr Richards turned to his mother.

'Would you see if you can find Mrs Bolter?' he said urgently.

Mrs Richards stowed away her napkin neatly and got up.

'She's probably being sick somewhere,' she whispered. 'She's had a lot to drink. I noticed.'

'I saw you noticing,' said Claire. 'I'll go and look for her.'

The best man raised his glass high in the air.

'And now let us be upstanding,' he commanded. 'A toast to the bride and groom.'

'The bride and groom,' muttered Mr Bolter and managed to get to his feet again. 'Let's cut the cake,' he said. 'Where's the photographers? Where's Phyllis?' He drank some more brandy, felt in his inside pocket and brought out another cigar, in a smart satin-finish aluminium tube, and sat down again. Everyone else seemed to be getting up. Everywhere he looked there seemed to be chaos, people scrambling around the table, the photographer approaching the cake, no bloody bride and groom of course, and the chatter of the well-lubricated, plates rattling, glasses clinking.

205

Faintly, in the distance as it were, faintly but unmistakably, he could hear the sound of police-car sirens and ambulances filtered through the closed doors and windows, those dreadful high-pitched sounds of the emergency services rushing regardless to the scene of some nearby fire or accident. A sound which one can hear from a great distance, clearly, and it wells up in volume. Fear travels in front of it, and relief picks up in the rear when the crescendo is reached and the sound begins to fade. Not your number on it this time. Not this time. But the sound was for someone, close to. Poor sods, bring them in here, he thought, and we'll give them a spot of the old eau de vie.

The rushing and scurrying about was still going on, like a bloody madhouse, confusing, noisy and disorientating all at the same time. It had been a great reception. Wished he'd spoken a bit longer though, cracked a few jokes instead of delivering an extemporary sermon. He'd had the punch lines written down on cards and then forgot them. What a bloody idiot! Claire looked beautiful. Young and fresh. Much too good for that middle-aged philanderer she'd married. They'd be off in a day or so to some bloody dirty old tent in the armpit of the Middle East. What a rotten start to a new life! Not much to do there, by all accounts, except get behind the mosquito-net curtains and get cracking. And you soon had your fill of that, he could tell them. He unscrewed the top of the aluminium tube and shook out the cigar wrapped in thin plastic film. He removed the film very carefully and held the cigar to his ear, rolling it between finger and thumb, listening with great satisfaction to the small noises produced by that action. His eyelids were getting heavy. When Phyllis came she'd take him home and make him something hot to drink and he could sleep. Sleep was what he wanted now. Say what you like about her, she was good to have around when you were under the weather.

He became aware abruptly that the immediate mêlée in

front of the top table had somehow dispersed. People were still in the room but gathering in small groups. There was no sign of Claire or Richard, or of any of the other Richardses in all their variety. He became aware too that Mrs Snow was approaching. He fought away the mists and fogs which were blurring his vision and threatening to seep over him. He blinked. Mrs Snow, the Colonel at her side, came back into focus and he could see her quite clearly now, coming towards him, leaning heavily on her frame, the white ribbons on it moving gently. They came closer and he smiled at them. His mouth and tongue felt dreadfully dry. Perhaps he should ask for coffee.

'Mr Bolter,' Mrs Snow said. Her eyes were shiny black stones.

He waved his cigar limply.

'So glad you could come,' he managed to get out.

Mrs Snow nodded over her frame.

'If we can be of any help, the Colonel and I,' she said. 'Any time. You know where to find us.'

He smiled. What an odd notion. Funny old bag.

'How very kind,' he murmured. 'Bless you.'

Mrs Snow nodded again and the Colonel half saluted. He watched them turn about and begin the long slow trek back to their table. And there was that Chief Inspector Jackson fellow taking her arm, and the Colonel's, helping them along. He wasn't such a bad sort, even if he did make it look for all the world as if he was arresting them! What a happy conceit, he thought, that they think they can be of service to me! He stood up suddenly. Once again his chair toppled over, but now there were no waiters behind to pick it up.

'Phyllis,' he called, and punched the table. 'Phyllis!'

He looked despairingly about the room. It seemed that the groups of people moved closer together, turning to face him, the circles tightening and contained silently amongst themselves, not hostile, not sympathetic, but neutral, silent.

207

'Phyllis,' he called yet again, but there was no answer.

Somewhere in the background he could hear the sound of someone weeping, crying the way Claire sometimes used to cry when she was a child, as if alone in a lonely place and her heart was breaking. When the sound stops I shall weep too, he thought, and he waited, but it went on and on, beyond time, and he knew then that for him it would never stop, and that the time for weeping – if ever there was a time – had long passed.